Entwined Publishing books by Sierra Cartwright

Mastered

With This Collar
On His Terms
Over the Line
In His Cuffs
For the Sub
In the Den
With This Ring

The Donovan Dynasty

Bind
Brand
Boss

Mastered

WITH THIS RING

SIERRA CARTWRIGHT

ENTWINED PUBLISHING

With This Ring
ISBN # 978-1-80250-753-9

Interior text design by Entwined Publishing
Published by Entice, an Entwined Publishing imprint

Published in 2025 by Entwined Publishing, United Kingdom.

Entwined Publishing is a division of Totally Entwined Group Limited.

WITH THIS RING

Dedication

Always, always for BAB.
In book one, *With This Collar,* I wrote that I can't imagine trying to do this without you. And now I have to. I miss your smile, your sass, your sense of humor, the way you'd kick my ass. Here's to endless cups of coffee, entire nights spent proofing, memories that will last a lifetime, and a friendship that enriched my life more than you will ever know.
I love you, Bev, and I miss you. Every single day.

A huge thank-you to the readers who found me when the first book in the series was released and are still with me today and asking for Gregorio's story.
Bethann, you're awesome.
And, Trish…woman, you are amazing!
Thank you all!

Prologue

Three years ago

Always the bridesmaid…

This was the fourth wedding where Sasha had been forced into a horrific, frothy, itchy gown that looked terrible on her and she would have never chosen to wear.

If she was ever the bride, she wouldn't make such awful choices.

She shoved the thought aside. The way her dating life looked, she would never receive a proposal.

Leah, today's bride, insisted there was a reason Sasha found every man lacking. She was measuring them against an impossible standard, one that had been set more than a decade ago.

Sasha had shaken her head as she'd informed Leah she was wrong. But deep down, in a place she didn't want to acknowledge, Sasha knew she was lying to herself.

Around her, the ballroom of the upscale boutique hotel in downtown Denver buzzed with conversation and laughter.

A band played in the corner. Obviously, the quartet with their smooth melodies had been chosen by Leah's grandmother, who was paying for the whole shindig. Sasha hadn't recognized a single tune yet, and the music was too refined for her tastes. She craved something with a beat, something she could lose herself in. Right now, she would even settle for a line dance.

Nursing a glass of champagne, she stood at a tall, round table off to one side.

Her whole life, she'd been a misfit. She wouldn't be here tonight if she hadn't been paired with Leah on a college project, when they'd become fast friends.

With a sigh, Sasha took a sip, and the bubbles tickled her nose. The stuff was okay, no doubt uber expensive, but she had little appreciation for life's finer things.

On the dance floor, the bride and groom swayed together, oblivious to everyone. They looked so happy, so in love. What would that be like?

Part of her envied them—a little.

But not enough to settle or give up the life she'd chosen.

"Sasha. Would you...would you like to dance?"

She glanced up at Tristan, the groomsman she'd been matched with for the festivities.

He sidled up to her, his shoulder brushing against hers. His expensive cologne was even more cloying than it had been earlier. How was that possible?

Tristan seemed harmless enough, even if all he talked about were his trips and cars. They had less than nothing in common, and in other circumstances she doubted he'd do anything other than look down his patrician nose at her.

Still, what harm was there in spending a few minutes in the arms of a man good-looking enough to pose for the cover of a Hampton's fashion magazine, something he'd managed to mention twice?

"Sash?"

Maybe it was the sudden melancholy, a longing for something she might never have or the urge to hurry time along, but she gave him a fake smile. "Sure." She slid her glass back onto the table.

The itchy fabric chafed her inner arms. With a sigh, she attempted to adjust the bodice of the gown.

"Let's go."

Instead of waiting for her, he headed to the dance floor. She trailed, seemingly an afterthought.

A pity dance for the wallflower?

Had Leah or her new husband put him up to this?

With a movement that wasn't as smooth as she'd expected, he turned to her then pulled her into his arms, a little too close for her comfort. His breath smelled of something much stronger than champagne. Whiskey, maybe, or tequila. No wonder he'd taken a second bath in his cologne. Something had to overpower the scent of alcohol.

How much of this song was left, anyway?

Without asking her anything about herself or making polite conversation, he extolled the virtues of his latest purchase, a car reported to cruise along at over two hundred miles an hour.

"Isn't the top speed in this country eighty or eighty-five?"

"My car can be shipped to other places in the world. Or tested on racetracks."

Schooled by the trust fund baby. "I see."

Resisting the urge to roll her eyes, she forced a smile as he launched into his next monologue.

"What do you say…?"

Realizing she'd completely tuned him out, she blinked to clear her head. "Sorry?"

Impatiently, he expelled a breath. "I said we should head somewhere quieter."

Before she could respond, the tiny hairs on her nape stood up, warning of danger.

Someone was watching her.

Surreptitiously, she looked around, scanning the crowd, but she noticed nothing amiss. And yet, the feeling persisted. It was like an itch between her shoulder blades, a prickle of awareness she couldn't shake.

"Are you paying attention to me?" he whined, pulling her closer and sliding a hand lower on her spine.

She stiffened and eased back a little, not quite ready to bring her heel down on his instep but getting closer.

From nowhere, a hulking presence appeared and forcefully tapped Tristan's shoulder.

"Get your fucking hands off her."

Both she and Tristan froze.

Sasha would know his voice anywhere. The deep, rich baritone danced through her dreams, echoed through her fantasies.

Gregorio.

God save her.

No.

"Who the hell do you think you are?" Tristan demanded.

Protector. Lethal warrior. Her fiercest defender. And biggest nemesis.

The man she measured everyone against.

Rather than answering, Gregorio leaned toward Tristan, getting in his face. When he spoke, his tone was controlled and steely, filled with threat. "Do you need me to repeat myself, pretty boy?"

Tristan's eyes widened, but ego—and maybe whiskey—propelled him toward recklessness. "Look, dude, I'll have you know—"

"Tristan," she urged, finally able to shake off her paralysis in order to act. "Don't."

He opened his mouth again, but then he looked at Gregorio, who stood several inches taller and was much broader.

His massive biceps strained against the sleeves of his suitcoat.

No polite, civilized veneer could possibly hide the power coiled in his frame, the barely restrained violence.

A diamond earring winked from one ear.

In a past life, he could have been a pirate.

Gregorio was thrilling and terrifying all at once.

Even though Tristan was lean, in a yoga or runner type of way, they all knew Gregorio could take him apart in a single move.

What *he* didn't know was that Gregorio would do just that, no matter the setting.

"I'll give you the count of three to get lost."

Immediately, Tristan released Sasha and stepped back.

He adjusted his tie as he cleared his throat. "Uh, yeah." He looked her up and down. "Bitch like you isn't worth the effort anyway."

Her mouth dropped from shock.

"You signed your death warrant."

Paling, Tristan pivoted and strode away.

Before she could recover, another song started. Gregorio swept her into his strong arms and moved them closer to the band, away from prying eyes.

"Interrupting my dance..." She could handle herself, and a man like Tristan wouldn't have posed much of a challenge. "That was uncalled for."

"Was it?"

He sounded appallingly unconcerned.

"I saved you, Sasha. Again."

For most of her teenage years, he'd repeatedly stuck his nose in her business. He'd been her constant shadow, always watching, always intervening. It had been equal parts comforting and infuriating.

In so many ways, he'd helped her become the person she was today. "I can save myself, Gregorio," she insisted. After all, she taught self-defense to others. She could lay out Tristan in the space of a heartbeat.

Gregorio swept a searing, appreciative gaze over her.

Then, before she could protest, he nudged her closer, leaving her no choice but to inhale his spicy, outdoorsy scent. It was familiar and foreign all at once, bringing back a rush of memories—late night conversations, shared laughter.

"I mean it, Gregorio." She tried to pull back, but he tightened his grip. "You had no right to do that."

"Hmm." He flicked a casual glance toward Tristan, who was making a beeline to the bar.

"He's not worth the time or effort."

"You don't get to decide that."

It's my life we're talking about.

"Pretty boy fucked up when he insulted you."

"Just stop. I don't need you to protect me."

"He's going to die tonight." As if she hadn't said a word, he continued, "Or at least regret being born."

She shuddered. Not from fear, but from a sudden, visceral awareness of his strength, his power. It was like being caught in the gaze of a predator—exhilarating and paralyzing all at once.

"Furthermore, *you* should be thanking me."

"*Thanking* you?" He thought he could show back up in her life and tell her what to do? "You need to get over yourself."

"He'd have been fun until he fucked you, then abandoned you. He'd have sweet-talked you into not using a condom, then refused to take responsibility."

She gasped.

"You're an investigator." He lifted a shoulder in a casual shrug. "Look up the men you're considering inviting inside your home." He paused. "Or your body."

Jesus. "I wouldn't have let that happen."

"Tell me he didn't try to take you upstairs."

Flushing, she looked away.

"He'd be good for a minute, maybe two."

She opened her mouth to speak but no words emerged.

"If he could get it up after consuming all that alcohol."

Sasha longed to argue, to tell him he was wrong, but the words stuck in her throat.

"Selfish bastard wouldn't have even gotten you off first."

Emotions crashed through her—longing, desire, the illicit, forbidden thrill that came from having this conversation with a man she'd had a crush on. "How is that different from most men?" *Why did I say that?* She was in dangerous territory with him, and she shouldn't poke the bear. Heat chased up her neck and settled on her cheeks. No way should she be in the arms of her former brother-in-law, talking about orgasms. Desperate to change the conversation, she narrowed her gaze. "Are you jealous?"

He chuckled, immediately dismissing her taunt—his sound one of pure male superiority. "Of him? Not a chance."

"What I do and with whom I do it is not your concern." She paused, then breathlessly rushed on. "And it never was, actually."

"Still telling yourself pretty little lies, Petal?"

Petal?

The nickname hit her hard, a flashback, a timeless moment. It was so much more suited to the teen she'd been than the fully capable adult woman she was now, and yet she liked it more than ever.

"You've always needed a protector."

Fuck off. "Just because—"

"Obviously, you still do."

That she didn't have an instant comeback was likely because she was reeling in shock from seeing him again. Even though Leah had talked endlessly about the people who'd be in attendance, Gregorio's name had never been mentioned.

Even though they worked at the same place, the irony of running into him at a wedding didn't escape her, considering she'd been seated in the front row of the divorce proceeding between him and her older sister—a place she wished she'd never gone.

It had been one of the most awful days of her life, watching two of the people she loved most in the world tear each other apart. She'd clenched her hands, body frozen, as the lawyers had laid out the sordid details of their failed marriage—the lies, the betrayals, the slow, painful unraveling of a love she'd once thought was forever.

"I was hoping for a memorable experience tonight," she lied.

"Memorable? Maybe I can help you out."

You?

"And I'll make sure you get off."

Almost missing a step, she blinked and searched his face for some hint of mockery but found only an intense sincerity that made her breath catch.

In an instant, he released her, only to immediately clamp a hand around her wrist and all but drag her from the packed ballroom and down the hall into a janitor's closet.

Never pausing, he kicked aside a bucket, sending the mop clattering to the floor, the noise so loud it echoed in her ears and covered the sound of a lock being ratcheted home.

In a single move, he slammed her up against a wall and raised her hands above her head to pin them in place.

"Gregorio..."

He leaned in closer.

Suddenly, the only sounds were her frantic breaths and thundering heart.

Because of her training at Hawkeye, she was also a competent bodyguard and security agent. People counted on her to protect their lives. But this close to Gregorio, she was helpless, ensnared by his masculine prowess. "What the hell are you suggesting?" She could escape his hold in a single move. Two at the most. So why wasn't she running away screaming?

"You want something memorable. I'll make damn sure this is an evening you won't soon forget."

Slowly, he traced his thumb down the column of her throat, bringing it to rest on the frantic pulse that thundered there. His touch was electric, shooting wildfire through her veins.

"Open your mouth for me."

Desperate to save herself, she shook her head.

"I won't force you." He quirked an eyebrow. "I won't need to."

What cocksure arrogance.

"You want this," he stated. "You want *me*."

Once more, she frantically shook her head. But even as she denied it, she knew it was true. She'd always wanted him, always craved his touch, his attention, his approval. It was a secret she'd carried for so long it had become a part of her, as essential as breathing.

He pressed lightly on her throat. "Your actions say one thing but your body says another. It's speaking to mine, isn't it?"

She should deny what he said.

"Right now, this moment, you're feeling compelled to spread your legs as wide as possible, right after you pull up your dress and show me your secrets."

Absolutely not. "No."

As if she'd said nothing, he went on in his hypnotic way. "Once you do that, you'll want me to slide my fingers inside your panties and give you an orgasm that would make you scream if we weren't in public."

He leaned impossibly closer and she stared at him, unable to look away. His eyes were dark, almost black in the dim light of the closet, and filled with a hunger that matched her own.

Protests sprang to mind, and each died before emerging. Instead, she was captivated by his air of confidence, worn as easily as the suit hugging his powerful frame.

"But since anyone walking by could hear you, I'd have to silence your cries with my mouth."

Sasha didn't want this. *Shouldn't.* Yet her body betrayed her. Her clit throbbed with need, and an ache built deep inside her.

"Tell me to let you go, Petal. Or use that beautiful mouth of yours to ask me to kiss you and bring you off."

His crudeness made her gasp.

"Or I can walk away right now and leave you wondering, turned on and frustrated."

Embarrassed, she worried her lower lip. But beneath the embarrassment was a thrill, a dark excitement at the thought of surrendering to him, of letting him take control.

Something she'd spent years longing for.

"I'm betting you'd stay behind for a while to masturbate to the fantasy of what you could have had but didn't have the courage to ask for."

Damn you.

"You and I would both know what you were doing, wouldn't we?"

He was impossible.

"Since I'm a gentleman..."

What a total and complete lie.

"I'll offer you the same courtesy I gave pretty boy. You've got three seconds to respond." He waited. "Three."

She vowed to remain silent.

"Two."

To keep herself from whimpering with need, she pressed her lips together.

"One."

True to his word, he released her wrists.

Helplessly, she left her arms in place. "Gregorio."

He turned toward the door.

Need consumed her. *"Gregorio!"*

Hand on the lock, he stopped.

"Kiss me?"

He turned to face her. "Now you'll have to use your manners."

Sasha squeezed her eyes shut. *Do you have to make me beg?*

"The words, Petal. Say them. I want to hear them."

With a gulp, she nodded. "Please. Please kiss me."

"Nice start."

Still, the determined bastard didn't move.

"Now, repeat after me—please, Gregorio, use your hand to bring me off."

If it weren't for him, she would never have gone into the personal security field, wouldn't have had the courage to take the risks that made life worth living.

This moment thundered with danger.

If she gave in and asked for what she needed, would her sister see it as a betrayal?

Yet she lacked the conviction to send him away.

"What will it be, Petal?"

She was powerless to resist the sway he held over her. Softly, she said, "Please, Gregorio, use your hand to bring me off."

"Very nice."

His approving purr thrilled her, made the awful words worthwhile.

"Now lift your hem and bunch the dress around your waist."

No man had ever been this outrageous with her, yet there wasn't a single part of her that considered denying him. Her hands wavered as she reached for the hem, and her heart pounded so loudly he had to hear it.

With a deep swallow, she lowered her arms to gather the ridiculous amount of pale pink chiffon and tucked it into place.

"Very nice." He swept his hot gaze over her, taking in her legs, her tummy, then settling at the apex of her thighs. The heat of his stare was like a physical caress on her skin.

Trying not to betray her nerves, she took a breath. "The thong's unexpected. In a nice way."

Sasha much preferred panties or boy shorts that offered full coverage, but Leah had been very vocal, insisting her wedding pictures would not be ruined by panty lines.

"Now take it off."

Heat flooding her face, she worked the material down her legs. Her hands trembled as she turned over the scrap of silk, the intimacy of the gesture making her feel exposed and vulnerable in a way she'd never experienced before.

"Good girl."

His approval made the room spin.

"Smell it."

The man offered no respite. Before she was finished being scandalized by one request, he made another. *"What?"*

"I want you to smell yourself."

Wishing the floor would open up beneath her, she followed his command.

"Now tell me about the scent."

In the distance the party continued, the music creating a backdrop at odds with her emotions. An occasional conversation or giggle from the hallway affirmed how absurd being in here with Gregorio was.

"I'm waiting."

The musky, heady aroma made her body flame with embarrassment and desire. After momentarily squeezing her eyes shut, she replied. "It's, ah…" She cleared her throat. "My arousal."

"Mmm." He nodded. "Is the material damp?"

You already know the answer.

Silently, he approached her, something that should have been impossible with a man as large as he was. But Gregorio had always been able to move with silent grace, a stealth that belied his size and strength.

And she'd seen him accomplish the impossible before.

"Now hold it to my nose."

Ready to die from his demands, she followed his outrageous direction.

"Intoxicating, Petal." He then plucked her thong from her and dropped it into his pocket. "I could mainline your scent and feed on it for days."

Who the hell are you?

She'd known he was lethal, but she'd never seen this side of him before. His raw, primal sexuality weakened her knees and made her heart gallop.

"Now, put one hand on the wall next to you and use the other to spread your labia, holding yourself open to me."

This time, she didn't protest. She couldn't, not when her body ached for his touch, taste, possession.

Right now, they both recognized the sway he held over her. She would do anything he wanted.

Once she'd complied, she remembered what he'd said earlier. Without being prompted, she spread her legs wide, made more difficult by her heels and the way her body wavered.

"You really are a good girl. *My* good girl."

She was indecently exposed to the man who'd once been her brother-in-law, and she'd never wanted anything as much as she wanted him in this moment, never craved anything as much as she needed his approval, his praise, his possession.

"Now open your mouth."

He claimed her lips, making it impossible to breathe. He plundered, taking before she offered, as if he had every right to do so.

Exactly the way it should be.

Burying the unwelcome thought in the darkest recesses of her mind, she closed her eyes and surrendered.

A moment later, he changed the tempo to make love to her with his tongue.

When her knees buckled, he was there for her, holding her wrist tight and keeping her steady. Then he slid a finger between her slick folds.

She gasped into his mouth at the sensation of his rough, calloused finger against her most sensitive flesh.

He pulled back long enough to gently nip at her earlobe and whisper, "You have such a beautiful little pussy."

Instantly, he took her mouth again and toyed with her clit, igniting pleasure in the tiny bundle of nerves.

Her body went rigid as he stroked and circled and teased, driving her higher and higher.

Suddenly, an orgasm overtook her, more powerful than anything she'd ever experienced.

Bucking her hips, she sought even more as the waves crashed over her. She rode his hand, grinding against him, chasing the pleasure only he could offer.

If it hadn't been for the way his tongue filled her mouth, she would have screamed aloud, as he'd known she would.

On and on he went, slipping a finger inside her, angling his wrist to find her G-spot.

Desperate for him, she lifted onto her tiptoes and rocked her hips, simulating sex. Her body wanted him to enter her, stretching her, completing her in a way no other man ever had.

Reading her as if they'd been together dozens of times before, he eased a second finger inside, filling her, fucking her.

Her mouth and pussy were full of him, and the world began to spiral.

As if sensing her need, he pumped his fingers faster, harder, driving her closer to the edge.

Gregorio pressed the heel of his palm against her clit and rubbed hard.

She was swimming in sensation and pleasure. *In him.*

Disobediently, she pulled her hand from between them and wrapped her arm around his neck, hanging on with desperation, praying the moment would never end.

How many years had she fantasized about this dark, enigmatic man who was more of a stranger than a brother-in-law? Someone she had probably never truly known, even though she thought she had.

Impossibly, he deepened the intensity by adding a third finger, spreading her wider, forcing her to accept his penetration.

The stretch, the fullness, the sheer presence of him overwhelmed her. But he was also perfect, everything she'd ever wanted.

God.

She was gone, surrendered in bliss.

A shocking, powerful climax rocked her as wave after wave of pleasure crashed over her, and she writhed, her pussy clenching him as she drenched his hand.

Only then, when she was shattered, did he release her mouth. "Yeah. That's right. You're my girl."

Still dizzy, she opened her eyes, struggling to bring the world into focus.

Gregorio filled her vision and her senses. In this moment, he was her everything. *Just like he'd always been.*

Taking his time, he withdrew his fingers, then held them to her mouth.

"Lick them. Taste yourself. Know that I did this to you…brought you this pleasure."

His request was so sensual she almost came again. Her pussy tingled, craving more of him, all of him, in every way possible.

Part of her was shocked that she'd done what he said, but how could she deny him anything when he'd just given her everything?

Once his fingers were clean, he lowered his hand to pull down her dress, sending the chiffon tumbling back into place.

She blinked.

Are we finished?

He leaned forward to kiss her lips. Tasting her orgasm?

With unbelievable slowness, he traced the plunging neckline of her dress, making her breasts throb with desire. Her nipples tightened, straining against the sheer fabric of her bra, begging for his attention.

For as satisfied as she was, he'd left her wanting and emotionally bereft.

He lowered her arm, and good thing he thought to do so because it seemed to be frozen in place.

Then, in a thoughtful gesture, he rubbed her shoulder, bringing sensation back into it.

"Ready to rejoin the party?"

What the hell had he just done to her? "Wait." *No. After that?* "I need my underwear back."

"Not a chance." Gregorio left her to unlock and open the door, then he checked the hallway in both directions.

When it was safe, he beckoned her.

On wobbly legs, her body still vibrating from the physical and emotional aftermath of what they'd shared, her mind reeling with the implications, she walked past him.

Possessively, Gregorio pressed his fingers against the base of her spine, his touch seeming to sear her even through the gown's fabric as he guided her back toward the reception.

His simple touch, the small claim, made her heart squeeze with longing.

"Remember not to make mistakes with pretty boys."

"So I can make bigger ones with dangerous men?"

His quick smile promised sin and salvation.

"Yeah." He ushered her back into the ballroom. "Shall we?"

Moments later, his touch was gone. And so was he.

She glanced over her shoulder, but he was nowhere to be seen…vanished into the crowd as if he'd never been there at all.

Stunned, she wrapped her arms around herself.

Gregorio had shown up unexpectedly, turned her life upside down, then disappeared as if the event in the janitor's closet had meant nothing to him.

If it weren't for her missing panties, the ache between her thighs, the lingering taste of him on her tongue, and the ghost of his touch on her skin, she might have believed she'd made up the entire event.

How am I supposed to go back to my real life now?

Chapter One

Three years later

I wish there was any other way.

With a disbelieving sigh, Sasha unzipped her suitcase and pulled out the glossy, faux-leather ensemble with big silver buckles.

The outfit seemed to mock her. She was in too deep and had no idea what the hell she was doing.

That wasn't the first time the thought had occurred to her.

Which was why she was standing in a hotel room of a fancy Winter Park, Colorado lodge.

A week ago, when she'd walked into the specialty novelty store filled with all kinds of skimpy clothing, items for bachelorette parties, and a dizzying array of toys for adult escapades, she'd stood there in shock.

The helpful young clerk, maybe noticing how wide and unblinking her eyes were, had taken pity on her.

Searching for calm, she'd informed him she'd be visiting a BDSM club for the first time, and he'd guided her to the far, forbidden corner of the store, hidden behind thick, red velvet curtains.

Quickly, she'd learned nothing could have prepared her for seeing the shocking items in person—gags, blindfolds, paddles, whips, clamps, and other items she assumed were supposed to go inside her rear. How they would fit, she had no idea.

Saving her from her galloping thoughts, the clerk had tipped his head to one side, as if studying her body shape, then he'd plucked a hanger from a rack and assured her it was the right look for the event.

He'd talked her into adding a crop with a small, puffy pink heart on the top.

If she played with anyone—which she didn't intend to—the implement would be a great introduction to impact play.

Because he made sense, she'd allowed herself to be talked into the purchase.

Desperate to escape the shop, she'd offered her credit card, then strode toward the exit as fast as she could, opaque plastic bag clutched in hand.

Now, as she studied the outfit, Sasha realized she was stalling.

She'd bought it for a single reason. To get Gregorio's attention.

Would it?

With a sigh, she transferred the outfit to the bed. The stark contrast between the white duvet cover and the shiny black material shocked her, and suddenly a whole new set of doubts assailed her.

In her years as a security specialist for one of the largest firms on the planet and now as the owner of her own private investigation firm, she'd adopted plenty of disguises.

More often than not, she tucked her long hair into a thick ponytail and donned a baseball cap, extra-large sweatshirt, and some sort of jacket to hide her weapons of choice, then slipped on a pair of oversize sunglasses and headed out. Invisible, blending in, she was able to surveil suspects who had security of their own.

Even if she was in a formal dress, pretending to fit in among the country's elite, it was as if she were wearing a layer of armor. *But this costume of sorts…?* This would be like slipping into a stranger's skin.

Before she could pick up the skirt, the piercing ring of her phone shattered the silence.

She jumped, testament to the fact she was on edge.

Her nerves had been frayed ever since she'd discovered her home office had been ransacked and case files had been strewn across the floor.

More disturbingly, several were missing.

The invasion was a violation of her sanctuary, leaving her feeling exposed and vulnerable in a way she never had been before.

With a deep inhalation to steady herself, she strode across the room to pick up the device.

Ashley.

Sasha's right-hand person and office manager of Pathways Investigations—a company she now owned by herself after splitting from her one-time business partner and love interest.

At least this wasn't a blocked number with heavy breathing and vague threats when she answered. Those calls had become more frequent, occurring more than once a day.

She'd considered ditching her main phone entirely, but clients still called it, and missing a lead could be catastrophic. Instead, she rerouted voicemails through a secure system, disabled GPS tracking, and kept a burner in her go-bag, powered off and ready. If things got worse, she could vanish off the grid in under sixty seconds.

Forcing her voice to be normal rather than rushed, she answered.

"I just got your message, Sash. Sorry I didn't get back to you before now."

"You deserve time off." Even if Sasha couldn't remember the last time she hadn't worked.

Still, if Ashley weren't on staff, there was no way Sasha or her three investigators would be nearly as organized or manage to keep the billing straight. Right now, Ashley's calm competence was a lifeline in the chaos of Sasha's life.

"What's up?"

"I'm working on a case, and I will be out of cell phone range."

"Oh?" Ashley asked, tone curious, as it should be. "Which client?"

"This is something personal." At best, her words were a half-truth. The invasion could be related to the Santos case, but maybe it was something else.

"You're making me nervous, Sash. Everything okay?"

She wasn't normally vague, but then again nothing about the events of the last weeks had been normal.

Ashley remained silent, waiting for more information.

Instead of offering it, Sasha changed the subject. "I'll be late on Monday morning." *Maybe.* Still, Pathways had clients who were counting on her, which meant this distraction had to be forced into the background. Nothing, nothing would stop her from doing the jobs she'd been hired for. "I have an appointment with Mrs.

Santos before coming in." Something she was not looking forward to.

On one hand, she had some good news for the woman who had hired Pathways to find out if her husband was having an affair.

He wasn't.

But Sasha had uncovered information that opened an entire Pandora's box filled with questions.

How had Felix been able to purchase the brand-new vehicle and have it delivered to his wife last week? From what Sasha had been able to ascertain, the man shouldn't have been able to afford even the big, fat red bow wrapping the luxury SUV.

And the Santos case file was among the missing ones. Could be a coincidence, but intuition told her it wasn't.

"I can open up the office, if you want me to."

"That would be great." Typically, she was first to arrive, by at least an hour. "And hold things down until I get there?"

"Of course." For a moment, Ashley remained quiet before asking, "You sure everything is okay?"

No. Nothing was. The admission would make it real. And she wasn't ready for that to happen, at least not until she had a better idea of what was going on.

Despite herself, Sasha crossed to the window for the dozenth time. Nudging back the blinds, she took in her surroundings, looking for any sign of trouble.

She'd constantly swept her SUV for scanners, just like she'd been trained—visual inspection, mirrors, magnet detector, even her handheld RF scanner. There were never any hits. She found nothing in the wheel wells, the undercarriage, or even hidden in the glovebox lining.

Since it was late summer, off season at the ski resort, the parking lot wasn't busy. Occasional shuttle buses passed by, taking vacationers to various parts of the town. Carefree laughter and chatter mocked Sasha's inner turmoil.

"Sash? You're worrying me."

"Everything's fine." She released the shade.

"*Oh*-kay." Ashley sounded as unconvinced as Sasha was.

"Promise."

"You're a terrible liar."

Which didn't always serve her well. She gave a small laugh to fill the awkward silence.

But obviously relenting, Ashley asked, "Do you need me to work tomorrow?"

"No." She tried to always give her staff Sundays off. Rest made people sharper. "But if you don't mind letting the answering service know to contact Justine if I can't be reached, I'd appreciate it." Pathways had hired a service so they appeared to have staff twenty-four hours a day, and Justine was the agent who'd been with Sasha the longest. "Oh, and give her a heads-up that I'm unavailable and that we'll move our weekly meeting to Tuesday?"

"Got it."

"You sure you don't mind? I know I'm interrupting your weekend."

"I've got you covered."

"Appreciate it." Aware of time ticking, she paced the room.

"Can I hope you'll at least get some relaxation?"

As if. "Maybe." Then, trying to be polite, she simply asked, "How about you?"

"Yeah. Jonah and I are going to grab some takeout and..." Ashley laughed. "Well, you know."

At least one of them would be enjoying a hot hookup.

Sasha's last one had been so long ago that she barely remembered it. The date, on the rebound after her hot, mind-blowing experience in the janitor's closet with Gregorio, had been disastrous.

She wouldn't have spent any time with the blind date except for the fact she'd been trying to prove to herself that Gregorio meant nothing to her.

Unfortunately, the sex had been so awful she couldn't recall the man's name.

And he'd done nothing to shove thoughts of Gregorio from her head.

Then came her boss, Toby.

If she hadn't been so obsessed with her girlhood hero, would she have made such disastrous decisions with Toby?

"Seriously, though. Don't work too hard," Ashley urged.

Sasha actually wasn't sure what she'd do if she had an hour to herself. Spend more time worrying was the most likely scenario. That's what happened during the lulls in her life. Which was another reason to stay busy.

Ending the call, she faced the waiting outfit once more.

No more stalling.

She'd set her course, and she needed to look the part, even if the outfit was ridiculously skimpy.

Because tonight's event at the Den was for ladies, particularly ones who were new and didn't have a sponsor, an informal event had been arranged. She was expected to meet others downstairs in the hotel conference room thirty minutes from now.

Rules and protocols would be discussed and there would be time for questions. Evidently the hosts were an actual D/s couple, Brandy and her Dominant, Master Niles.

Doubtless all the attendees were being vetted, which was smart, and something she appreciated. After all, people would be getting naked together, and no doubt some of the profiles contained lies or half-truths.

Hers certainly did.

In it, she'd claimed to be a submissive named Petal.

Stupid, stupid.

After all, *he'd* called her that.

Gregorio.

Her crush.

Her potential savior.

The only man she trusted to help her.

And the current caretaker at the Den, if her research was accurate. Which she prayed it was. After all, seeing him was the reason for this elaborate ruse. She had to get to him somehow. Since he was no longer an employee of Hawkeye, she'd had to use all her resources to track him this far.

She would never have tracked him down if she didn't need him.

Squaring her shoulders, she dropped her robe to the floor, pulled on a thong, then squirmed her way into the tight skirt. No way would she be able to take her usual big strides. The material acted more like mummification than clothing.

Somehow she managed to pull the top over her head. Then she began to tug the tiny piece into place.

The faux leather had cap sleeves and laced up the front. Horrifyingly, the garment was so short her midriff was left bare.

Precariously balancing, she slipped into four-inch platform sandals. At least those weren't as dangerous as some of the stilettos she'd eyed.

Being methodical steadied her nerves and had saved her life.

After a breath, Sasha ran through her pre-mission checklist, unzipping her oversize duffel bag to confirm its contents. Running shoes. Leggings and a sweatshirt. Panties that covered far more than the butt-floss confection currently buried between her ass cheeks.

In case she might have her bag searched on the way in, she'd added a bottled water and the crop she'd been talked into purchasing.

Her ops bag also had a secret compartment that hid her burner phone, first-aid kit, extra chargers, and her firearm. The burner wasn't active yet, but she had it prepped with encrypted apps and prepaid minutes. If anyone *was* tracking her, they'd have to work harder than this.

Sasha debated bringing her main phone at all. But if she ghosted, clients would panic, and she couldn't afford to look flaky. Ultimately, she tucked it deep into the hidden compartment—just in case she needed to prove she hadn't disappeared off the face of the earth.

Additionally, she also had a small purse with her real phone, an ID, room keycard, a few dollars, and a credit card.

Once all that was done, she walked across the room to fetch her coat from a peg on the wall.

The sight of her reflection in a full-length mirror stunned her.

Who the hell am I?

In this BDSM-friendly getup, legs and abs bare, and wearing tons of makeup and mascara to exaggeratedly highlight her eyes, this was her best disguise ever. Sasha barely recognized herself.

Maybe Gregorio won't, either.

All she needed, though, was to capture his attention. And hopefully he'd listen to her, for at least a few minutes.

One of the final things he'd said to her echoed through her memory.

"You've always needed a protector."

She'd hated the patronizing tone in his deep, rich voice, and she'd despised his smug certainty. But right this moment, she resented the hell out of the fact she was going to prove him right.

Squaring her chin, she shrugged into her coat.

The email she'd received from the Den yesterday said all people at the gathering had to be dressed suitably while in the hotel public spaces. *Don't scare the 'nillas,* they'd warned.

Which, she'd discovered, was shorthand for vanillas—people who weren't in the BDSM lifestyle.

She'd learned all kinds of things about consent, and the club's safe word had been mentioned in every communication.

Rules she appreciated, because they let her know what to expect in life. Sometimes she even followed ones she agreed with.

After securing both her bags over her shoulder, she looked through the peephole, then she cracked the door slightly to ensure the hallway was empty before leaving the room.

Usually, she preferred to jog down the stairs, but in these shoes she might kill herself if she tried.

Hyperaware of her surroundings, head on a swivel, she made her way to the elevator.

She'd parachuted into war zones with fewer butterflies than were flapping around inside her stomach right this moment.

This was about far more than being a fish out of water.

Each second ticking past brought her closer and closer to looking a long way up to meet the enigmatic, dark, mysterious eyes of a man who dressed all in black. For as long as she could remember, a diamond in one ear had refracted prisms of light wherever he went.

Do you still wear it, Gregorio?

No doubt he did. It served as a reminder to him of all the things he'd lost—just like the tattoo on his well-honed biceps.

But she'd do what she needed to.

Resolved, Sasha pushed the Call button.

Showtime…

Chapter Two

Under the stark lighting of the garage gym attached to his caretaker's cottage at the Den, Gregorio struck the heavy punching bag with a rhythmic thud, the power and precision honed by years of trying to outrun the past.

Shirtless, slick with sweat, he focused on each jab instead of the slight limp that left him a little off balance and the white bandage on his abdomen—a nasty fucking reminder of a recent mission gone south.

With each punch, pain flared, a soul-sucking contrast to the dull ache of his exertion. Ignoring it, he pushed through, just like he did with everything else.

Hell, he'd done it for so long it might as well be his life motto.

Endure.

This afternoon, he'd opted for silence over music, which meant the only sounds in the room were the repetitive echo of knuckles against canvas and the breaths burning his lungs.

Well-earned sweat dripped down his face, stinging his eyes.

On and on he went, clearing his mind with each combo, narrowing his world to a physical, brutal rhythm.

With a final, vicious jab, Gregorio stepped back to grab a towel.

As he wiped sweat from his face, the movement pulled at his wound, yet another in a long line that he'd needed to have stitched.

He was too old for this shit.

On rare occasions, and only on days the Den was closed to the public, he still freelanced for Hawkeye Security. But this one had been unsanctioned, and no one had known about it. He'd left a loose end when settling a recent score, and that bothered him enough to do something about it.

The bastard had died at his hand, but not without catching him with a knife and carving out a jagged chunk of flesh.

He'd allowed the doctor to do her work, as long as she skipped anesthesia. He was a physical man and wanted to feel every moment of his life. It reminded him he was still alive.

Muscles burning in a satisfying way, he headed back inside to get ready for the evening—ladies' night at the Den. More newbies than ever were planning to attend. So many, in fact, that he'd marked the event as sold out.

Inside his small, stark home, he jogged up the circular metal steps leading to the loft that served as his command center. In addition to his desk and a computer, he had a bank of security monitors which shared a feed with the ones in the main house. A specialized app made by a genius ensured Damien and

Gregorio were able to access every camera from their phones and watches.

Since everything was calm for now, he headed for the bathroom, ripped off the bandage, gave his wound a cursory glance—he'd probably pull out the stitches tomorrow, and have another scar to add to his collection—then took a quick, cool shower.

After toweling off, he slapped on fresh gauze and tape before dressing in his usual attire.

The moment his boots were on, his watch vibrated.

He touched a blinking icon. The catering service was at the gate.

Right on time.

He buzzed them through.

Their van was quickly followed by a shiny, oversize truck towing a trailer bearing a nearly full-size image of singing sensation Zephyr 'Zeph' Rockwell.

Unfortunately, this was likely the star's last appearance here.

With Zeph's meteoric rise to success, a tour bus was in his imminent future. Maybe as soon as next summer, he'd be a headliner, looking for bands to open for him.

After closing his front door and setting the alarm, Gregorio headed for the Den to open up.

For the next couple of hours, the Den—one of Colorado's premier BDSM clubs—was a beehive of activity.

Countless small details went on behind the scenes to ensure guests and members were able to focus on their experience without anything dragging them out of the world Damien had masterfully created.

On the main level, a check-in table had been set up, and Lillith—a fairly new house sub—was preparing for the first arrivals. She'd set up two electronic tablets and organized wristbands which would be assigned according to the role each attendee was assuming for the event—Top, bottom, house submissive, and more. Additionally, several House Monitor armbands were also stacked nearby.

"Going to be a busy evening," he observed.

"We're as ready as we can be." She nodded. "Susan will be here soon to help. And luckily Master Niles and Brandy already checked in the ladies who attended their event. All we'll have to do is assign wristbands."

Good plan since all the people would arrive at once, on the same shuttle bus.

Next, he greeted the woman in charge of the coatroom and ensured the valet stand was in place with extra personnel on hand.

Satisfied, he continued to assess progress.

Three bars had already been erected—one on the main level, another on the patio, and the final downstairs, near the dungeon.

The one outside had several blenders in place where frothy mocktails could be concocted.

Nearby, Zeph's bandmembers tuned up, though the man himself hadn't yet made an appearance. Planning a special entrance?

The catering staff began uncovering platters of small desserts, including chocolate-covered cheesecake on a stick.

Looking at the sweets for too long would result in a cavity, he was sure.

Satisfied everything was under control, he headed upstairs to a private area—the Den's unseen hub of security.

There, he had an office of his own, as did Damien and Catrina—for the rare occasions the couple visited the club.

On a monitor, the owner himself keyed the gate open.

"Well, well."

Less than five minutes later, Damien climbed the stairs to join Gregorio.

"Boss." They shook hands. "Surprised to see you here."

"Catrina is at a conference."

Explains a lot.

A lifetime ago, Gregorio had been married. Maybe he still would be if he'd paid half the attention to his wife as Damien did to Catrina. "When is she back?"

"Monday night."

By unspoken accord, they moved into Damien's office.

"Whiskey?" Damien offered. "Cheap-ass owner of the company finally sent me a bottle."

Gregorio schooled his face. Cheap-ass Damien could afford as much of the world-renowned single malt as he wanted. Maybe that hadn't been true for a time, but Damien had pulled himself back from beyond the brink of disaster to reach even higher levels of success, something Gregorio admired.

"Thanks." He shook his head. "No." Because he wasn't a cheap-ass, Gregorio had his own bottle of the limited release in his cottage.

Sometimes the fine distillate was the only thing that got him through the night, but because he wanted to be as sharp as possible, he never drank while on duty.

Damien nodded. "Don't mind if I do."

He pulled out the exquisite bottle and a glass, then measured out a couple of fingers. Drink in hand, he took a seat behind his desk and leaned back. "Update me."

Gregorio dropped into a nearby chair.

Because Damien had been busy, they'd missed their last couple of weekly meetings, which likely said something about how much he trusted his second in command to keep things running smoothly, confidence Gregorio appreciated. "First cabin was finished this week."

Damien lifted his glass in Gregorio's direction. "Ahead of schedule."

"Ready for your inspection." The designer would be adding final soft touches in the coming days.

Plans to expand the property and add more amenities had been underway for years. Focused on that goal, Damien had methodically acquired adjoining pieces of land.

Not only did he plan on maintaining the Den's status as the premier BDSM club in a five-state region, but soon members would be able to stay overnight instead of being shuttled back and forth to Winter Park.

"Bunkhouse is almost done." And it was looking good. "The hall should be finished within the month."

"Impressive."

The gathering space with a full chef's kitchen would be an ideal setting for weddings, collaring ceremonies, special events, parties, maybe even slave auctions.

Which meant Gregorio would be assuming a bigger role, but he wasn't always around to fill it.

Recently they'd hired Ryder Wolfe, a young Dominant who'd turned out to be a great asset, even if he was too damn cocky for Gregorio's tastes.

As if following the direction of his thoughts, Damien asked, "How's the pup doing?"

"You mean the internet sensation?"

Damien sipped his beverage.

A BDSM video production company filmed at the Den, and Wolfe was their new super star. The videos he appeared in had more downloads than almost all of the other talent combined.

No doubt the Dom was part of the reason this ladies' night had sold out.

But Gregorio wasn't complaining.

The production company had just signed a new contract, booking additional days every month. As a result, he'd bumped the fee substantially. Wolfe's appeal was putting cash in everyone's pocket, which had been part of the reason they were able to speed up development of the rest of the property. "He'll be doing a demo with Lillith."

The woman was beautiful and willowy. He'd watched Wolfe interact with professional submissives in videos. Even though Lillith was not an actress or model, the pair promised to make a captivating team.

Beauty and elegance were secondary, however, to safety.

"I'll look forward to being in the audience."

Damien was a gifted teacher whose classes were legend in BDSM circles. "Unless you'd like to do it yourself, since you're here?"

"Not tonight." Damien shook his head.

Respecting your relationship with your wife-to-be? Of course, with how much the two were in love, they didn't have eyes for anyone else. Gregorio respected that. And he fought back the uncomfortable nudge of jealousy that told him he might have had something similar. If— He shook off the uncomfortable intrusion. "Want a tour of the cabin while it's still light?"

Damien nodded.

Since the man was on the hook for well over a cool million in construction loans, he deserved the opportunity to see the building before anyone else.

Damien's phone chimed. "Excuse me."

While he checked it, Gregorio scanned the monitors, then strode to the window.

A couple of very high snow flurries swirled in the wind. There'd be no measurable precipitation from the small flakes, even if they made it to the ground.

But the dancing crystals whispered winter was on its way. Short days and endless nights suited him fine.

"Ready?"

Nodding, Gregorio turned.

Slipping his phone into a pocket, Damien stood.

The two walked toward what had once been the western perimeter of the property.

A temporary privacy fence was in place to prevent construction from interfering with views from the Den.

They walked through a gate, and Gregorio pulled it shut behind them.

"Bunkhouse is farther along than I expected."

"I want the crew to be able to use it so work can continue through the winter."

Damien nodded. "Good plan."

With how remote the Den was, and the lack of access to paved roads, getting contractors from town could be a challenge. Offering housing was a bonus.

Next they toured the completed cabin.

The log structure had been decorated in rich, earthy colors.

A sturdy O-ring was attached to an overhead beam, and apparatus had been screwed into the walls making the place a BDSM-lovers paradise. The bed's posters were perfect for securing a sub, and the rustic, hand-carved wardrobe was stocked with luxury toys, all crafted by Master Marcus.

The bathroom was spa-like, and the kitchen was well-equipped. "Still a few finishing touches needed."

Including towels, pots, pans, coffeemaker, candles, and a couple of throw rugs that were still on backorder.

"You're welcome to move in here," Damien offered.

Gregorio shrugged. "Happy where I am." He lacked the time and energy for anything other than basic necessities. In a perfect world, he'd be able to load his oversize SUV and walk away from his life in under ten minutes.

"Offer stands, if you change your mind."

I won't. He nodded politely. "If you remember, this was supposed to be the owner's cottage," Gregorio reminded his boss. Which would give him and Catrina more privacy when they were in attendance.

"I can always make a reservation."

For now, Damien still kept an apartment at the Den. But there had been discussion about turning the set of rooms over to Wolfe.

Gregorio's watch vibrated, and he checked the gate. *Speak of the devil.* "And he's here." Earlier than expected, which was a point in his favor.

As they approached the Den, Wolfe braked, bringing his black SUV to a stop in front of the valet stand.

He emerged, then jogged over to join them.

"Understand you're doing a demonstration tonight," Damien said, shaking the man's hand.

"Gregorio warned me he'll be watching." Wolfe gave a quick smile. "I have big shoes to fill."

Gregorio all but snarled. "You won't be filling Damien's shoes. No one can."

Chastened, Wolfe nodded. "No offense meant, sir," he said to Damien.

"None taken." He studied the apprentice. "Bring your unique approach to the evening. I'm looking forward to watching."

The boss was far more generous than Gregorio.

Once they were all inside, Wolfe headed for the dressing room, and Gregorio watched him go.

"He'll be okay," Damien said. "Reminds me a little of myself at that age."

"Wolfe is nothing like you, boss." Then he excused himself. "I'll make my rounds." He started to walk away, only to be stopped by the quietness of Damien's voice.

"Do you need some time off?"

With a furious scowl, he turned back to face his friend. "The fuck you talking about?"

"You got injured again."

Damien knew him too well for Gregorio to attempt to deny the truth.

He'd been convinced he was disguising his limp, but obviously he was wrong. "Should see the other guy." Not that there was anything left of him.

"It's no hardship for me to step in. A week, a month." Damien shrugged. "Take some time off."

If he didn't keep moving, soul-sucking remorse for his life choices would drop Gregorio to his knees.

"At least consider taking tonight off," Damien suggested. "I'm here and, frankly, looking for something to do."

"Appreciate the offer."

Damien held up a hand. "I'll say no more."

As long as there was breath in his body, Gregorio would not abdicate his duties. "See you around."

Each man went their separate ways.

Restless, Gregorio headed back to the dungeon.

If he was smart, he'd find a sub to play with later.

Or he'd bare his back for a thrashing that would take him out of his own head. On occasion, for the right Top, he'd be a bottom. With the way he lived his life, he sometimes craved release and that was one way to find it.

Another was by totally being in the moment with the right submissive.

Focusing on the job at hand, he checked the private rooms. In addition to being sparkling clean, they'd been stocked with water and sanitizing wipes.

Since there was nothing else to be done here, he headed back upstairs and outside onto the patio.

Zeph's crew was ready with a stage and impressive backdrop.

Tall, round tables had been draped in white, and caterers had even added candles. Battery-operated, it appeared.

Ten minutes before seven, he lit the firepits and gas heaters.

Then the first guests arrived.

Within an hour, the place was filling up.

Zeph took the stage, glimmering in the spotlight.

Along with a couple of House Monitors, Gregorio kept an eye on the action in the private rooms, and he stopped to answer questions from a couple who were new to the club.

Back upstairs in command central, Damien was nowhere to be seen, so Gregorio scanned the monitors.

The bus carrying Master Niles and Brandy, along with the first timers who'd met in Winter Park, lumbered through the entrance.

Since two people were at the check-in desk, his help wasn't needed—at least not right away.

One guest paused at the entrance.

Others were paired up, chatting, but she was alone, and she looked around, scanning her surroundings before glancing overhead.

She looked straight into a camera at him, her shockingly emerald-colored eyes wide and unblinking.

No one else had eyes that color.

Sasha.

Petal.

My Petal.

The only woman on the planet off limits to him.

The one woman who haunted his nights.

Playing with her that night at Leah and Jon's wedding had been the biggest mistake of his life.

Forbidden fruit.

Once he'd skimmed his work-calloused fingers over her silky skin, tasted her desire, inhaled the jasmine-scented promise of hope, listened to her tiny whimpers as she begged for him…

He'd fucking become obsessed.

To protect her—and save himself—he'd had to walk away. And stay away.

Otherwise he'd have yielded to his baser nature and claimed her forever.

Gregorio knew one thing for certain. Sasha was too good of a person for someone like him.

He'd killed without compunction—recently, even—and considered it a good night's work.

And that night at the wedding, he'd taught Tristan a lesson he wouldn't soon forget. Pretty boy would be minding his manners around Petal in the future.

Before he'd walked off, Gregorio had suggested the man catch a ride to the emergency room since he wasn't fit to drive himself.

That was the kind of man Gregorio was. And Sasha deserved happily ever after with a man who would come home at night.

He should find a House Monitor, maybe Wolfe, and have his former sister-in-law's curvy derrière put right back on a bus and hauled back to Winter Park. Where she was safe from men like Gregorio.

For a moment it seemed she willed him to make eye contact.

As if he could look away.

What in the fuck are you doing here, Petal?

With a tiny shrug, she severed the connection she couldn't possibly have known they'd shared.

Moments later, she selected a white band.

White?

The actual hell?

Scowling, Gregorio folded his arms. She was here as a submissive?

She wanted to be dominated?

Anger, hot and molten, seeped through him, picking up speed.

No fucking way, Petal.

No man is touching you. Except for me…

Chapter Three

"Don't scare the 'nillas."

Now that she was at the Den, Sasha realized the word actually referred to her. And if she were honest with herself, she'd admit she was plenty scared.

Though Brandy and Master Niles had been welcoming and casual, Sasha was still unnerved.

Knowing she would soon see Gregorio only added to the uncertainty chugging through her veins.

The white band settled around her wrist, and she traced the symbol that signaled that she was a submissive and available.

If Gregorio was here, that would get his attention...unless he'd stopped caring since she'd last seen him, three years ago at Leah's wedding.

"And before I can let you inside, I just need to be sure that you're familiar with the club's safe word," Lillith said.

She appreciated the attention to safety and consensual play. "Halt."

"Enjoy your visit."

"Thank you." Clutching her duffel bag, Sasha walked past the check-in table and entered what appeared to be the main floor of a spectacular, large mountain home.

In a sweeping glance she took in everything she could immediately see. Living room, kitchen, dining room—including tables laden with all kinds of miniature desserts and salty snacks. Near that was a makeshift bar that she'd been informed served up nothing stronger than sugar and caffeine.

Dozens of people filled the spaces, all in various stages of undress. She had to give it to the clerk at the novelty store. Even though her tiny two-piece outfit scandalized her, no one here even gave her a second glance.

Brandy stood near a stairway, and Sasha made up an excuse to see her.

In reality, she wanted to see the second level.

As she neared, she noted an open door with a light on. Maybe a bathroom? But there was another door past it, blocking her. Private area for the owner and Gregorio? *Is that where you are? Are you watching me?*

When she'd checked in, she'd stared straight into the security camera.

She'd connected with Gregorio—instinct told her that, even if she had no way of actually confirming it.

Drawing her eyebrows together, pretending to be a little lost, she asked Brandy, "Can you point me in the direction of the locker room?"

"As long as you promise you won't hide in there all night," Brandy teased.

She winced. "Am I that obvious?"

"Believe me, I totally understand. I was a bundle of nerves the first time I attended."

Skeptically, Sasha raised an eyebrow. Brandy seemed so controlled, and she was both classy and poised.

"I swear. I was so nervous, tripping over my tongue as well as my feet." Then, reassuringly, she added, "If I can do it, you can do it."

Sasha appreciated the pep talk. But if Brandy had any idea why Sasha was really here, she would never have been allowed to walk through the door.

"I'm here all night if you need a friend."

"Thank you." Sasha forced a small smile. "I appreciate that."

"Jeff runs multiple shuttles back to town. And the shuttle is on a loop. If you want to leave at any point, just let the valet know."

"You think of everything."

"Honestly, I'm a bit of an introvert. I love spending time at home with my menagerie." She shrugged. "So I understand being more comfortable if there's an escape plan."

Sasha never entered a place without noting all the ways she could get away, in case things went horrifically wrong. More than once, they had.

"Locker room's that way." Brandy pointed. "Remember to enjoy yourself. This is supposed to be fun."

Fun wasn't the word she'd use. "Thanks again."

As she turned to walk away, Brandy's voice stopped Sasha.

"And Petal?"

She glanced over her shoulder. Again she wondered what had possessed her to use that as a scene name.

"Chocolate helps."

This time she smiled. "That definitely couldn't hurt."

After finding the locker room, she stashed her gear and double-checked that her outfit was still covering her naughty parts. Then she checked her makeup.

When she smoothed her hair, she realized Brandy had been right. Sasha was stalling, something unusual, even when she was in a new situation.

Slowly, she clenched and unclenched her fists before pushing through the exit.

Rock music thumped erotically in the air.

Erotically?

Shaking her head, she shoved the fanciful thought aside. She was only here to get Gregorio's help.

She wandered through the house, resisting the petit fours as she exited onto the back patio.

Why haven't you found me yet?

Even though the calendar said it was the end of summer, a chill blanketed the night.

Needing something to occupy her hands, she crossed to the bar and scanned the menu. All the drink names were creative, making her smile, helping her to relax.

"What'll it be?" the woman behind the bar asked.

Sasha wrinkled her nose. "I can't decide. Something…" Her gaze landed on the Safe Word. It had blood orange and other juices, along with coconut cream. "Sounds a little like a piña colada." She pointed to the description. "But different." *Better?*

"With a spicy kick."

Spicy. That certainly fit the vibe of the evening.

The glass was supposedly rimmed with a blend of cayenne pepper and sugar.

"Sure you can handle it?"

Feeling like the question was a bit of a challenge, she grinned. She was already here, out of her comfort zone. Why not go all the way? "Bring it on."

When the bartender was done mixing the beverage, she added an orange slice and a tiny red pepper as a garnish.

"If it's too much, you can always use your safe word, and I'll make you something else."

Wrinkling her nose, a little nervous, she licked the rim. A shiver went through her.

The bartender grinned.

I can do this.

Her first taste was a wicked contradiction—silky, yet with an afterbite, making a slow heat curl at the back of her throat.

"What do you think?"

"Damn."

"Is that good or bad?"

"Amazing." Her lips tingled. The only thing that could make it better was a couple of shots of rum...*served by a man with a dangerous smile and a voice that whispered promises that had haunted her for years.*

"You *are* brave." The woman moved off to help others.

After another sip to fortify herself, Sasha glanced around. Thankfully she recognized a couple of women she'd met earlier in Winter Park, and she walked across the patio to join them.

"Isn't he dreamy?" one of them asked, referring to Zeph Rockwell.

He was talented, for sure. And if she were attracted to blond-headed men with crooning voices and gyrating hips, she'd be gaga like everyone else.

Unfortunately for her, she only had eyes for a Mediterranean god with a shaved head and dark, haunted eyes.

A gust of wind hit her.

"Brr!" one of the women said.

The group of them hurried toward one of the firepits to warm up.

When the conversation turned toward which Dom they each wanted to play with, she suddenly became the fifth wheel.

After listening for a few minutes, she gave a polite smile and excused herself. Near the house, she glanced around one more time. The man she wanted to see was definitely not around.

Why hadn't he made a move? Gregorio had to know she was here.

A thousand times, she'd gone over tonight's plan. But it never occurred to her that Gregorio would ignore her.

Maybe he was just busy?

Or perhaps he wasn't here after all. That thought, she dismissed. She *knew* they'd connected earlier.

She went back inside and double-checked each room.

With a sigh, she put down her empty glass on a tray.

The only place she hadn't looked was the dungeon. Dare she go down there?

After swallowing her fear, she gripped the banister and began to descend the staircase.

With each step, the atmosphere became more and more charged with tension.

Different music thumped here, the tones deeper, resonate, more primal than she'd experienced before.

Goose bumps traced up her bare arms.

Needing to steady her nerves, she paused at the bottom before venturing on.

A bar was in a far corner, along with several tables.

An open area was filled with couples, threesomes, even moresomes.

Nearby, a woman was on her knees, chained to the wall. Though her head was bowed, she occasionally glanced up at the tall man standing near her, an expression of adoration on her face. Other than that, she was beautifully still, in a way Sasha wasn't sure she'd ever experienced or was capable of.

Farther into the dungeon, before reaching the private rooms, a submissive lay on her back, her thighs parted, her hands beneath her buttocks. She wore a blindfold, a thong, and pasties with black tassels.

A man was knelt between her legs, and he talked to her soothingly as he kept a large, plugged-in vibrator pressed against her clit.

The sub whimpered and begged, but her Top was relentless, driving her to orgasm after orgasm.

Other than the amazing time she'd had in the janitor's closet, Sasha had never experienced anything like that.

Reeling from everything she was seeing and hearing, she moved down the hallway and lifted onto her tiptoes to peer inside one of the private rooms where a Top had his bottom bent over a desk.

She was dressed as a schoolgirl, complete with knee socks and a short skirt that was flipped up to her waist. Her face was turned toward the window, making it possible for Sasha to see the tears streaking down the woman's cheeks.

Her Top held a wicked-looking ruler in hand, and he was bouncing it off her buttocks.

Still, the woman wasn't tied or secured in any way. Which meant she was a willing participant.

Part of Sasha longed to run away, go outside and drink in a breath of fresh air, but instead, she remained where she was, transfixed.

The man pulled down the woman's panties, exposing her already reddened bottom.

And the sight aroused Sasha.

Frantically, she shook her head at the realization. No way could the idea of a spanking be turning her on. *No way.*

Inside the room, the Top trailed his fingers down the woman's spine before moving to one side to swipe her bare ass once more with the piece of wood.

In commiseration, Sasha winced.

The woman lifted a single finger. When the Top repeated his stroke, slightly lower on her butt, the woman raised a second finger, counting out her spanks.

How many more did she have to take?

Suddenly, the air around her crackled as if electrified, and Sasha froze.

He was near.

The unmistakable scent of him—power and confidence mixed with masculine spice—surrounded her. An involuntary and undeniably feminine response crashed through her, making her knees weak.

The frantic flutter of her heart warned she was in danger. Not physical, but far, far worse. Emotionally.

She drew on her inner resources to protect her emotions from the man standing behind her.

Suddenly, his hands—strong and unyielding—clamped on her shoulders.

Against her ear, his voice flat with steely calm, he said, "You don't belong here."

Chapter Four

His voice…

Awareness skittered through her, igniting her nerve endings.

Suddenly she remembered the gruff notice in his tone that night when he'd ordered her to do all those wicked things.

As soon as she'd been able to escape from the wedding, she'd gone back to her hotel room and taken care of herself in the shower.

That had only taken the edge off long enough for her to get into her bed…where she'd brought herself off the second time.

Even that hadn't diminished her craving to have Gregorio fill, stretch her, claim her completely.

"You need to leave."

"Still trying to tell me what to do?" Last time they'd been together, she'd done everything he ordered. In retrospect, it scared her how willing she'd been to turn over control to him.

"I don't recall you objecting."

A shudder rippled through her and his knowing laugh proved he'd felt it as well.

"Why are you here, Petal?"

She longed to turn and face him, but he held her prisoner, forcing her to watch the scene.

In front of them, the Top dipped his fingers between the bottom's thighs.

Even through the door, the man's words rang clear. "You're wet."

How is that possible?

That ruler had to hurt, and the nasty red welts on her ass proved it.

The Top tossed the ruler to the side, and it clattered onto the desk near the submissive's head.

Were they done?

Thank God. Maybe now she could deal with Gregorio.

But he didn't release her.

As she watched, Top stepped back to unbuckle his belt. Sasha told herself she didn't want to watch—simultaneously, she couldn't force herself to look away.

When she'd decided to come here tonight, it had been for one purpose only. To find Gregorio. She'd never expected to be captivated by everything that was happening.

"I'm waiting for your answer. Why are you here, Petal?" Gregorio's warm breath was on her, making her shiver with anticipation. "Did you come to bare your ass so I can give you the spanking you want?"

"No." Frantically she shook her head.

"That's what your wristband says."

She closed her eyes against the hot rush of anticipation that flooded through her.

"Or is it the service part of BDSM that interests you? Perhaps you enjoy doing little things for your Top?" he suggested softly. "Scrubbing his back in the bathtub? Stroking him off in the shower?"

God no. She'd never done any of those things, had never wanted to, and suddenly images of her doing what he suggested blazed through her mind.

But it wasn't for just any man.

Only him. Only Gregorio.

"You were studying the submissive you saw out there in the dungeon. The one who was kneeling, chained to the wall, waiting for scraps of attention from her Master."

So he had been watching her.

"Would being required to do something like that make you happy?"

Scandalized, she gasped. "No." *Not ever.*

"We could go back and watch them for a few minutes."

She tried to shake her head, but his words held her immobile.

"He loves running his hand down the back of her head, cradling it."

Sasha told herself to end this conversation, right this moment.

"Then he'll turn to her and lower his zipper."

A shiver ran through her.

"He'll stuff his cock down her throat, gagging her, enjoying the fact tears are streaming down her face while he carries on a conversation with someone else."

His words turned her insides molten, and she hated that.

Sasha reminded herself that she knew the club's safe word. And Gregorio was the Den's biggest enforcer.

If she even breathed it, he would take his hands off her and step back.

Yet no matter how dangerous he was, she hadn't felt this safe in a very long time. She needed to be this close to him.

Inside the room, the Top blazed the schoolgirl's behind with the belt that was no doubt warm from his body.

Shocking her, the woman didn't struggle at all. In fact, the harder he wielded it, the more relaxed she seemed to become.

"Your first visit to a club, Petal?"

Of course not. Fast and furious, the lie sprang to her lips. But she held it back. He would see through it and no doubt raise the stakes.

Is that what I want?

"She's a pain slut."

"A what?"

"The more she gets, the more she wants. Which is why I'm glad she is paired with Master Dimitri. He will set limits where she would not. He knows what she can endure better than she does."

After several more strokes, the belt clattered onto the table next to the ruler.

The Top—Master Dimitri—crossed to the wall and returned with a long, thin strip of rattan.

A cane?

Half a dozen times, he bounced it off her flesh like he had with the ruler, lightly teasing, taunting.

Through the door, the whoosh from the implement knocked the air from Sasha's lungs.

"That's okay here?" she asked Gregorio around the knot in her throat.

"I'm watching. They've been coming here for a very long time." He paused. "Too extreme for you?"

"Some of this looks interesting. But this…?" She shuddered.

"Guessing you're not a pain slut?"

That much, she was certain of. "Absolutely not."

Methodically, the Top marked the bottom, starting just above the backs of her knees and working his way up.

A few times, the woman moaned. But she continually pressed her hips back. Asking for an orgasm? For harder strokes?

Gregorio might be right. This wasn't a place she belonged.

As if reading her thoughts, he asked, "I'll repeat myself a final time, Petal. Why are you here?"

"I was looking for you."

Finally, he loosened his grip, and she turned to face him.

Breath left her body.

She thought she'd been prepared to see him. After all, the wedding reception had been a very long time ago, long enough to get over her physical reaction to him.

But the truth was, a lifetime wouldn't be long enough.

As always, he was dressed in his signature all black clothes, but he seemed different…broader, more muscular.

His normally sun-kissed skin was darker than she remembered, as if he'd spent time beneath the torturous sun. Up here in the mountains? Or somewhere else?

He was as shockingly gorgeous as always—maybe even more so—with his single diamond earring catching the light.

At one time, he'd worn a veneer of civility, but it was gone, and she barely recognized him as the brother-in-law he'd once been.

As she looked closer, she noticed his cheekbones were even more finely chiseled, and his jawline seemed sharper. Subtle lines were grooved next to his dark, wary eyes. Their depths appeared haunted, as if he'd seen something awful in the intervening years.

What happened to you, Gregorio?

And why did she ache to soothe the pain from his features?

"Petal?"

His hands were still on her, but the way he lifted one eyebrow penetrated the haze he'd wrapped her in. "I need help."

Tightly, he nodded. "You've got it."

Until that moment she had not been one hundred percent certain what his reaction would be when he saw her.

But he didn't ask what she needed help with. He automatically agreed.

Every part of her knew she had made the right choice in coming to him.

"I'll get Wolfe to cover so we can talk in private."

"Thank you." His help might come with a cost, but whatever price he demanded, she'd pay.

As they made their way through the dungeon, a couple of people stopped him to talk. He did not introduce her. Though it was completely against her normal nature, she remained where she was, not drawing attention to herself, even though several members shot her some curious glances.

The submissive that Gregorio had referred to was still chained in place, and she appeared just as serene as she had been earlier.

The Top turned to her and snapped his fingers.

With the small, satisfied smile, she knelt up and opened her mouth as she tucked her hands behind her neck.

This cannot be happening.

But as he lowered his zipper and fed his cockhead between her lips, she opened her mouth even wider.

Wave after wave of awareness crashed through Sasha.

As Gregorio had said, the Top continued his conversation with a woman whose bottom was attached to her leash.

She'd leapt into an alternate universe.

Would she wake up at home in the morning to find this had been nothing more than a terrible, erotic dream?

"Petal?"

The shortness in Gregorio's voice jolted her from her thoughts. Evidently, he'd spoken to her more than once.

"Shall I put you on a leash, my Petal?"

Yes.

No. No, no, no, no, no. She couldn't imagine anything more horrific.

Dragging her gaze from the erotic scene in front of her, she frantically shook her head, her hair cascading over her shoulders.

"In that case…" He angled his head toward the exit.

Obediently, silently, she followed, reassuring herself she was not behaving like a submissive.

On the Den's main level, he asked her to wait while he talked to Wolfe.

With a nod, she watched the check-in desk and people interacting in the living room.

Less than two minutes later, he rejoined her, possessively placing a hand on her lower back like he had that night at the wedding as he guided her toward the staircase.

"Gregorio."

A man, tall, also in black, long, sleek hair held back with a thin strip of leather, stepped in front of them.

"Boss."

Damien, she guessed. The club's owner.

He was classically handsome, with an air of confidence and charisma. His piercing eyes held a depth that hinted at untold secrets, and he seemed to see right into her.

She imagined the two formed a powerful alliance.

"You heading up?" Damien asked.

Gregorio nodded.

"Unusual."

"It is."

"And you are?" Damien prompted when Gregorio didn't perform the introduction.

"Petal," Gregorio said.

At the exact moment, she supplied, "Sasha."

"I see."

Judging by the way he scowled and looked at Damien, she wondered if he truly did.

Had Gregorio mentioned her?

The thought was wild, absurd, and she shook her head to clear it. She didn't mean anything to him.

"Are you consenting to be alone with Gregorio"—he looked between the two of them—"Petal?"

She appreciated him honoring her anonymity.

"There are no cameras in the offices," he went on. "No one to check on you."

Brandy and Master Niles had obviously meant it when they said the club looked out for all members. That even seemed to apply to the owner's second in command.

"She's fine," Gregorio snapped.

Damien raised a hand. "I'm speaking to Petal."

She met his gaze. "In answer to your question, yes. I was hoping for a word with Gregorio."

"I'll give you fifteen minutes."

Gregorio opened his mouth as if to object, but Damien smoothly said, "Seems to me someone even looked out for Catrina."

Gregorio angled his head to the side. A warning tic flickered in his temple. "Acknowledged," he said tightly.

Who was Catrina? Someone special to Damien? Regardless, Damien's pointed words evidently had meaning to Gregorio.

Apparently satisfied, Damien stepped to one side.

As she passed, he nodded. "Petal."

"Sir." *Is that what I'm supposed to say?* The word had fallen out easily, almost automatically, shocking her.

Upstairs, they passed a couple of powder rooms, and he continued to a door set at an angle to block anyone from going farther.

He touched a few keys on the wall, and a lock released.

After pressing down on the handle, he ushered her inside.

She'd stepped into yet another world, this one crafted of thick glass walls and masculine furnishings, along with banks of monitors with security feeds showing every bit of the club, from the dungeon to the patio, even as far away as the entrance to the property and the main road beyond it.

Here, surrounded by technology, she was comfortable. Now that she was on familiar ground, she could breathe more easily.

Gregorio took a seat behind a large, sturdy wooden desk that had a computer on it and nothing else. No snapshots, no pens, nothing to mark it as his.

With a nod, he invited her to sit across from him. But she preferred to remain standing.

"You went to a lot of effort to find me."

The task hadn't been easy. "Called in some favors."

Like him, she wouldn't reveal sources. To his credit, he didn't ask.

Gregorio leaned back in his chair, the dim light casting shadows across his features, making him look intimidating.

She shivered, glad he was an ally rather than an enemy.

"I'm waiting."

His gaze was fixed on her with an intensity that made her skin prickle.

Taking a deep breath, Sasha steeled herself for what she had to say next. "Strange things have been happening recently."

"Such as?"

"About two weeks ago, while I was out for a run, my home office was ransacked, and several files were taken. A few days ago, I noticed I have a constant tail. I can't always shake it. Black sedan. Sometimes a white SUV."

"Anything else?"

This unnerved her more than anything. "Before leaving the office every day, I rinse my coffee mug." One that Toby had bought for her to celebrate the grand opening of their agency almost three years ago. Her name was in green—the color of money—along with their company logo. "I leave it next to sink, right by the coffeemaker."

He nodded.

"Monday and Wednesday, I found it in the middle of my desk."

"That sounds personal."

Which was exactly what she thought.

Gregorio didn't ask if she'd been confused. He knew her too well for that. But that wasn't all. Her pictures had been rearranged, and one had been turned backward.

"No signs of a break-in?"

She shook her head. "Nothing on security cameras." With an exhalation, she went on before he asked. "We're old-fashioned. Regular keys for entry."

"No extra copies floating around? A disgruntled employee, maybe?"

"I change the locks when someone leaves the company."

His jaw clenched as he processed her words. "Keypad or card swipe is more secure. I'll have Hawkeye see to it."

"I'm a step ahead of you. I've already contacted them, and I'm also having them install an alarm system."

"Were you followed today?"

"No. The drive to Winter Park is so long that I would have noticed if I had a tail."

He nodded.

"When I rode the shuttle up here, I sat in the back to ensure no one was behind us."

"Smart."

"Still..." Her voice faltered, revealing her vulnerability. Now that she'd said it aloud, the walls seemed to close in around her.

Sasha had been in war zones, served on protective details, and she could handle herself. But now that she and Toby were no longer partners, she didn't have anyone to back her up—not that he'd actually been on her side. The illusion that she could count on someone other than herself was just that. A fantasy. "Honestly, Gregorio?" She folded her arms across her midriff. "You're the only one I trust."

"Who else knows you're here?"

"No one." She shook her head. "I kept it off my schedule." *Just to be safe.*

"You think this is related to a current case?"

"That's the only thing that makes sense." Since the drama surrounding the dissolution of her partnership with Toby, her personal life had become dull and boring.

"Anything stand out?"

"Only the Santos investigation." Everything else the firm was dealing with was straightforward. "Mrs. Santos—Brenda—suspects her husband of infidelity."

Palms pressed together, Gregorio leaned forward. "And?"

"Surveillance shows he's not cheating." She shrugged.

"But?"

His perception didn't surprise her. "Felix is definitely hiding something. Has secretive conversations in people's cars. Takes a lot of phone calls outdoors." Talking this through helped her relax, feel more in control. "He owns several businesses...nightclubs, a restaurant, a coffee shop, but the couple appear to be having financial issues. A couple of days ago, he bought his wife a brand-new vehicle, and paid cash, from what I can find. According to Mrs. Santos, they don't have that kind of money. She had to get a loan from her sister to hire me."

"That's one of the missing files?"

She nodded.

"What are the others?"

Though he didn't take notes as she gave him the information, she knew he was cataloguing every detail. "Anything else I should know?"

"No." Sasha shook her head. "I have another meeting with Mrs. Santos on Monday morning to go over what I've learned."

With a tight nod, he said, "Tell me about your business. Employees. How long they've been with you. Anyone you've had to fire or let go of?"

"We've been relatively stable." Or at least since she'd managed to get Toby out of her life. "Pathways is a small firm. Besides me, there are three other investigators, and we have an office manager."

He frowned. "I thought you had a partner."

So he'd kept up with her since she saw him last? Surprised—in a good way—she answered, "Past tense. Ended a little over a year ago."

"Any hard feelings?"

"Shouldn't be." Unease traced across her shoulders, making her shrug. "Maybe." At the time they'd started their own agency, she'd thought she knew him. But crossing ethical lines wasn't something she was willing to do. They'd had a heated argument, and it had ended with him storming out of the building. "He came out the winner. Cost me every last cent I had to buy him out." Even though she was working harder than ever to make the business a success and pay bills, keeping her integrity had been worth it.

"Give me his full name."

When she did, he scowled. "The same Toby who worked for Hawkeye?"

The same company where Gregorio had gotten her a job. "That's where we met." She shrugged. "He was my boss."

Gregorio fell silent for a few moments, then asked for the names of everyone associated with her firm.

"I don't think—"

"Things have happened in the office that don't make sense," he reminded her. "And you've seen nothing on the building's surveillance cameras." He continued to regard her. "That would seem to indicate an inside job."

"But why?" She frowned. "We're a close team, and we all like working with each other. That just doesn't make sense."

"Unless it's someone close to you who knows how to get around your security measures."

The only one that could apply to was Toby. But why, after this long?

Gregorio lifted a shoulder. "I am serious about this. Give me the names of your employees."

Hating that he was right, she scribbled down the list.

With a tight nod, he told her, "Coming here...you made the right decision."

She exhaled. What other option was available? She was too close to the situation to see all the nuances. The fact she pushed back when he wanted the names of everyone at Pathways proved that.

Abruptly, Gregorio stood, his chair scraping back against the floor. He moved around the desk, closing the distance between them in a few powerful strides.

He pulled her to her feet, his hands firm on her shoulders, overwhelming her. "You'll be staying the night with me."

Shocked, she blinked.

Absolutely not.

She wasn't sure what she'd expected, but his reaction wasn't it. "That's not necessary. I have a room in Winter Park." She shook her head. "I'll be fine there. All I need is someone to bounce my ideas off, come up with a plan, see what I'm missing. Maybe we can have breakfast in the morning to discuss this further and I can pick your mind, see what I'm—"

"You came to me, Petal." His grip tightened, not a lot, but with determined intent. "That puts you in my world and makes you my responsibility. Tomorrow, I'll take you back to your room."

"But... No." Sasha shook her head. "My luggage is there, and I need my gear."

"Such as?"

"All the things." In frustration, she sighed. "Something to sleep in."

A hint of a smile played around his lips. "Naked is fine."

She opened her mouth, but no words emerged. His words were a dream, an impossibility.

"Or you can borrow one of my T-shirts."

So he'd been kidding about wanting her naked. She should have guessed that. "I also need girl stuff. Makeup, soap. Shampoo. Brush." *And I need to be away from you for my sanity.*

"We'll go in the morning." His voice was ice, implacable.

Resolutely, he folded his arms across his chest.

"Gregorio—"

He silenced her with a kiss that was so hard and deep he bruised her mouth and left the room spinning.

"My way, Petal. Or no fucking way at all." Then he folded his arms across his chest and studied her hard. "What will it be?"

Chapter Five

Like it always is.

Reeling from the unexpected kiss and his insistence that she stay with him, Sasha struggled to regain her composure. Before she could formulate a response, a knock on the door jarred her.

Gregorio released her and stepped back, putting some much-needed distance between them right as the knob turned. His touch, his possession, was overwhelming.

Damien entered the office. In an instant, he took in the scene before him. Studying them intently, he asked, "Everything all right in here?"

"Fine," Gregorio replied tersely.

Had the kiss affected him? Or was it a meaningless, yet effective way of making a point?

"I'll be off duty for the rest of the night," Gregorio said, voice flat. "I hate to ask, but I'm going to need you to fill in. Have something important to take care of."

"I see." Damien's gaze flicked to Sasha briefly before returning to Gregorio. "Anything you want to tell me?" His tone made it clear it was not really a question.

"No." Gregorio's voice was flat and final, making it obvious he wouldn't tolerate arguments or prying.

Damien held up his hands in a gesture of reluctant acceptance.

He looked at Sasha again, a furrow between his eyebrows. "Petal, are you sure you're okay with this? You're under no obligation to go anywhere you don't want to."

Sasha appreciated his concern. And it wasn't all that misplaced. "I'm fine, really." She forced a small, lying smile. "Thank you, though."

Damien studied her for a moment longer before nodding. "In that case, I'll leave you to it. Let me know if you need anything." He leveled a look at her. "Same goes for you, Petal."

"Thank you."

With that, he exited, pulling the door shut behind him. Sasha released a breath, once more aware of her frantically pounding heart as Gregorio swept his hot, maybe appreciative, gaze over her.

"You had a duffel bag with you when you checked in."

Proving he *had* been watching her and her intuition was correct.

"Go and get it," he instructed. "I'll meet you downstairs in five minutes."

She turned toward the door.

"Sasha?" His voice was hard, a whiplash of intent running through it.

Despite herself, she paused and looked back at him.

"Don't try to run. You won't get far."

She'd seen the monitors. Cameras were all over the property. And no doubt he could communicate with the shuttle driver. "I won't."

He inclined his head, as if unsure whether he believed her or not. "Five minutes."

Without responding, aware of his hot, calculating gaze on her, she turned the knob and left, glad for the temporary reprieve.

Since he hadn't given her enough time to change, she settled for shrugging into her coat, then grabbing her bag and slinging it over her shoulder, grateful to have a weapon close by.

In the living room, Brandy and Gregorio were next to the window, talking quietly.

As if sensing Sasha's presence, he looked in her direction, and Brandy followed suit.

A few seconds later, Brandy headed up the stairs, and Gregorio strode toward Sasha. "I'll take your bag."

"Thanks. But I've got it." She tightened her grip on the strap.

Without a protective-male argument, he nodded agreement then he led the way outside.

Shocking her, he took her hand.

"The patio is smooth enough, but the path to my place is rocky and uneven. And in those heels…"

"Maybe I should change them."

"You have other shoes?"

"I do."

"So you have a go bag." He flashed her a grin. Voice filled with approval, he added, "Smart girl."

Without another word, he guided her to a bench, away from other people. "Sit."

Zeph, the musician, must have taken a break because the sounds of laughter and conversation drifted around them.

Sasha placed the bag next to her and unzipped it, and he knelt in front of her to unbuckle her shoes.

At the trace of his thumb on her bare skin, she shivered. "Gregorio." He was taking his responsibilities far too seriously.

"The sooner this is accomplished, the better."

So it was about expediency and nothing more?

Once the laces of her sneakers were tied and her club heels were tucked away—hopefully for good—he took her hand once more.

"Let's go."

Her eyes struggled with the dark, but he seemed to have no problems at all. Soon, all sounds from the Den receded, leaving them beneath an inky, star-filled sky with high, drifting clouds.

Moonlight cast a silvery sheen over the mountains, a surreal backdrop to the evening's events.

The cold air nipped at her bare legs, and she shivered.

In this distance a twig—maybe a branch—snapped, making her jump.

"An animal," he reassured her.

No doubt he recognized the nocturnal sounds around them.

Gregorio was just aware of threats as she was—maybe more so.

"We'll be there in less than a minute," he promised.

Good, because if they went much farther, she planned to dig out her cell phone to turn on its flashlight.

Seconds later, a bright light flashed on, making her blink. "Motion detectors?"

"Yeah."

The brightness reassured her, and a small structure came into view.

Moments later, on the patio, Gregorio pressed a finger against a pad. "I'll get you programmed in."

"No need. I won't be here that long."

"Do us both a favor and stop fucking arguing with me."

His response unsettled her.

After opening the door, Gregorio flicked on a light and guided Sasha into the cottage, his hand steady on her back.

Gregorio ushered her inside, then the click of the deadbolt echoed off the high ceiling.

The warmth was a welcome contrast to the crisp mountain air, and she appreciated the quiet.

As she expected, his space was utilitarian. Yet the cottage was surprisingly cozy, with its honeyed pine walls and flooring.

A small kitchen occupied one corner, and a counter had a couple of stools positioned beneath. He also had a wooden table with two chairs.

The living area had a large, comfortable-looking couch, along with an oversize chair, both of which faced a stone fireplace.

A staircase led to a loft with a computer and an array of monitors. His office—command central—no doubt.

There was more to the Den than she'd originally imagined. Not that she should be surprised where Gregorio was concerned. Everything she knew about investigations and security, she'd learned from him. And he took no risks with anything.

He turned to face her, his eyes dark and intense in the dim light. "Make yourself comfortable." His voice was low, controlled, making the words an order, rather than an invitation. "I'll take your coat."

"Thanks." After putting her duffel bag down, she shrugged out of her jacket, then felt exposed once she had.

Being dressed for BDSM at the club was one thing. But revealing this much skin while alone with Gregorio in his intimate space was another.

"Thank you," she said when he hung the garment on a peg.

"Bathroom is through my bedroom." He motioned toward the far side of the cottage. "Feel free to freshen up. You'll find towels in the linen closet."

Grateful for the chance to wash away her tension and change into fresh clothes, she grabbed her bag and hurried away, pausing once she'd crossed into his room and flipped on the overhead light.

The king-size lodgepole pine bed occupied the center of the room, taking up most of the space. In addition to one nightstand with a lamp, he had a single chair. Here, like the rest of his home, not one thing was out of place.

She continued to the bathroom. Though it was small, it was functional, with a glass-enclosed shower and simple fixtures. But the tile work on the floor was gorgeous and high-end, adding an unexpected touch of luxury.

As hot water cascaded over her shoulders, the tightness in her muscles began to ease.

From the living room, voices reached her.

Curious, she strained to hear words but couldn't make them out.

She picked up the soap nestled on a built-in shelf.

Of course it smelled of rich, masculine cedarwood and crisp mountain air. If she used it, she'd be enveloped in Gregorio's rugged essence with every breath.

With a soft sigh, she slipped the bar back into its spot.

A few minutes later, a soft knock on the door was followed by the turning of the knob.

Her heart pounding, she covered her breasts with her forearm, and she placed her free hand lower, trying to hide as much of herself as she could.

"I won't look," he promised, voice low.

Through the misty haze on the glass, she made out his silhouette—sexy and strong, and reassuring. Coming to Gregorio was the right decision, no matter what he did to her libido.

"Brandy brought over a few things for you."

"Oh?"

"Damien's fiancée, Catrina, keeps a lot of things in their apartment."

So she'd been right that Catrina was someone special to Damien. Had Gregorio tried to protect her, as well?

"She's happy to share."

Before Sasha could express her gratitude, he added, "I'll set them on the vanity."

"Thank you."

"I'm also hanging up a robe for you."

True to his word, he left without seeming to glance in her direction.

Simultaneously relieved and a little disappointed, she closed her eyes.

Her reaction to him was so feminine, leaving her aching with longing.

Which was ridiculous, she chided herself.

She was here because she needed help. Nothing more.

That decision in mind, she banished her wayward thoughts and pushed open the glass door.

A small, round basket waited for her, filled with everything she might need—a hair clip, ponytail holders, lavender-scented shower gel, shampoo, lotion, face wipes, even moisturizer.

Brandy had also thoughtfully included a toothbrush and toothpaste.

She hoped to have the chance to thank both Brandy and Catrina at some point.

Goose bumps covering her, Sasha picked up the small bottle of body wash and hurried back under the warm spray.

A little later, feeling much more in control, she turned off the knobs, then dried herself.

The robe he'd left for her was oversize—obviously one of his.

After a moment's hesitation, she pulled on the garment and snuggled into its comfort.

The mirror was steamed over, and she wiped a path so she could see her face as she removed her dramatic makeup.

Within a minute, she appeared more like herself again.

But her eyes, wide and apprehensive, were unfamiliar.

Part of her had hoped Gregorio would be reassuring, telling her she was overreacting to the situation.

But the way he'd instantly been on guard and taken control had left her shaken.

After cinching the belt a little bit tighter around her waist, she pulled back her shoulders and walked through to the living room.

A small fire crackled in the hearth, inviting her to relax even more.

She found Gregorio in the kitchen, an electric kettle nearby, and two mugs in front of it.

Sasha had been alone for so long, fighting her own battles, that his anticipation of her needs meant the world to her. This tenderness was a side to him that she hadn't expected, one that contrasted sharply with his hardened, black ops persona. "Thank you for everything."

"Brandy did the work."

"But you asked her to. And I appreciate it." Resting her hips against the counter, she studied him.

"Tea?" he asked. "I'd offer wine, but I figured you might want to keep a clear mind."

"You're right about that. Something hot sounds great, thanks." Not that she could keep a clear mind around this man, no matter what she drank. She noticed an assortment of tea bags scattered on the counter. "Chamomile?"

"Supposed to be soothing. Help your sleep or something."

"Did Brandy bring those over, as well?"

His lips twitched. "How did you guess?"

"As I recall, you only used to drink coffee. Thick enough for a spoon to stand up in it. I can't imagine you've changed that much."

"You know me." He grinned as he shrugged. "And she gave me directions, so I shouldn't mess it up too badly." After placing tea bags into mugs, he filled them both with water. Then he slid one toward her.

Needing something to do to occupy herself, she curled her hand around the warmed ceramic and lifted it.

Steam rose, creating a miniature cloud, and she breathed in the delicate floral, honeyed scent.

Comforting. Appreciated. Almost allowing her to forget the uncertainty that brought her here.

A few moments later, she pulled out the tea bag. After it drained, she threw it away. He followed suit, as if he'd been waiting to see what she did.

The slight hesitation from this fierce warrior charmed her, lowering her guard.

"Join me?" he invited.

With a nod, she followed him to the living room.

Thankfully, Gregorio took his chair, allowing her the couch.

Holding her mug carefully, she snuggled up, tucking her legs beneath her.

In the grate, the fire hissed and popped, and she stared into the flickering flames.

"You must be tired."

This situation had drained her more than she'd realized.

She looked over at him. In the dim light and crackling flames, he was cast in an amber glow. "I think I've been running on adrenaline." And now that it had faded, her energy was depleted.

"Get some rest. We'll come up with a plan in the morning."

Maybe it was being with him, or the tea, or the hot shower, or the sensation of being safe, but she nodded.

For tonight, just tonight, she could give up control.

"Take my bed. I'll sleep on the couch."

"No." She was the unexpected and uninvited guest. "Absolutely not."

"I insist."

Sasha shook her head. "I can't let you do that. You've already gone above and beyond. Asking you to sleep out here isn't fair."

"In case you are confused, that wasn't a request, Petal. And you didn't ask." He stood. "If you don't agree, I'll have no choice but to carry your ass into the bedroom and cuff you to the headboard."

Shocked, she slowly blinked. *Are you serious?* From what she'd seen at the Den, he was definitely a Dominant. Maybe tying women to the bed was something he did regularly.

The thought should disturb her.

But it didn't.

"And to be safe, I'd join you."

Her pulse revved into overdrive. Surely that was his mad idea of a joke.

"What will it be? Are you going to bed alone?" He studied her. "Or with me?"

Chapter Six

She couldn't speak.

"Petal?"

How could she confess the truth? That she ached to be in his arms and snuggle against his strength, and more, that she wanted to be beside him, beneath him.

But a very real sense of self-preservation urged her to remain silent. Giving in to temptation with him a second time would only lead to heartbreak.

Three years ago, when he'd walked away from her without a backward glance, she'd been shattered, and she wasn't sure she'd recovered.

After him, she'd made really bad choices with Toby that she was still recovering from.

How much worse would the devastation be if she surrendered to her emotional and physical needs again?

Despite the warmth, she shivered.

"Petal?"

In the fireplace, a log cracked, making her jump. "I..."

Waiting, he arched a single, dark eyebrow.

Her admission lodged in her throat as she struggled against the desire threatening her resolve.

"Are you going to sleep with me?" he asked again.

She was mad. But resisting him, and her own desires, was impossible. "With you." She met his inscrutable gaze. Taking a deep breath, she quietly admitted, "But you won't need to tie me up."

"Fuck." His curse was soft with repressed need.

In an instant, he was across the room, standing in front of her.

A muscle worked in his jaw as he regarded her. "Damn it, Sasha..." He reached out and traced her cheekbone with a fingertip.

Instinctively, she turned toward him.

"Tell me," he urged.

Her heart thundered as he gently captured her face in his hands.

His gaze was intense, searching.

Like their last time together, his eyes were filled with desire. Unmistakable, raw desire.

She swallowed hard.

Here, with him, she was safe from the real world and its outside dangers. At least for now.

"Petal—"

"Take me to bed, Gregorio," she whispered. "And I'm suddenly no longer tired." Bravely, she met his gaze. "I want you. If you want me."

"Jesus. Fucking hell, Petal." His eyes darkened, making him even more formidable. "How can you wonder that?"

Her heart went into a freefall.

"Forgetting you—the way you taste, the way you respond—has been impossible." His confession was gruff, filled with emotion.

Her mouth parted slightly. *Do you mean that?*

"You were my sister-in-law. I don't want to fuck up your family life."

She nodded, sharing the same fear. Yet... This attraction, this consuming need, was undeniable, despite the potential consequences. "No one has to know." She wished her voice weren't so wobbly.

"You deserve someone better than me."

"That's not true." Sasha studied his face, memorizing his features. "You're amazing." One of the few people she'd ever been able to count on. "I want this." Then she added, "You."

For a moment, as if warring with himself, he frowned.

Finally, with a sigh, he managed, "I'll protect you."

"Thank you." She was grateful he was thinking clearly because birth control would never have occurred to her.

"You know the Den's safe word."

"Halt," she told him.

"Do you want a separate one for you and me?"

"That one is fine."

"I will always honor it."

Wildly, maybe recklessly, she wanted to know where this went. If she stopped playing with him now, she'd never know how it ended.

"Just so we're clear"—he leaned in a little closer—"if we do this, there's no turning back. You're mine."

She shuddered.

This was the Gregorio she recognized. Terrifying. Thrilling.

He offered a hand, and she slid hers against his much larger, stronger one, rife with calluses from hard, dangerous work.

After he'd helped her up, he continued to draw her toward him.

Then, purposefully, he leaned forward to capture her lips in a savage kiss—this time an explosion of sensation that deepened her need. He touched an emotional place in her that no one else had or could.

She'd never be able to get enough.

When he finally eased back, she couldn't breathe, and she couldn't look away from him.

Before she could think, he swept her up in his arms, wincing a little as he did.

"Are you okay?" she asked as he rolled her slightly toward him.

"Fine."

Though she was skeptical, she looped her arm around his neck.

"The years I've dreamed of this…" Purposefully, he strode toward the bedroom as firelight cast its shadows around them.

"But you're injured!"

"Never so badly that I can't hold you." After he crossed the threshold, he stopped, and his gaze locked with hers. "Nervous, Petal?"

Beyond words. "Should I be?"

"Yeah."

Always the truth. Because of that, a shiver danced through her.

He lowered her slowly, sliding her down his body, the hardness of his cock unmistakable between them.

The knowledge that he craved her as much as she did him gave her a euphoric buzz.

But instead of releasing her right away, he held her waist. Slowly, intentionally, he leaned forward.

Possessing, demanding, tasting of hunger and fire, he took her mouth again.

She melted under his relentless, sensual onslaught, and she responded with equal urgency, threading her fingers into his hair.

She moaned, her body melting into his, craving the sensation of skin on skin.

Impossibly, he pulled her even closer, and he eased one hand down her back to cup her rear. His erection, hard and ready, pressed against her abdomen.

It wasn't enough. Not nearly enough.

He broke away, ending the kiss, leaving her emotionally bereft.

"Soon," he vowed.

Every motion economical, he turned back the blankets before facing her to strip off his T-shirt.

She gasped at the sight of the gauze taped to his abdomen. "You *are* hurt."

"A scratch. Nothing more."

This time…a lie.

"Hazard of the job." He shrugged.

His job—one of the reasons her sister had hated her relationship with him.

"You know how it is." Studying her, he added, "You've had more than a few of your own."

But not in the last few years.

Gently, Sasha placed a palm on his chest. "We don't have to—"

"This won't stop me from fucking you the way you deserve. The way I want." Gregorio's voice held a deep, gravelly rumble that sent shivers down her spine, holding hints of danger and control, intimidating as well as seducing her. "I promise you that."

He ensnared her wrist and lowered her hand to her side. "Finish undressing me."

"I..."

Rather than arguing, he raised an eyebrow in quiet expectation.

Dominant demand.

This man tilted her world off balance. She'd never dealt with anyone like him, and she wasn't quite sure how to behave.

This close, she became more aware of his scent, cedarwood and wild, moonlit nights.

She allowed her gaze to wander over his battle-scarred upper body, taking in his broad shoulders and the way his honed muscles rippled with each movement.

A perfect smattering of hair dusted his chest, trailing downward to disappear tantalizingly into his waistband.

Sasha licked her dry lips.

For a flash of time, he'd been hers, but that suddenly seemed like an eternity ago, and he was once more a stranger who both intrigued and intimidated her.

"Waiting for something, Petal?" He considered her. "Or perhaps you've changed your mind?"

"No." With determination, she shook her head. "Not at all. I just..."

He waited.

"I don't know what to do. This is all..."

"New?" His lips twitched with a smile. "So tonight was your first visit to a BDSM club."

Caught. At least she hadn't lied out loud.

He drew a thumbnail across her upper lip.

"Don't you worry about a thing, Petal. I'll tell you what to do. And you'll be perfect."

She wished she could believe it was easy.

"I can't tell you how much it pleases me that no other man has dominated you."

And he'd done that before, hadn't he? At the wedding. Now she knew for sure that he'd been exerting sensual control over her.

"Start with my boots." He sat on the side of the bed and nodded toward the floor.

The words were a command. Not a question.

Maybe she should be grateful for his guidance.

Heat rushing through her, she knelt.

This evening, she'd seen a lot of things at the Den, but she'd never imagined she'd be in this subservient position in front of any man.

Still... She didn't hate it. The startling thought shocked her.

"Get on with it, unless you want to earn a spanking."

Mouth open, she glanced up at him. "You don't mean that."

He clamped his hands on her shoulders. "Don't I?"

Hoping he was joking, she removed his sturdy motorcycle boots, her hands shaking the whole time.

God help her. This felt natural—the way things should be.

Moments later, she tucked the socks inside the footwear and slid them out of the way.

"Good girl."

She sucked in a deep breath and looked up at him.

"You like that, don't you?" He captured a lock of her hair and wound it around his hand. "Being my good girl."

No.

Yes.

Impossibly, she did.

Like the first time they were together, he forced her to explore parts of her personality she never knew existed.

"Admit it."

"I..." With uncertainty, she licked her lower lip. "You know I do."

Triumph and possession in his eyes, he released his grip and stood, bringing her face within inches of his crotch.

What was she supposed to do now?

"Remove my pants."

Again, it seemed as if he'd read her mind.

Sasha reached for the mattress to steady herself as she rose, but he held onto her upper arms, forcing her to remain in position.

"Did I tell you to stand?"

"Uhm." Her stomach plummeted. "No."

"But I did issue a direct command, did I not?" His words were filled with deadly quiet.

"You did," she whispered.

"I told you to remove my pants. Now give me the response I want to hear."

Her pulse fluttered.

Into the thick, sizzling night air, she softly complied. "Yes, Gregorio."

"Yes, Sir," he corrected.

How could she?

How could she not?

"Yes, *Sir.*" The honorific undid her, melting her insides.

"*Fuck.* I love the sound of that word on your tongue."

The purr of approval in his voice spiked her adrenaline. At this moment, she was under his control, yet simultaneously, she was stepping into her own power.

Fingers shaking, she fumbled with his belt buckle.

"Take your time. Stop overthinking. Get out of your head and trust your instincts."

To center herself, she momentarily closed her eyes.

He was right, and this should be no different from practicing yoga or firing her pistol at the range.

A moment later, nerves steadier, she finished what she was doing, then she unfastened the button at his waist and reached for the zipper's tab.

Tooth by tooth, she lowered it, the metal on metal and rustling fabric seeming to echo in her ears.

Finally, his pants fell to the hardwood floor, stealing her breath.

Gregorio wasn't wearing underwear, and the sight of his fully erect cock heated her lungs.

She'd had no idea he'd be so big, so ready.

The damp tip of his manhood brushed against her cheek. Sasha yearned to take the lead, wrap her hand around him, maybe lick the drop of pre-cum from the tip.

Or was she supposed to wait for instructions? "Gregorio, I want to touch you." She hesitated before adding, "May I?"

"Soon enough."

"But—"

"That was a no." His voice was edged with implacable demand.

Sasha had never begged for the honor of stroking her partner. In fact, at times, she considered it a chore. But Gregorio—her temporary lover—was no ordinary man.

"We're doing this my way."

Like they had at the wedding reception.

Yet now that he'd denied her, her inner ache intensified.

A little chastened, she sat back on her calves.

His lips quirked into a half-smile, and he released his grip to offer his hand. "Stand for me, Petal."

When she was upright, he set her away from him, just a little. "I want to see you. Take off the robe."

This would be so much easier if he'd do it himself then make love to her. That way, she could just close her eyes, helping her get over her first-time nerves.

"I'm waiting."

Somehow, even with the rush of emotions chasing through her, she managed to unknot her belt.

"You're doing fine."

Had she ever been with a man who was more approving?

"Keep going."

She drew apart the lapels of her robe. Then, glancing away to hide her embarrassment, she opened it all the way.

"Beautiful breasts, Petal. I should never allow you to hide them from me."

When she had the courage to look back at him, heat simmered in his darkly enigmatic eyes.

"Now finish removing it."

Her fingers nerveless, she shrugged and released the thick material, allowing it to swish to her feet.

For a moment, he took her in. "You're exquisite, Petal. Everything about you."

Was this really happening? She was in Gregorio's bedroom, both of them naked, anticipation thumping through her.

"Your nipples are hard."

And not from the cool whispers of night air. "Yes, Sir." *Am I truly saying these things to him?*

"Begging for my touch?"

Unable to find her voice, she swallowed.

"You want them sucked, Petal? Played with? Tormented?"

Her legs wobbled.

"Answer me."

"Yes." *Please.*

"That will happen. All of it. Until you can't take any more."

Her entire body was on fire.

"Now turn around so I can look at your ass."

Clenching her hands at her sides, she spun, so much more exposed than she'd ever been in that small closet so long ago.

"Even better than I imagined."

Finally, she faced him again.

"So fucking hot."

With a low, sexy, guttural sound, he pulled her against him, his steel-hard dick pressing into her. Suddenly, he captured her mouth once more, this time more insistently, his lips parting hers, his tongue plunging deep, tasting every inch of her.

They moved together, the heat between them becoming a living, breathing thing. Despite how forbidden he was, she was again consumed with a sense of rightness.

His intention was clear.

He was taking control, dominating her completely, giving her the experience she'd craved since he walked away from her three years ago.

She writhed, the need to feel his body against hers overwhelming.

He slid a hand up her thigh to glide his fingers over her most sensitive spot, leaving a trail of demand in their wake.

Desperately, she moaned.

Responding to her need, he dipped inside her.

With a gasp, she jerked, instantly arching into his touch.

He was not gentle, not hesitant. Instead, he claimed her with a raw and primal possessiveness that left her breathless and shuddering.

Her whimpers became lost between them, and the unmistakable scent of her arousal filled the air.

With one hand pressed against her back, holding her in place, he finger-fucked her, each stroke more demanding than the last, driving her closer and closer to the edge.

Abruptly he ended the kiss and he set her back, just slightly.

He seemed to know what she needed—the surrender, the abdication of control.

He pressed a thumb to her clit, teasing her until she struggled for air.

"Please," she begged, the word barely more than a whisper.

"Please, what?"

Desperate, all vulnerability and need, she looked at him. "Please make me come, Sir."

"My pleasure." He slipped another finger into her, stretching her wide open, and she cried out at the invasion. "That's it, Petal. Ride it."

Her body trembled, and her heart pounded.

Tormentingly, he continued to toy with her clit, rubbing circles around the sensitive nub, and her climax built, threatening to overwhelm her.

Gregorio thrust his fingers into her, quickening his pace, pushing her ever closer to the edge.

Her body shook, and she reached for him so she didn't fall.

Impossibly, he slid a third finger inside, stretching her wide, preparing her for what would happen later.

As she cried out, her knees buckled.

"Now, Sasha. Give it to me." He growled. "Don't you dare fucking hold back."

Convulsing, spiraling into bliss, she came all over his hand.

But he was relentless, driving her on and on until she shattered again before taking pity on her.

Gently, he eased out of her, then he licked his fingers, reigniting the sensual flames burning in her.

She struggled for breath, and she looked up at him. He smiled triumphantly.

"You're mine, Petal."

He was protector and predator, primal and unyielding, and she'd die for his touch.

This was a dangerous game they played, but the thrill—the aliveness—only made her crave him more.

"I'm going to claim every inch of you, mark you as mine, and no other man will ever touch you again." His voice was thick with promise and warning, a stark declaration of ownership. "Do you understand?"

Chapter Seven

Surely this was nothing more than the heat of the moment.

He couldn't actually mean what he said.

And yet his face was set in implacable lines.

Heart thundering at the intensity of their exchange, Sasha managed, "Yes, Gregorio." She cleared her throat. "I understand."

Gregorio nodded. "Stay right there."

He disappeared into the bathroom, and she wrapped her arms around her middle to ward off the sudden chill—one as much from the night air as well as the way he'd rocked her world.

Moments later, cock erect, powerful muscles rippling, he returned and tossed a couple of condoms onto the nightstand.

Then he faced her, desire flaring in his eyes.

She'd dreamed of being wanted in this way.

"We'll start with you on the bed."

Start?

Without waiting for her compliance, her strong protector scooped her up and placed her in the middle of the mattress, then he pushed her down on her back.

Instinctively she reached for him, but he shook his head.

"Raise your legs."

Confused, she drew her eyebrows together.

"Don't make me repeat myself or you won't like the results."

She exhaled a shaky breath.

"Hold them all the way up, Petal. I've seen you do yoga, and you're fit."

Another reminder of their shared past.

"Stop stalling."

Aware of how exposed she would be, she closed her eyes and did as he said.

"Very obedient."

With her shallow breaths, her chest rose and fell quickly.

"Now open them wide."

No one had ever demanded anything like this from her. Though some of her friends had shared their sexcapades with her, part of her had wondered if they were making it up.

"Gregorio..."

"Use your safe word." He tipped his head to one side. "Or do as you're told."

"I..."

"I'm waiting."

With a sigh, she spread herself for him.

"That's my good girl."

Kneeling, he lowered his head toward her pussy.

A whirlwind of desire surged through her as he skimmed his fingers up and down her inner thighs. Frantically, she dug her fingers into the sheets.

"You want this."

"Yes." Needed it, as much as oxygen. "But it's—"

"Ask me for it." With his gruff words, he cut off her automatic objection. *"Fucking ask me."*

Was he determined to demolish all of her inhibitions?

"I'm waiting."

"Please," she whispered. "Please, Gregorio."

"That's not good enough. Be specific."

He was far too demanding, too carnal. "I want to come."

He feathered his touch a little closer to her pussy, but then he confoundingly pulled back.

"Tell me how you want me to do this."

Scandalized by his statement, she gasped.

He'd be satisfied by nothing except her complete capitulation.

Unable to believe she was going to do this, she breathlessly managed, "Lick me."

"That's a start. Keep going."

"And…" She couldn't.

"I'm waiting."

"Fuck me with your fingers."

"So damn good, Petal. But there's one thing you're forgetting."

What?

"Put it all together, for you. For us."

The pieces clicked.

Stunning herself, she pushed past her comfort zone. "Please," she whispered. "Lick me, fuck me, Gregorio. Make me come." *Make me yours.* "Please, please, please."

Intentionally, he pressed his thumb against her clit, igniting a desperate flame. "You're so close to getting what you want, Petal."

Understanding dawned.

Suddenly, she knew what he wanted, and she was willing to give into his demands in exchange for the satisfaction that he held just out of reach. "Gregorio, please. Lick me, finger-fuck me, please. I need this so much." She looked at him. With everything in her, she added, "Please, *Sir.*"

"Holy hell. Yes." He growled. "That's my good girl." He leaned in, and the warm, wet heat of his mouth enveloped her, sparking erotic excitement through her body.

He was masterful, flicking and darting his tongue, awakening her to sensations she'd never before experienced.

Moaning, she bucked her hips against him.

She was close… So close. "Don't stop," she pleaded.

As he continued his teasing torment, tension swelled in her, and the world began to tip off its axis. She whimpered. "I can't take this anymore. I need to come…"

Then suddenly, he pulled back, causing her to cry out in frustration.

"Not yet." His eyes were intense, and his expression was dark.

This was going to be on his terms. "But—"

"I know you need it." His gaze never left her. "And I'm going to give it to you when I'm ready."

With that, he slid two fingers inside her, slowly at first, exploring her wet-hot core.

At the sensual intrusion, she sucked in a deep breath, and her pussy tightened.

"That's it," he murmured, his voice low and rough.

He moved in and out, his motion a slow, steady rhythm that drove her wild. "More," she whispered, begged.

Gregorio smiled his satisfaction.

He twisted his fingers, stretching her, and her body clenched around him.

"I can't hold back any longer." Yearning for completion, she arched her back.

"Fuck, Petal…"

But on and on he went.

Ready to sob, she closed her eyes against the tears.

How much more was she expected to endure?

She was his to command, and it was on his terms only. "I—"

"Trust me, Petal," he said, his voice deep with demand.

With those words, he once more leaned forward and used his tongue to tease her throbbing clit, even as he continued to finger-fuck her.

Every nerve ending flared with anticipation.

But the terrible, terrible Dominant continued to hold back, keeping her in the throes of pleasurable agony, tossing her head as release teased her, remaining just out of reach.

Gregorio withdrew his fingers, leaving her slick and swollen, yearning for the final push.

Then, as if to prolong the torture, he trailed his tongue down the length of her pussy, bring a hand up to press against the entrance to her rear.

"Tell me yes."

"Yes." She could deny him nothing. "Yes, Sir."

At the gentle invasion, she trembled, clenched her muscles. *Oh… My God…* "Gregorio!"

As if he'd been waiting for her cries, he plunged his tongue inside her damp pussy.

Screaming, lifting her hips off the bed, waves of pleasure crashing over her, she shivered.

But he wasn't done with her.

The echoes of her screams faded, and he pulled back momentarily, and then another climax claimed her, this one even more stunning.

Suddenly, she spun into a dizzying white haze and consciousness drifted away, leaving her floating.

She had no idea how much time passed, moments—minutes—but from beyond her awareness, she realized he was gently stroking between her folds.

Without her noticing, he'd eased his fingers from her pussy and her ass, leaving her satisfied, but strangely yearning for more.

"You okay, Petal?"

He mastered her body, making her respond in ways she had never imagined.

Her aftershocks subsided, leaving her with a sense of peace that she didn't remember ever experiencing before. "That was…" Words didn't exist to describe the soul-deep world he'd shared with her. "Spectacular."

And that thought was quickly followed by another, chilling one. Walking away from him after this was over might destroy her.

"Spectacular?" With a slow smile and satisfied nod, he took in her reactions. "I'm afraid that's not good enough. Time to raise the bar. Are you ready for what's next?"

Chapter Eight

"Next?" Sasha's voice contained an adorable squeak.

Her beautifully vibrant green eyes darkened into a deep, forest green, and her mouth parted with shock and desire.

Watching her reactions, seeing her surrender, hearing her breathless gasps, sent a wave of masculine satisfaction through him.

How the hell had he stayed away from her for so long?

Maybe, just maybe, avoiding her had something to do with the risks he'd been taking since the night he'd first tasted her forbidden deliciousness.

Fucking her—making love—might be a nail in his coffin, something he'd never recover from, but he was no longer capable of giving a fuck.

He brushed a knuckle across her trembling lower lip. "Stay in the bed, Petal."

Blinking sleepily, she said, "I'm not sure I have the energy to do anything else."

For a minute, he left her to wash his hands and to grab a cool washcloth.

He returned to find her rolled onto her side, watching him.

"On your back," he said softly. "And spread your legs."

She blew out a small breath as she complied.

Such an amazing submissive, exactly the way she'd behaved in his vivid and constant dreams.

His eyes locked onto hers, he pressed the damp material against her heated pussy.

"That's cold!" She wiggled, trying to get away, but he clamped a hand around her ankle, holding her steady. "Is this necessary?"

Goose bumps traced up her arms.

"Yeah. It'll soothe." He paused. "I don't want you too sore. This night is just getting started."

Even while wrinkling her nose in distrust, she sighed.

A few moments later, the temperature warmed, and she relaxed.

"You really are a good girl, Petal."

She looked at him.

"*My* good girl."

"Gregorio…" Sasha reached a hand up to trace her fingertips down his jawbone.

After removing the cloth, he tossed it toward the closet, then he grabbed one of the condoms. "Do you want this, Sasha?"

Much as it would kill him if she denied him, he respected her choice.

"Yes." Nodding, she whispered, "I do."

Her beautiful, breathless response made his cock throb even harder.

Being with her was even more spectacular than he'd imagined—and over the years he'd imagined plenty. Even when he had no business thinking about her.

"Earlier you said you wanted to touch me." Standing next to the bed, he offered her the small, foil-wrapped package. "Put it on me."

Her gaze flicked to his face, then back to the condom. "I've never done this before."

"Then it's about time you learned, isn't it?"

Tense silence hung between them.

"Having you do little things like this for me brings me pleasure."

She might not think that acts of service were fulfilling, but she'd learn. Caring for his submissive—*her*—satisfied him on a deeply personal level.

Finally, she nodded and sat up, then she scooted toward him.

Hands shaking, she accepted the package and tore it open. "Now what?" she asked, dropping the wrapper back on the nightstand.

"Come closer." He took her wrist to guide her hand. "Put it on the tip and roll it down. I want to feel you doing this for me."

Her gaze was filled with equal measures of uncertainty and determination. Then, slowly, she followed his directions. This was more than just a physical act, it was a gesture of trust and surrender.

"That's it, Petal." *Fuck.* Having this beautiful, desirable woman servicing him... *Yeah.* This was the stuff of dreams. And memories that would fuel his fantasies.

When she'd finally finished, she released her grip and looked up at him, her eyes wide.

"Excellent."

"What next?" she asked, her voice shaky.

He played a hunch that she wanted to take at least a small amount of control. "Tell me what your instincts are saying."

"I want to stroke you."

"Good. Do it."

Hesitatingly at first, she curled her hand around him, then traced her way down his length. As she looked at him, she drew her hand up.

"Keep going."

She began to stroke with an age-old rhythmic precision, and he gritted his teeth together as he struggled against his climax.

He wanted this moment to last, to savor every touch, each glance, all of her sensual sounds.

As she continued, she tightened her grip.

Shit. How much longer could he last?

From beneath her long lashes, she looked up at him, seeking reassurance that she was doing it right.

Once he gave a small nod of approval, she sped up, her movements becoming less tentative, more confident.

Her touch was exquisite torture.

Gregorio gritted his teeth, forcing himself to hold back as every muscle in his body tensed and his nerves stretched to breaking point.

Sasha continued, squeezing a little tighter and shortening her strokes.

"Fuck." He groaned, and his balls drew up.

Knowing he couldn't last, he clamped a hand around hers to stop her.

"Problem?" she asked softly with feminine power. "Sir?"

Vixen.

After prying apart her fingers, he pressed her down onto her back. Then he positioned her where he wanted her, on the edge of the mattress, thighs as far apart as possible.

"If you keep this up, I may need to add a more advanced yoga class, Sir."

"Too demanding?" Not that he wanted to change anything, but he didn't want her to get muscle cramps that would ruin their time together.

"Nothing a hot shower or a massage won't fix."

"I can arrange both." Maybe both together. In fact, he looked forward to having his hands on her body.

With two fingers, Gregorio parted her labia, making her suck in a shallow breath. "Now I want you to masturbate yourself."

She blinked.

"You heard me, Petal."

"I..."

"Would you like me to spank your pussy to ensure your obedience?"

"What? *No.*" Frantically, gasping, she moved her hand, placing hers over his to protect herself. "You can't mean that."

"Oh?" He arched an eyebrow. "Are you seriously contemplating challenging me?"

"You'd actually..." She shook her head. "I mean, spank me? *There?*"

"Any number of places, actually." He tried—and failed—to hide his grin. "Because you're new to my way of life and I'm feeling particularly generous, I'll give you three seconds to follow my order."

"I..." With a doubtful frown, she searched his gaze. "Does my safe word still work?"

"Of course," he reassured her. "Always."

But he was betting she wouldn't use it.

His beautiful little Petal was enjoying her first taste of submission.

By telling her what to do, she could abdicate responsibility. He was giving her permission to enjoy herself, shove aside the dozens of reasons that they shouldn't be doing this. "Three," he warned.

"Gregorio..."

His grip firm, telegraphing his seriousness, he captured her wrist and moved her hand to her belly, exposing her gorgeous, still-swollen pussy.

Then, still keeping her labia parted, he pulled back the hood of her clitoris. "This will sting, Petal."

"I—"

"Two."

All of her muscles tensed.

"Last chance to start playing with yourself."

Though she didn't move, her gaze was miserable, pleading, a combination of dark desire and nerves.

Refusing to be swayed, he gave her pussy a spank.

"Gregorio!"

But instead of trying to escape, she arched toward him, her body begging for more.

How could he deny her?

Leaning forward, he used his tongue to take away the slight sting. "That was a gentle tap." A slight reprimand, a taste of what might follow. "If you don't want to another one, much harder, get busy."

She squeezed her eyes shut, then he lifted her hand and sucked two fingers into his mouth, wetting them—not that he needed to do so. Sasha was already wet, and the musky scent of her heat filled the air. Sweet, sweet intoxication.

His precious little Petal had enjoyed her light, tiny spank.

He placed the damp fingers on her clit. After teasing her, he lowered his hand. "Play with yourself."

As if her closed eyes weren't enough, she turned her head to one side.

For now, he'd allow her a slight bit of modesty.

Gently, she stroked her clit, jerking a little bit as she did.

"That's it. Keep going."

Softly moaning, she continued.

Gregorio's cock throbbed, and his pulse pounded in his ears. A single touch would make him explode. "That spank makes the sensations so much more intense, doesn't it?"

"Yes."

"Relax for me."

Sasha moved her shoulders, sinking deeper into the mattress, and as she did so, she seemed to lose some of her inhibitions.

Her motions quickened, making her clit swell even more. "So perfect." *So damn beautiful.*

He sucked in a breath at the sight of her touching herself.

Sasha gasped, her body trembling and shaking. "*Gregorio!* I need..."

Her movements increased, showing how close she was to the edge. "You may come, Petal. Any time."

Her body tensed, and a fierce furrow buried itself between her eyebrows.

She clenched her free hand into a tight fist. But he was having none of that. "Pinch your nipples."

Though she tensed, she cupped one of her breasts.

He could start and end every day watching her get herself off.

Her breaths came in desperate, tiny bursts. Frantically, she lifted her hips to rub herself against her hand.

Needing to be part of this, he slid his fingers inside her tight pussy.

She screamed, jerking and shaking as she clenched around him.

Wanting her to ride the climax as long as she could, he continued on until finally she shuddered, and her body went limp.

Sasha, his Petal, had been worth the wait.

Slowly, she blinked open her eyes. A sensual haze glazed their green depths, proving how much she enjoyed the experience. Maybe, just maybe, as much as he had.

"You..." She swallowed. "No one... I mean, I've never experienced anything like that. Like you."

As far as he was concerned, he was her last. No one else would be allowed to touch her. "We're perfect together." He eased his fingers from inside her, then brushed the dampness across her mouth. "Lick it off," he instructed. "Taste yourself."

Tentatively, she traced her upper lip with the tip of her tongue.

"I love the way you come for me."

Meeting his gaze, she said, "You're a generous lover."

"Have you been with some selfish bastards, Petal?" Gregorio took the hand she'd used to pleasure herself, and he sucked her fingers clean.

She went still. "I want you, Gregorio."

Good thing, because his cock ached with insistent demand.

He was incapable of denying her—or himself—a moment longer.

Scooping her up once more, he moved her to the middle of the mattress and placed her head on a pillow. "Open yourself for me."

Welcoming him, she spread her thighs, and he positioned himself between them.

Then, fisting his cock, he guided himself to her entrance. "Take me."

"Yes."

Slowly, he began to sink into her heat.

She tensed. "You're so big!"

"We'll go as slow as you need." Restraining himself, he stilled, letting her body accommodate his girth and length.

"I thought after…what we've been doing…"

"Stretching you?"

She nodded.

To distract her, he kissed her, the heady taste of her on their tongues making his senses swim.

When he ended it, they were both breathless, staring into each other's eyes. She was so right for him. So perfect.

With a deep exhalation, she finally relaxed. "I'm ready."

Taking great care of her, ensuring she was wet for him, he began to move.

With a whimper, she dug her heels into the bed. "More," she pleaded.

"Hold onto the headboard slats." Which meant she'd be stretched, with her arms above her.

"That will be a lot."

"Yeah." For both of them.

Gregorio captured her hands and positioned them where he wanted.

Now that she was helpless, he sank in all the way. *"Jesus."* The fit was tight, forcing him to grit his teeth.

"God above. *Gregorio!"*

Driven by her urgency, he picked up the pace, thrusting his hips in a primal rhythm.

Her breaths ragged, she arched up to meet his every thrust.

"That's it. Give me everything, Petal."

In perfect response, her pussy clenched around him, pulling him in deeper.

The sensations, the pleasure, overwhelmed him. It wasn't just the sex, it was her.

Sasha.

The woman he'd obsessed over.

He intended to claim her, make up for lost time, possess her in every possible way. "Fuck..." The control he'd fought for began to crumble.

"I want to touch you."

He nodded tightly, giving permission. "Wrap your legs around my waist. I want even more of you."

With a tiny sob, she released her grip to encircle his neck, and she maneuvered herself into the position he'd requested.

"Oh my God!" she cried when the angle allowed a more intense penetration.

Determined not to come without her, he reached between them to touch her swollen clit.

"I..."

"That's it."

With a scream, she clamped around him, raising her hips higher and higher, bucking against him.

She squeezed her eyes closed, and her climax came in waves, her internal muscles tightening in powerful contractions, almost making him come.

Instead, he pulled back.

Only when her shudders subsided did he allow himself to move again.

"Oh..." She gasped. "That was..."

Then, filled with possessive hunger, he thrust forward, matching the rhythm of her contractions.

Suddenly, he couldn't hold back any longer.

"Fuck!" He orgasmed, his cock pulsing inside her.

Her pussy clenched around him, draining every drop from him.

Finally, arms shaking from the sexual exertion, he propped himself up on his elbows, lifting himself so he didn't suffocate her.

Their breathing slowed and their movements became less frenzied.

She reached up to stroke a finger down the contour of his jaw. "That was..."

His Petal didn't finish, and he didn't have words, either.

The most intense pleasure he'd ever experienced. Fiery. Fucking consuming.

He'd fantasized about this moment for years. And it was so much more than he'd imagined.

When he'd recovered somewhat, he rolled to one side and tucked her against him, protecting her in the comfort of his arms.

He captured her chin and held it firmly. Gregorio wasn't sure what the actual hell he was thinking, but now that he'd been inside her and she'd come apart in his arms, he owned her.

"Gregorio?"

As long as he could shove aside the fact she was his ex-wife's little sister and that there would be hell to pay for taking her as his, everything was fine.

"Gregorio?" she asked again, frowning. "Is something wrong?"

Chapter Nine

Shall I tell you the truth?

Or lie to both of us?

Shaking his head, Gregorio brushed wayward strands of hair back from her face.

For now, he'd savor the moment, relishing the heady taste of her on his lips, remembering the way she looked at him and the feel of her pussy and legs as she wrapped around him.

The morning was soon enough to deal with reality.

Tonight, he wanted to be lost in her. To believe their future was a certainty.

"Everything's fine." With a soft kiss, he promised to return.

As he slipped out of bed, and she propped herself on her side, her eyebrows still drawn together, as if she wasn't sure whether or not she believed him. She was right to have those questions.

He left her to dispose of the condom and to restore his equilibrium.

In the bathroom, he splashed cold water on his face, trying to clear his head.

He'd fucking been married to her older sister. But now, with the feelings he was experiencing for Sasha, he had to wonder whether or not he'd ever truly cared for Adriana.

Shucking away the droplets, he turned the tap on again, this time to hot.

After drying his face, he returned to her, carrying a warm washcloth, his cock already half-hard again.

He pressed the soothing warmth to her red, swollen pussy, and she purred. Instantly, his dick demanded he possess her again.

What was it about her that got inside him this way? Not just his physical responses, but his emotional ones, as well.

He couldn't get enough.

Gritting his teeth against his demanding arousal, he vowed to let her recover. At least for another couple of hours.

Sasha had come to him for advice and comfort, not to be fucked ragged.

Too bad he couldn't convince his body of that fact.

Her gaze took in his erection. "You're ready again?"

"Perpetual state of being where you're concerned." He grimaced before gently picking her up and scooting her over. "Need a T-shirt to sleep in?" He'd prefer she snuggle up to him, naked.

"You don't want to make love again?"

"Want to? Hell, yes. But you need rest."

"Being sore would be worth it."

His cock pulsed. This woman… "When was the last time you slept well?"

Softly, she sighed. "I can't remember."

"Figured." He climbed back in bed and gathered her close.

For the moment, he was content to hold her while he figured out a plan.

She placed a hand on his chest and spread her fingers wide. Then slowly, her eyelids fluttered before finally closing. Moments later, she sighed, and her breathing changed, letting him know she was asleep.

To be sure she was out completely, he remained where he was for long minutes, replaying what they'd shared, then reminding himself she would never have sought him out if she wasn't in danger.

Keeping her safe was his number one priority…even more important than satisfying his consuming hunger for her.

Careful not to disturb her, Gregorio eased out of bed.

She murmured softly in her sleep but didn't wake.

Unable to help himself, he gazed at her for long moments, drinking in her beauty and peacefulness. There was nothing more he wanted to do than climb back in bed and hold her tight.

Still, he dressed, then turned off the bedroom light and pulled the door mostly closed before setting the house alarm and heading back to the Den.

The night was quiet and dark, the only sound his sure footsteps on the path.

Keeping to the shadows, he crossed the patio.

Once he was inside, Lilith glanced up from where she was standing near the sliding glass door. "Wasn't expecting to see you back here, Sir."

"Won't be here long." Already, he was anxious to get back to Sasha. He hated leaving her alone even for a few minutes, despite how secure the property was.

A couple of guests snagged his attention, and he bit back his impatience to chat for a few moments before excusing himself and heading upstairs.

In the private offices, Damien still sat behind his desk, staring at his computer screen. "I've been expecting you."

Gregorio wasn't surprised. They'd been friends and associates for too damn long not to read each other's minds.

"How's your guest doing?" Damien asked, leaning back in his chair.

Gregorio dropped into the chair opposite him. "Exhausted."

Studying Gregorio closely, Damien nodded. "She came to you for help and protection." It was a statement, not a question.

"Someone ransacked her office." Gregorio ran a hand over his head. "And she's being followed."

"If my guess is right, the woman in question is your ex-wife's little sister."

Gregorio tensed. "And?"

"You sure you know what you're doing here?" Though Damien's voice was calm, controlled, his eyebrows were drawn together with skepticism. "With her?"

Much as he despised the reaction, if the tables were turned, he'd be asking the same questions. Made Damien a good friend. And annoying as hell.

"Given your history…"

"Fuck off," Gregorio snapped.

Damien held up a hand.

"She needs my help."

"I saw how you looked at her." He paused. "The way she looked at you."

"The hell does that mean?"

"Only a fool would have missed the tension. There's more to this story."

Which he planned to keep to himself. No one needed to know that she completely came apart for him. Or that he'd thought of her constantly since that first night that he'd had no businesses touching her. Or that he planned to keep her forever.

"Don't let your feelings cloud your judgment."

"They won't." It was a total fucking lie. And Damien was right to caution him.

His history with Sasha was beyond complicated. She'd witnessed the good and the bad between him and Adriana. And Sasha had been the only person with a front-row seat for their ugly divorce. He'd never forget the sight of her that day—the stricken way she'd looked at him, tears falling down her cheeks.

And yet...

He could no longer fight his need for her.

Until she'd come to work at Hawkeye, she'd strictly been his wife's little sister.

Then one day, she'd left the workout room after an intensely physical training session. Her chest had been heaving from the exertion, and she was glowing from sweat. Even though she was wearing a sports bra, her nipples had been hard. And she'd been grinning.

Light from a nearby window had played with her hair, and he'd nearly been brought to his knees.

She was absolutely fucking beautiful and totally unaware of it.

Not seeming to care who was around, she'd run to him and thrown her arms around his neck and thanked him for helping her get the job.

She'd pressed herself against him, and pulling away from her had taken every bit of his self-control.

"You're welcome," he'd told her before pivoting and striding away, telling himself she was a new recruit and his former sister-in-law, not to mention a junior employee. She was totally off limits.

But most of all, he'd needed to hide his erection.

His attempts at nobility had been somewhat successful…until the night at the wedding.

All his baser needs flared, and he'd been helpless to stop them. A taste wasn't enough. In that instant, he'd been determined to take what was his. After him, she wouldn't want anyone else. Why should he suffer alone? She was the only one he had ever obsessed over. If that made him an asshole, he didn't care.

Realizing Damien was staring at him, he shook his head, trying to pick up the thread of the conversation. "I won't turn my back on her."

"You know people who can help her. Protect her. Without the complications."

"Fuck that."

Regarding Gregorio, Damien fell silent. "So that's the way of it."

"Yeah."

"Understood." He nodded tightly. "Tell me what you need from me."

"Hope to resolve it quickly. If I need Wolfe to cover, I'll let him know." He shrugged. "And you."

"See that you do."

Without another word, Gregorio left the office.

He managed to avoid other people as he made his way through the Den and headed back out into the night—and back to Sasha.

As he walked, Damien's warning reverberated in his head,

His friend was right. Pursuing something serious with Sasha was risky, maybe even foolish. The fallout with Adriana and her family would be hell. And if he failed Sasha, hurt her in any way... He'd never forgive himself.

But letting her go was impossible.

Consequences could get fucked. He wanted her. Needed her. He'd do whatever it took to protect her and keep her.

Resolved, he let himself back into the cottage.

Sasha was still sleeping peacefully, her face relaxed, vulnerable in the dim light.

Exhaling a relieved sigh, he headed up to his office to check the security cameras and to review the entire evening's feed of every vehicle that approached the gate or that hesitated on the main road, looking for any anomalies.

More than an hour later, satisfied, he expanded the range on standard notifications. If anyone attempted to step foot on the property tonight, he'd know about it.

Next, he entered a secure portal and did a search on Brenda and Felix Santos to see what he could turn up. Probably not much more than she already had, but he had contacts far and deep and wide.

Methodically, he began a search of her former business partner.

Not satisfied when the search turned up nothing, he grabbed his phone. Toby Renshaw seemed to have gone to ground. Living off the money he got when Sasha bought him out of Pathways? Or was he involved in something else?

Moments later, Gregorio's call was answered.

Despite the late hour, Hawkeye, his boss and the owner of the world's leading security firm, answered.

"Surprised to hear from you."

Often, the two men went months without talking, and Hawkeye almost always initiated contact since he'd quit working there in favor of finding some sort of healing at the Den. After Sasha had quit her job, going to headquarters no longer appealed to him. "Need to know what you've got on Toby Renshaw."

Silence echoed back before, "He's a piece of shit."

Gregorio had figured as much.

"I fired his ass."

Hawkeye only kept the best agents. With ruthless efficiency, he got rid of the rest.

"Started a new company. Hoping to compete with us." He gave a low laugh. As if that was possible. "But he took Sasha with him. Hated to lose her. You were right to suggest we bring her aboard. She made an excellent addition to the firm. I would have liked to have kept her long term."

"Sasha's the reason I'm calling."

Hawkeye was quiet for a moment. "I'm listening."

Gregorio outlined the details Sasha had provided earlier, ending with, "I want to know where he is, what he's up to."

"Surveillance?"

"Yeah." He'd pay any price to keep her safe. "While I've got you, need to know what you have on Felix and Brenda Santos." He gave a list of the other missing files. "Along with whatever you can find on everyone who works for Pathways." Though she had a company website, there was no information on any employees.

"Where's Sasha now?"

He hesitated. "With me," he reluctantly admitted.

"I see."

Before ending the call, Gregorio added, "When are you planning to increase security at Pathways?"

In the background, a keyboard clacked. "Monday."

"Make it tomorrow. Noon. I'll meet the crew there."

"Consider it done."

"While you're at it, I want a system installed at her house."

"Address?"

Gregorio gave a half-laugh. He had no idea. "I'm sure you can figure it out."

"Anything else?"

"Yeah. I won't be available for assignments anytime in the near future."

The line was silent for a few moments, then Hawkeye hung up.

Still needing to burn off the angst churning in him, Gregorio headed downstairs to wash their mugs.

Then, telling himself he was just doing his job, he checked on her.

His Sasha looked perfect, innocent, with her hair spread across on his pillow. Faint shadows from the stress she'd been under were painted beneath her eyes.

Everything in him tightened.

This was where she belonged.

"No one will hurt you, Petal." *Not even me.*

Restless energy churning in him, he set the alarm then headed to the garage gym.

Once inside, he tipped his wrist and opened the security app on his watch. If anything—anyone—came near her, he'd instantly know.

Then he stripped off his shirt and once more positioned himself in front of the heavy punching bag.

With a deep breath, he began striking it with precision and force, the dull thuds echoing in the otherwise quiet room.

Faint sounds from the Den reached him—people laughing on the patio, vehicles leaving.

Each of his punches was fueled by his anger at whoever had dared to threaten her. Intentionally, he shoved aside his own complicated emotions and instead channeled that tension into his precise movements. Within minutes, his face dripped with sweat and exertion made his muscles burn.

Time vanished as he lost himself in the physical sensations.

Finally, with one last powerful strike, he stepped back, breathing hard.

But his mind was clearer, his emotions under control—the way they should be.

After snatching up a towel, he made a halfhearted attempt to dry himself off before pulling on his shirt and jogging back to the cottage.

His beautiful Petal was still asleep, her hair fanned out on the pillow. So fucking right. She belonged here. With him.

But the fact she was in danger filled him with seething rage.

On the other hand, that's what had finally brought her to him.

Careful not to wake her, he moved silently past the bed and into the bathroom.

He turned on the shower, letting the steam fill the small space as he undressed.

After removing his bandage, he stood beneath the hot spray, he closed his eyes and let the water soothe his aching muscles.

Moments later, the temperature in the room dropped, and he instantly tensed.

"Gregorio?"

He exhaled. *Petal.*

With his hand, he cleared steam from the glass door. She was gloriously naked and walking toward him.

"Room for one more?"

"Yeah."

Moments later, she stepped into the shower, pressing her body against his as the water cascaded over them both.

"Insomnia?" she asked.

"A few things on my mind. So I worked out."

"I fell asleep right after we had sex."

Fucked. Made love. Sex was far too tame a word for what they'd shared.

Eyes wide, fastened on his, she picked up the soap. "May I?"

"Pleasure will be mine, Petal." *Sub.* Acts of service. She might think she didn't want to perform them, but the way she'd removed his clothes, then masturbated him nearly to completion, proved otherwise. This sealed the deal.

Slowly, she lathered his arms with gentle strokes. When she moved to his chest, she took great care to avoid his wound.

Her touch was both soothing and arousing, and he gritted his teeth against the rush of desire that almost dropped him to his knees.

Taking her time, she glided over his wet skin, following the contours of his muscles.

His cock arrowed toward her, and she paused for a moment, looking to him for guidance. With a nod, he said, "Do it."

She stroked, and his dick jumped in response.

Casting her gaze downward, she tightened her grip.

Then, as she continued, his balls drew up. He ensnared her wrist. "Petal." His voice was raw with need and warning, but she paid no attention to him. "You're playing with fire."

Through her fringe of lashes, dotted with drops of water, she looked up at him.

Desire, equal to his own, radiated from the emerald depths.

Slowly, taking charge, she dropped the soap back into its dish then leaned in, her lips just inches from his. "I'll take the risk."

He sucked in a breath.

Then, surprising him, she lowered herself to her knees.

She licked pre-cum from his tip and made a soft, approving sound before taking his cockhead into her mouth.

As she sucked, she stroked his length, then she used her free hand to cup his balls.

He groaned.

Hell's pleasure.

How many times had he imagined this?

Looking up at him, water sluicing down her face, she sucked him deeper into her mouth.

Desperate to remain at least somewhat in control, he placed one palm on the tiles and held onto her shoulder with the other.

"That's it." So damn good. So fucking perfect. "Just like that."

The sensation of her lips and tongue shot electric shocks up his spine.

As she took more of him, his hips bucked involuntarily. "You don't need to—"

"Need to, Sir?" she prompted.

The fuck had I been going to say?

His knuckles went white as he fought to keep from thrusting into her mouth. He watched, transfixed, as she began to increase the pace of her movements.

Tension thumped through him. "Petal…" It was the last warning he was capable of.

Continuing to ignore him, she persisted.

Suddenly, his control snapped, and he went rigid.

With a long, deep moan, he came, ejaculating down her throat.

Choking, she still refused to stop, using her mouth and hands to drain every drop from him.

"Jesus." He shuddered.

Eventually, she stopped.

She looked up at him, eyes filled with adoration and trust.

He vowed to deserve both.

When he could breathe, he helped her up, then he drew her against him. "Petal, you're…" He had no words.

Her lips curled in a private smile. "Wanted to return the favor from earlier."

"We're more than even."

"I'm not finished washing you," she protested.

"Yeah. You are." He soaped her up, then he took down the handheld wand and moved it over her body, rinsing her properly. "Spread your legs."

Wide-eyed, she did what he said.

"Such an obedient Petal." His voice was gruff with approval. "Now part your labia for me."

"Gregorio—"

"Do as you're told, Sasha."

At his sharp tone, she followed his order.

"Keep holding yourself wide for me." He directed the shower spray between her thighs and adjusted the pressure to a gentle pulse as he sent the warm water cascading over her pussy.

"Oh my God." With a small jerk, she gasped.

"That's it." He kept his gaze locked on hers. "Let the water tease that beautiful pussy of yours."

As her legs trembled, he slid a finger inside her, and her tight heat clenched around him.

"Gregorio." She moved her hips in rhythm with his hand.

"Do you like that, Petal?" He brushed a soft kiss against her ear. "Do you like me fingering you while you're getting all that pleasure?"

She nodded, and her breath came in tiny gasps.

"Tell me." Her voice, so soft, trembling with need, fed an unholy place deep inside him. He had to have her words, her confession.

"Yes," she whispered, giving him life. "I love the way you're fingering me, Sir. And—" She cried out as he increased the pressure against her clit. "This is too much!"

Not nearly enough.

He added another finger, stretching her, filling her. Her moans grew louder, echoing off the shower walls.

"God!" She arched, surrendering totally to him.

"And what about this, Petal? Did you like it earlier?" He made sure his finger was wet, then pressed it against her anus. Nice girls didn't always admit to liking this kind of thing. But with the way she'd responded earlier, he was betting she loved it.

He hoped so because he wanted to claim her—own her—in every way possible. Getting her to the point she'd beg him to bury his cock in her sweet ass would require patience. As well as persistence.

"I..."

"You'll want to tell me the truth so I don't have to punish you."

Her breathing changed, becoming ragged. Oh, yes. Sasha—his Sasha—was made for him.

"Punish?" she squeaked out.

"Absolutely. Trust is essential. And you can't have that without being totally revealing." For a moment, he moved the spray a little farther away from her slightly swollen pussy. He wasn't letting her come until she gave up all of her secrets.

"Yes." She squeezed her eyes shut for a moment. Then she opened them wide and looked at him. Embarrassment stained her cheeks. "Yes. I liked it."

He smiled, letting her know how much he appreciated her. "Are you saying you want me to finger your ass?"

She swallowed deeply and nodded.

"Bear down a little for me." The angle was slightly different than it had been earlier. "Makes it easier. Let me in." Murmuring praise, he eased forward. "That's it, Petal. Such a perfect girl." The tight ring of muscle gave way, and he slipped in up to his first knuckle. If he had lube, he'd insert a second finger, but for now, he was satisfied with letting her get accustomed to the intrusion. "Let yourself go."

He pressed a gentle kiss along the column of her throat as he began to thrust in and out of her ass, working himself deeper with each stroke.

He brought the shower spray closer to her clit again, and she moaned, her body beginning to move with the rhythm of the pulsing water.

"Does that feel good, Petal? Having my finger all the way up in your ass?"

Frantically, she nodded, and her breaths came in passionate, short bursts. "Yes…yes, it feels amazing, Gregorio."

"Tell me what you want." While he loved her being so perfectly obedient, he wanted her to unleash her hidden naughty girl. "Tell me," he urged again. "Or we can stop this right here."

She gyrated her hips, and he took the opportunity to push his finger deeper into her rear.

"Fuck me, Sir. Take me. Make me yours."

His cock leaped in response. *Hell and high water.* How could he have walked away from her that night at the wedding?

"Make me come apart for you."

She had no idea all the things he wanted to give her.

He curled the fingers inside her pussy, seeking that sweet spot that would send her over the edge. "That's it, Petal. Let me hear you scream my name."

Once more, he increased the intensity of the water on her clit. Her body trembling, she bucked against his hand.

All of her muscles tensed, and her breaths came in desperate bursts.

"Gregorio…"

"You've earned it. Take it."

He gently nipped her shoulder, sending her over the edge.

The scream he wanted echoed through the shower as her body convulsed around his fingers.

Relentlessly, he kept the water where it was, drawing out her orgasm, until she sagged against him, her knees buckling.

While supporting her weight, he carefully removed his fingers from her and turned off the water. Then he wrapped his arms around her, holding her close as she shook with the aftermath of her release.

"You're so perfect, Petal. So beautiful. So responsive to me."

Looking at him with her bright green eyes, she whispered, "Only for you."

Possessiveness rocked him. *Yes*. Only for him.

"That was..." She let out a shaky exhalation. "I don't have words for what just happened."

Good. "It's a promise of what else is to come."

"You scare me a little."

He should frighten her a lot. "I'm going to know you in ways no one else ever has." Or ever would. He intended to lay her bare before him, emotionally as well as physically.

Starting now...

Chapter Ten

The sound of footsteps on the hardwood floors behind her broke the silence.

Gregorio's presence filled the room like a gathering storm—dark, electric, inevitable. His scent, that of untamed power and sandalwood, wrapped around her, making her pulse quicken. The air hung supercharged, crackling with tension, thick with everything they'd done the night before.

Trying to tame her racing heart, she turned to him.

He was leaning against the doorway, his hair tousled, his intense, dark eyes fixed on her.

He wore black cargo pants and a fitted black T-shirt that emphasized his broad shoulders. The diamond in his ear caught the morning light. Even like this, relaxed, unguarded, he was commanding, and her knees weakened.

Gregorio moved next to her to grab a mug.

As he reached past her for the coffee pot, his arm brushed against hers, sending a shiver through her body that had nothing to do with the morning chill. "Sleep okay?" His voice was scratchy from sleep, so sexy she couldn't stand it.

When she didn't answer right away, he looked at her more closely.

He seemed to see straight through her, making it hard to breathe.

To break the spell, she glanced down into the depths of her coffee.

Last night, as she'd arrived at the Den, she'd been a bundle of nerves, wondering if he was watching. Then later, the feel of his hands on her shoulders as she'd watched the couple through the window in the door.

She'd gone from being turned inside out to telling him about her ransacked office, the missing files, and the constant feeling of being followed.

Because she knew him so well, she'd known he would volunteer to help her out. But that he'd insist she stay…? In her wildest dreams, she hadn't expected that.

And then…

Her knees weakened as she recalled everything they'd done once he had her alone.

He was her hero, and her sister's former husband. Because of their family dynamics alone, being with him in that way should never have happened.

Yet she wasn't sure she could resist him if he lifted her up onto the kitchen counter right this moment and slipped his amazing cock deep inside her.

The way she reacted to him, calling him Sir, turning herself over to him completely, terrified her.

She prided herself on being in control, but with Gregorio, she abandoned everything and wanted more.

Realizing he was still waiting, she gave herself a mental shake. "I slept better than I expected." How could she not when she'd been snuggled against his hard body, protected by his arms? "I think I was more exhausted than I realized."

"No doubt."

Meeting his gaze, she said, "Thank you."

"For?" He raised an eyebrow.

"For letting me stay."

His eyes darkened, becoming endless pools of midnight that threatened to draw her in. The muscle in his jaw tightened, and when he spoke, his voice was rough with emotion. "I don't think you understand, Little Petal. There's no way I would have allowed you to walk away."

In a vain attempt to steady herself, she took another sip of coffee. Then she turned back to the window, watching as the first rays of sunlight painted the trees in shades of gold and amber. "I was thinking about going for a run," she said after a moment, her voice careful. She'd wanted to do that all morning, and she'd regretted not taking Gregorio up on last night's offer to program her fingerprint into his security system. "Clear my head."

"We can do that."

She tensed, her shoulders stiffening as she turned to face him. "I meant alone."

"Not happening."

"Gregorio…" She exhaled. "I can take care of myself. As you know, I've been doing it for years."

"And yet you're here," he said, his tone calm but unyielding. "You came to me because you knew you weren't safe. Nothing's changed since last night, Sasha. You're not going anywhere alone."

Frustration bubbled to the surface. She hated feeling trapped, hated that he was right. "Fine," she said, setting her mug down with more force than necessary. Unable to help herself, she tossed him a challenge. "Try to keep up."

"Oh, Sasha. You're going to regret those words." He shot her a grin that made her tummy turn over. "You're on."

The run was both relief and torture.

She set a steady pace through the wooded trails behind the Den, their breaths forming small clouds in the crisp morning air. Sasha was acutely aware of Gregorio's presence near her, his footfalls matching hers, close enough to protect her, but far enough away to give her the illusion of freedom.

Every so often, when she glanced back, she caught him scanning their surroundings, his protective instincts never wavering. The physical exertion was welcome, but it didn't banish her memories of last night or the need clawing at her again this morning.

Despite his response to her challenge, he didn't close the gap between them, helping her relax.

A few minutes later, she rounded a tree, ready to head back.

Then suddenly, a strong arm wrapped around her waist and she was yanked to a stop. Breath whooshed from her as she was pulled against a hard, immovable chest.

"I'll always accept your challenges, Petal." Gregorio spun her around and pressed her back firmly against a tree.

Had she really thought that Gregorio would let her get away with her comment about keeping up?

Her heart roared as he pinned her wrists above her head. Even though he only used one hand, his grip was firm.

"Are you going to pretend last night didn't happen?"

That was the only way she could survive him.

He leaned toward her purposefully, his gaze on her, possessive and intense. "Hmm, Petal?"

Instead of waiting for an answer, he brought his mouth down onto hers, kissing her deeply, claiming her, exploring her.

Lost in him, she moaned, instinctively arching toward him. Even if her mind shouted no, her body screamed yes.

He grasped her chin and tilted her head to deepen the kiss. Then he lowered himself against her, trapping her. His arousal was hard and insistent, pushing into her.

Suddenly, he wedged his knee between her legs and forced them apart. Then he broke the kiss to trail his lips down her neck, nipping and sucking at her sensitive skin.

"Ride my leg, Sasha," he commanded, his voice rough with desire. "Let me feel you grind yourself against me."

She hesitated, but he captured her hip and guided her forward.

"Do it."

"Gregorio..."

"Do it."

When he used that gruff, commanding voice, she was lost.

Slowly, she began to rock her hips, riding his thigh. The friction rocked waves of excitement through her. Her breath came in ragged little bursts, and she dug her fingers into the bark above her head.

Eyes sparking with passion, he studied her. "That's right. Such a good girl." His voice had a note of satisfaction. "You're mine, Sasha. Mine to protect, mine to pleasure."

As much as she wanted to, she couldn't deny the truth in his words, the connection between them.

"Don't fight me. This. Let yourself go."

As she rode his leg, her body tightening with each movement, she knew she was in danger of truly falling for him.

The realization stunned her. And with the way he was holding her, demanding her surrender, forcing her to grind against his thigh, she cried out his name. Desperately she grabbed his shoulders as she spiraled over the edge.

Gregorio held her firmly, offering his silent strength and support. His gaze never left hers as she rode out the climax.

"You're the most beautiful woman I've ever seen." His voice was graveled, and he pressed his forehead against hers. "I can't get enough of you, Sasha. I won't let anyone or anything hurt you."

She looked into his eyes, seeing the raw emotion there. Her heart raced, not just from the physical exertion, but from the emotional intensity. "Gregorio," she whispered. "This is…"

"Go on."

"You're scaring the hell out of me."

"Am I?" His voice held no apology.

She absolutely had to get some distance between them. "This…" *How much I want you, need you. And how impossible it is.*

He lived in the shadows and risked danger at every turn. Even her sister hadn't really known what he did for a living. Special assignments was all he'd ever tell her. Once Sasha had joined Hawkeye, she'd learned he was in a specialty black ops unit that did the dirty work no one else was capable of.

Over the years, the Hawkeye family had mourned the deaths of numerous operators, and there was a plaque at headquarters honoring them. She'd prayed she'd never see his name there.

During the time he'd been her brother-in-law, Gregorio had rarely been home. That was part of the reason the marriage had ended.

Even though he was no longer employed by Hawkeye, he freelanced. His work was maybe even more dangerous now. Only people with nothing to lose took those missions.

Was that what she wanted? To care about a man who risked his life every day, who came and went like the wind? Who tore her emotions to shreds?

After the exchange in the janitor's closet, she'd been obsessed with thoughts of him. But he'd ghosted her.

Ultimately, that was the reason she'd agreed to help start Pathways. Living and dying based on whether or not she saw Gregorio or fretting about how he'd react to her was too much to bear.

She shook her head to clear it. That kind of uncertainty wasn't for her.

"Stop thinking."

His voice brought her back to the present. He was close, so close. He filled her vision and her senses.

Maybe searching him out hadn't been such a good idea. "I need to get going." *While I still can.* "I have a long drive back to Denver."

When he gave her some space and released her hands, she desperately brought them up between them and placed them on his chest, giving a little push. But of course her efforts were useless. Gregorio wouldn't budge until he was ready.

She used the rest of the run to try to focus on her case, not her reaction to the man close behind her.

When they were back inside his cabin, her phone buzzed. Grateful for the distraction, she grabbed it and answered.

"Hey," Ashley said, her voice bright but tinged with concern. "Just wanted to check in. You seemed… distracted yesterday."

Sasha tightened her grip on the phone. "Everything's great," she said, forcing herself not to look at Gregorio. He was near, barely winded from their run, and he was studying her with absolute focus. "Thanks for checking."

"You sure?" Ashley pressed. "It's not like you not to let anyone know where you are, Sash."

She paced to the window, more to distance herself from Gregorio than anything else. "I'll be back in Denver in a couple of hours."

"And I bet you're not even trying to have fun."

Fun? Sasha couldn't help but glance over her shoulder at Gregorio.

Her dark, dangerous protector was wicked and intense, and toe-curlingly demanding. But fun? She wasn't sure that word applied. "I'll see you tomorrow after I meet with Mrs. Santos."

"In that case, I'll get back to Jonah."

After ending the call, Sasha set the phone down. "That was my office manager."

"She seems overly concerned."

Does she? Or was he grasping at straws? Seeing something that didn't exist? "Can we get going?"

"You have time for breakfast first."

It wasn't a question, and she blew out a frustrated breath. "We can grab something on the way."

Rather than argue, he pulled eggs from the refrigerator. The man was an unmovable force of nature.

Knowing that she didn't have a prayer of winning, she settled for starting a second pot of coffee while bacon sizzled in a pan.

Then, wanting to put space between them, she headed to the bedroom to gather her belongings and repack her duffel bag.

A few minutes later, he joined her, carrying a fresh cup of coffee. "Breakfast is almost ready."

"Thanks."

She remained behind for a few more minutes before joining him.

He'd set two plates and silverware next to each other on the island, and she slid onto a barstool.

As always, his movements were economical. Was there anything he couldn't do? "You're competent in the kitchen."

"Necessity."

While they were eating, his phone chimed with a notification.

Excusing himself, he headed up to the loft.

While he was gone, she finished her breakfast and washed the pans.

"That was Inamorata," he said when he came back down the stairs.

Hawkeye's right-hand person, the woman who was the heartbeat of the organization. Sasha had immense respect for her brains and talent.

"A team will be at your office for the security install today at noon."

"But..." She scowled. "They're scheduled for tomorrow."

"I changed it." His words were flat, as if he had every right to do that. "And another crew will be at your house this afternoon at three."

"At...? What?" *My house?* He was taking over her life. "Gregorio—"

"If we're going to be there when they arrive, we need to head out."

She held up her hand. "Look... Stop."

As if annoyed, Gregorio quirked an eyebrow.

"I don't need you handling all the details of my life." *Running roughshod over me.*

He moved in closer, strides wide, each step echoing dangerously off the wood floors. "Too goddamn bad, Petal. When you came to me, you sealed your fate. I'm going to protect you."

With her arms folded, she forced out a shaky breath.

"Go ahead and argue with me." He regarded her steadily. "Tell me that moving up the day of the install is a bad thing."

As he knew, she couldn't.

"Or that knowing your house is secure is a bad idea. Tell me, Sasha."

"Look—" She raked back a wayward lock of hair. "You could have asked me."

"You were sleeping."

Always so calm, unruffled, even though he'd been making decisions about her life. Did anything ever get to him?

"Deal with it." He moved in closer and clamped his hands on her shoulders. "Or fucking try saying thank you before I turn you over my lap and spank your ungrateful ass."

Mouth open, she blinked. "You made that same threat last night. You know you wouldn't actually do it."

"Go ahead and try me." He dug his fingers in deeper.

Oh hell no. He was focused on her, his eyes seeming to dare her to push him just one step further.

After being in the Den's dungeon last night, she realized her former brother-in-law was a full-on Dominant. No doubt he was experienced and knew all the things to do that would make her cry and beg for mercy.

"Okay. Fine." Still, she couldn't bring herself to say thank you. "You're right. Extra security is a good idea." But that didn't mean he had to go to Denver with her. "I need to get back to my car." She set her chin stubbornly. "Or I'll call for a ride." With that, she wiggled from his grasp, recognizing she would never have gotten away if he didn't allow it.

While he tucked a weapon into his waistband and pulled on a buttery soft leather jacket that devastated her, she rechecked her duffel bag, moving her gun into her purse. Feeling more in control, she headed to the front door.

The drive from the Den to the lodge in Winter Park didn't take as long as it had last night, and the morning sun danced with the long, thin clouds, casting long shadows on the road.

Her car sat exactly where she'd left it. A couple were loading luggage into their vehicle while juggling to-go cups of coffee. Two men were lifting mountain bikes onto a rack in the front of a nearby shuttle bus, while a family with small children boarded the vehicle.

Everything was normal, a typical day in an off-season tourist town.

Tension eased from her shoulders.

Instead of dropping her off, he parked his SUV under the canopy directly in front of the revolving glass doors.

When the valet approached, Gregorio shook his head sharply.

"I appreciate you letting me bounce things off you. If there are any new developments, I'll reach out to you." She flashed him a half-smile as she reached for the door handle. "Thanks for everything. I've got it from here."

Unsurprisingly, he didn't respond. Instead he exited the vehicle.

"Gregorio..." She started to protest, then she clamped her mouth shut. Why waste the energy? Once she'd packed up her belongings, she'd be on her way.

As soon as they entered her room, unease crept up her spine.

She gave the room a quick glance, then she froze when she saw her luggage. A shirt wasn't rolled exactly the way she'd left it, with the logo up.

"What is it?"

She grabbed her gun. "Someone was in here."

He didn't ask how she knew, he simply gave a tight nod. Then he nudged aside the blinds to glance outside before checking beneath the bed, the wardrobe, and the bathroom, each movement fluid, precise, reminiscent of the predator she sometimes glimpsed beneath his controlled exterior.

Finally returning to her, he slid his gun back into place. "Clear."

"There's no way I could have been followed yesterday."

Gregorio inclined his head toward the door. "Let's check your car."

"I've been doing that more than once a day."

"Good."

"Even with an RF scanner." She shrugged. "I haven't found anything."

Outside, he grabbed a bag from his SUV. From it, he pulled out a sleek black case. Inside was a compact device she didn't recognize.

"New toy?" she asked, arching a brow.

"Military-grade spectrum sniffer. Picks up low-emission transmitters—stuff you don't find just anywhere."

He powered it on with a soft beep and began a deliberate sweep of her vehicle, pausing near the rear quarter panel.

The handheld vibrated.

"Got it," he muttered. A moment later, he pulled a tiny device—no larger than a postage stamp—from beneath the weatherstripping near the taillight.

Sasha's stomach dropped. "That's not consumer tech."

"No," he agreed, examining the tracker. "Whoever planted this knew what they were doing. Passive until pinged. Encrypted. Tiny emission footprint. You wouldn't have caught it unless you stripped the whole car."

Mouth set in a grim line, he crossed the parking lot and pressed the tracker onto the metal frame just under the luggage compartment. The bus rumbled to life and pulled away.

"That'll throw them off for a time," Gregorio said. "Leave your things here. We'll go to Denver in my car."

Her frustration mounted.

"This is bigger than you, Little Petal."

As much as she hated to admit it, he was absolutely right.

Taking charge, he pressed his palm to her spine and led her back inside. "We're staying a few extra days," he told the clerk.

She blinked. Even though she wasn't paying ski-season rates, the hotel was expensive.

Once an extension was arranged, he told the woman he wanted to see the head of security.

With a frown, the woman reached for her phone and summoned the man.

When he arrived, Gregorio took him aside, and pressed money into his palm.

A few moments later the guard glanced over his shoulder at her. Then with an understanding nod, he headed back behind the front desk.

"Let's roll," Gregorio told her.

As they exited the parking lot, making the right turn that would lead them back to Denver, her gun dug into her back.

One unspoken question lingered… How far was her stalker willing to go?

Chapter Eleven

On the outskirts of Denver, Sasha's phone rang.

After checking the display, she glanced over at Gregorio. "It's Brenda Santos."

The look he shot her said everything. *Interesting.* After all, they had an appointment scheduled for tomorrow.

She swiped to answer, but before she could give her name, Mrs. Santos was speaking, her voice shaking with barely contained panic. "Sasha, thank God I reached you."

"Mrs. Santos. How can I help you?"

"Felix just told me he's taking a trip. He wouldn't say where or when he'd be back. I'm afraid he's with *her.*"

Sasha's chest tightened at the barely contained panic in the woman's voice.

As he navigated the growing I-25 traffic, Gregorio shot her a glance and a nod. No longer surprising her, he seemed to read her mind.

"Would you like me to come over?" she asked her client.

"Yes." Brenda gave a shaky exhalation. "I don't know what I'm going to do."

"Just stay calm. We'll figure it all out together. Can you do that for me?" Her compassion battled with her professionalism.

"I'm losing my mind, Sasha." Brenda's voice cracked.

"I'm not far away. I promise."

"Will you hurry? Please?"

"As quick as I can."

"Thank you."

Then, before she could change her mind, she said, "I have an associate with me."

Across the compartment of the SUV, Gregorio scowled at her, and she changed her focus to stare out of the side window.

"I suppose that's okay."

"Good. I'll see you in less than twenty minutes."

"Thank you." Brenda choked back a sob. "I'll let the gate guard know you're coming."

As the call ended, Gregorio's eyebrow lifted. "Associate?"

"What would you like me to say?" *Lover? The man who my sister divorced? Someone who made me scream his name last night? A Dominant who had a finger up my ass and made me admit I liked it. The crush I've never gotten over?* Instead of answering, she sighed and asked, "Do you mind meeting her? You don't have to."

"Petal, try keeping me in the car."

His tone held the weight of a vow, reminding her that this dangerous, compelling man had appointed himself her protector whether she wanted one or not.

To cover her reaction, she kept the conversation focused on business. "Maybe you'll catch something I miss."

He didn't respond to that.

She looked up the address and gave it to him, and he told his onboard system to redirect them.

They parked around the block and walked the rest of the way.

Mrs. Santos greeted them at the door of her sprawling home, a Tudor-style mansion.

"Come in. Come in." Her face was pale and drawn, her eyes red-rimmed and swollen. She wrung her hands nervously, her wedding ring catching the sunlight and throwing prisms against the wall.

Her gaze darting to the driveway, she stepped aside.

"This is Gregorio," Sasha introduced once the door was closed behind them. "The, uhm, associate I was mentioning."

"Ma'am." His voice was pitched low and reassuring, though Sasha caught the underlying steel.

"Please, call me Brenda." She tried to force a smile that came out more of a grimace.

"Brenda."

He gave the woman a kind smile, something Sasha had never experienced from him.

In response, Brenda blinked several times. Then with a sigh, her shoulders rounded once more, and she led them toward the back of the house to the kitchen.

The last time Sasha had been here, the place had been immaculate. Today, the space was a bit messy, with several pairs of shoes left in a pile near the foyer, and a stack of unopened mail piled on the console table. A throw blanket was on the floor near a sofa, and the scent of burned coffee lingered in the air.

"Thank you for coming." Her voice wavered, threatening to crack. "I'm sorry I had to call you, but I don't know what's happening with him anymore." She dropped down into a chair, and they followed suit. Two different coffee cups had been abandoned, half-full.

"He's never been like this before," she went on. "Secretive. Argumentative. And then buying me stuff I don't need…that vehicle, flowers, jewelry. He has to be feeling guilty about something." The words tumbled out, as if she'd been holding them back for too long.

"We'll do everything we can to help," Sasha assured her. "Tell me what happened. Step by step."

Beneath the table, Brenda knitted her hands together. "We were supposed to go out to dinner with friends tonight. But this morning, he started throwing his belongings into a bag." Desperately, Mrs. Santos tried to blink her emotions away. "He's never packed his own suitcase. Not once in all these years." A tear finally fell. "Then he said he had to leave town. And he didn't say when he'd be back."

"Or where he was going?"

Mrs. Santos shook her head. "Oh, Sasha. I'm so scared."

Gently, she reached forward to touch the woman's hand. "I know you need answers, and I can tell you this…" She glanced toward Gregorio, who gave her a small nod. "I've had surveillance on Mr. Santos."

The woman straightened her back, and her eyes were wide, unblinking, like a rabbit caught in headlights, as if she was bracing herself for what Sasha might say.

"I have found no evidence that he is having any kind of affair."

Her breath caught on a sob. "Really?"

Sasha nodded. "Now that doesn't guarantee that he's not, but what I've found so far suggests something else is going on."

Squeezing her eyes shut, she sighed.

After processing the information, she looked at Sasha again. "Then…? I don't understand."

"Do you want to know what I have found?"

"Yes." She curled her hands around one of the abandoned cups and dragged it close. "I have to."

"I'm happy to tell you everything, but first, would it be okay if we took a look in Felix's office?"

"Why do you need to do that?" She hesitated for a moment. "I don't know what you think you'll find."

"I'm not sure, either," Sasha admitted. "Hopefully something that will help make more sense out of all of this so I can totally put your mind at ease." With the way he'd been giving his wife an SUV and jewelry, she doubted that. But she wanted answers herself.

Mrs. Santos twisted her wedding ring. "I suppose that would be okay." With a trembling hand, she gestured toward the hallway. "It's the third door on the left."

"Thank you." Sasha squared her shoulders, hyperaware of Gregorio's solid presence at her back as they stood and made their way down the hall.

Felix's office was exactly what she'd expected—rich mahogany furniture, leather-bound books lining built-in shelves. But the meticulous precision of the space set off warning bells. Every pen was aligned, every paper perfectly stacked. It wasn't just tidy—it was obsessively perfect.

With his elbow, Gregorio closed the door behind them. Then he pulled a pair of latex gloves from inside his jacket pocket and locked the door.

"I'll start with the desk," she said.

"I've got the bookcase."

She donned a pair of gloves that she kept in her purse.

The first two drawers yielded nothing but ordinary office supplies, arranged with the same level of organization as everything else.

When she reached the third, she brushed against an inconsistency in the wood. "I may have something."

Gregorio joined her.

She pulled out the drawer and carefully pried up the false bottom, revealing a sleek black ledger bound in leather. "Bingo."

After flicking a glance toward the door, just in case, she flipped open the cover.

The pages were filled with small, meticulous handwriting—columns of numbers, dates, and coded entries. Some names she recognized as businesses that Santos ran. And others she recalled from an investigation at Hawkeye.

But one word stopped her cold.

Jesus. "Gregorio," she said softly, beckoning him over.

Instantly, he was beside her, leaning over her shoulder, reassuring, protective.

He swore in a language she didn't recognize. *"Argentum?"*

To the rest of the world, the company was a philanthropic one. But she knew better, as did Gregorio.

They were organized crime, with enforcement arms all over the world.

What the hell was Santos up to?

The ledger was more than evidence—it was a roadmap of Felix Santos' secrets, and possibly a death warrant for anyone who found it.

Her mouth dried, and she met Gregorio's gaze.

How much danger was Santos in? And did this have anything to do with who was stalking her?

"May I?"

"Go ahead." She stepped aside.

While Gregorio flipped through the ledger, she dug out her cell phone.

"Good idea." He placed the book down on the desk, and she began snapping pictures of each page.

"Sasha?" Mrs. Santos called, trying the door.

Shit.

"I'll take care of her," Gregorio said.

At that moment, she appreciated having him with her.

While he unlocked the door and opened it a crack, she replaced the leather-bound book and slid the panel back into place.

"What's taking so long?" Mrs. Santos asked.

"Being thorough. You don't happen to have coffee, do you?" he asked. Charm was laced through his rich baritone. "Sasha was anxious to get over here to see you, so she didn't let me stop for a cup. Can't function without my caffeine."

"I…"

She imagined the woman trying to peek past him. But she might as well be trying to see around a mountain.

"Of course," Mrs. Santos said eventually.

After sliding the drawer closed, she did another quick sweep of the bookcases before removing her gloves and pocketing them alongside her phone.

Then she returned to the kitchen.

A fresh pot of coffee was spitting and hissing, and she smiled at her client.

"Black or cream?" Mrs. Santos asked, her voice wavering slightly as she reached for mugs.

"Black for me," Gregorio replied. The way he handled the situation—redirecting Mrs. Santos' attention while giving Sasha time to process what they'd found—showcased his tactical expertise.

"And you, Sasha?"

"Cream. Thanks." Trying to appear calm, she took a seat at the table, across from Gregorio.

The Argentum connection stunned her. If Felix Santos was involved with them, his sudden departure might have taken on a much darker meaning. Was he running from them? Or carrying out some kind of assignment?

Mrs. Santos' hand trembled as she set a mug in front of Gregorio a couple of minutes later.

Then Sasha accepted hers.

"You think something's wrong, don't you?"

"I think your husband may be in over his head with some business dealings," Sasha said diplomatically.

"Business dealings?" Brenda sank into her chair and curled her hands around her earlier, abandoned cup. "He's been having a lot of meetings. Sometimes late at night. It's not unusual for him to get home after midnight, with the restaurants and nightclubs, but he never used to get out of bed to answer phone calls."

"Has your husband mentioned any new business partners recently?" Gregorio asked. "Or received any unusual phone calls?"

Mrs. Santos twisted her wedding ring. "He's been taking a lot of calls in Spanish lately. And there was a man who came by the house last week—I'd never seen him before. Felix seemed...afraid of him."

Sasha and Gregorio exchanged quick glances.

Gregorio leaned forward, and when he spoke, his words were gentle. "Can you describe him for me?"

"Do you think it's important?"

"Just following up on everything," he assured her.

As Mrs. Santos gave a brief description, Gregorio paid close attention. But like before, he didn't take notes.

"Anything else at all that seems odd?" Sasha asked.

"As I've already mentioned, the gifts." For a moment, she stared ahead vacantly. "We've always been careful with money. We do well enough, but..." She gestured vaguely at the luxurious house around them. "This was a gift from my family. Felix has always been sensitive about that."

"I'd like to increase surveillance on your husband," Sasha said carefully. "With your permission, of course."

"Is that really necessary?"

She chose her words with care. "The more we know, the better we can help. You. And maybe your husband."

As if it were a lifeline, Mrs. Santos pulled her cup closer to her.

"Maybe I'm overreacting."

Definitely not. "No," Sasha assured her. "Your instincts that something is wrong are valid. But let me do my job and investigate properly before we jump to conclusions."

Sasha's phone buzzed. "Excuse me." She glanced at the screen, expecting another update from Ashley or perhaps a notification about Hawkeye's security team.

Mind your own business. Or the old woman dies.

The phone nearly slipped from her fingers, and Gregorio reached across the table to grab the device.

Outside, a car door slammed.

Mrs. Santos paled and jumped up. "That's Felix's car."

Chapter Twelve

"I have no idea how many years it's been since I had to scramble over a fence," Sasha said with a small wince.

AsFelix Santos had entered the house, Gregorio and Sasha had hustled out the backdoor of the mansion and made a mad dash for the far end of the property.

Close escapes were a constant in his life. Maybe too constant.

With a half-smile, she accepted the wineglass he offered. "Appreciate it."

Holding a glass of Bonds whiskey, he sank into the chair close to her. On the Den's patio, flickering flames from the firepit cast shadows across her face, making her skin golden and catching the highlights in her hair.

After they'd sped away from the Santos' neighborhood, Sasha had said very little.

Then they'd met with the Hawkeye teams, and she'd sent the new office codes to her staff.

During the drive back up the mountain, they'd debriefed with Inamorata. Sasha had been efficient. Professional. Keeping it together.

But he'd noticed the way her hands curled into fists in her lap, the way she kept her spine straight as if she was bracing for impact.

But even here, where they were safe, the vast Colorado sky stretching above them and the crisp mountain air biting at his skin, the tension in his shoulders refused to ease.

This mission wasn't like the others. No clear orders. No defined threat. Just a tangled web of questions and half-truths, and the gnawing sense that someone—maybe everyone—was lying. Gregorio hated not knowing. Hated the way his instincts itched, like he was walking blindfolded through a minefield.

He took a breath. Then another.

The Santos mess was handled…for now.

Hawkeye had what they needed…for now.

Her discovery of Argentum's involvement confirmed Sasha was caught up in something big and dangerous, and it redoubled his determination not to let her go it alone. Despite her protests that she didn't need to be sheltered away at his cabin, that was exactly where she was going. Not just because she'd been family at one point. And not just because she'd come to him for help and his integrity wouldn't allow him to walk away.

After last night, Sasha was in his heart.

With other women, even her sister, he'd been able to keep his emotional distance. He was always in control, always able to walk away without a backward glance.

But Sasha…?

Fuck it to hell.

She demolished his defenses with a single look. The way she surrendered to him, trusted him, became wild and uninhibited in his arms—he'd never experienced anything like it before. She wasn't any woman.

She was…everything.

His everything.

Fucking her, making love, had been a mistake. One he wasn't sure he'd recover from.

She tipped her head back, and his gaze was drawn to the elegant line of her throat. Above them, a shooting star streaked across the inky sky.

"Do you believe that wishes come true?" she asked quietly.

He wasn't sentimental. Didn't believe in anything other than hard work and persistence. Right and wrong. Rather than darken her mood, he took a sip and countered with, "Do you?"

"Used to. When I was a kid." Her voice held a note of wistfulness that made his chest tighten. "Before…"

Before her parents' restaurant had been held up at gunpoint, and she'd been huddled up, frightened and unable to do anything to help them during the robbery. "And now?" he asked.

"Like you, I just believe in getting the job done." She took another sip of wine, then turned to regard him. "I've been thinking…"

In the firelight, he studied her, wishing he could see her eyes more clearly.

"It started after I saw Mrs. Santos in person."

He looked at her sharply. "The stalking?"

She nodded, and her fingers tightened around the stem of her glass. "I'd been working the case for a while, but nothing happened before we met in person."

"Where did you meet?"

"I went to her house."

So Mrs. Santos was being watched. Made sense, especially considering Felix showed up at home, less than twenty minutes after he and Sasha arrived. Not bad for a man who was supposedly out of town.

Before they'd left, Sasha made the woman promise she'd call the moment it was safe. So far, the phone hadn't rung.

"So who was in my office?" Despite the fact she was bundled up and had a blanket around her, she shuddered. "Argentum?"

That was the only thing that made sense. Santos was mixed up with them, and if he were in trouble, surveilling their home made sense.

And that meant the risk to his Petal was even greater.

They spent the next few minutes talking about other angles to the case, things they'd discussed a dozen times on the drive back to Winter Park, looking for things they'd missed.

Until they heard back from Inamorata or Mrs. Santos, they were at a dead end. "Tell me about your former partner." Especially after what Hawkeye had said, Gregorio had no reason to trust the guy. "About Toby."

"I doubt he's involved. That just doesn't make sense."

"We need to look at every connection. Humor me."

She shrugged. "He was my boss at Hawkeye. I thought he was good at what he did. Smart. Capable. The kind of person people trusted." Her knuckles went white around the glass.

Fuck. He should have seen this before. "You loved him?"

The wine sloshed in her glass, but she didn't respond.

Jealousy ripped through him, primal and possessive. He clenched his jaw as images flashed through his mind—another man touching her, holding her, sharing her bed. Coming home to her every night.

His thoughts were irrational. Dangerous. He had no claim on her past.

"I wouldn't call it that." She considered. "I mean... We started Pathways together, which meant we spent a lot of time with each other. On some level, we fell into a relationship. We were living together, trying to save money by sharing expenses while we got the agency running. But it wasn't like a burning, passionate love." She closed her eyes. "Regardless. It's still stupid, right?"

"Don't." The word came out harsher than he'd intended.

With a small frown, she turned to face him. "Don't what?"

His voice dropped, rough with emotion he couldn't hold back. "Call yourself stupid for trusting someone who didn't deserve it."

"Thank you for that."

Her eyes held a fragile vulnerability, and he curled a hand into a fist, wanting to slam it into the man's face for hurting her. If he ever saw him, he wouldn't be responsible for his actions.

"I had to leave everything behind," she continued softly. "The place we'd shared. The life we'd built. All because I wouldn't compromise my ethics." She lifted a shoulder. "I moved back into my parents' house while I tried to scrape together enough money to buy him out of the Pathways agreement."

Her words were a knife in his gut. The thought of her struggling while that bastard lived in their home…

"Like I said. I was stupid to trust him."

"Emotion makes us blind." He kept his voice steady despite the rage building inside him.

A gust of wind swept across the patio, and she shivered.

The fire's warmth wasn't enough anymore—not for this conversation, not for what lay between them. And it sure as hell wasn't enough for the possessive need consuming him.

Standing, he held out his hand. "Let's go inside, Petal."

Her gaze met his.

"Gregorio…"

"Take my hand." When she finally placed hers in his, he closed his tightly.

No other man would ever hurt her again.

Because there was little light, he turned on the flashlight on his phone as they made their way down the path.

As they neared his place, the motion-sensor lights switched on. In the near distance, a coyote howled.

Once inside, with the alarm set and the door locked, he released her hand and turned her to face him.

"Strip for me."

Her eyes widened.

"I want you."

She wrapped her arms around herself, but she made no move to protest.

"You're going to be mine."

"This…" She hesitated. "I mean…" She looked around the room. "You mean right here? Not the bedroom?"

"You know who I am. What I want." He came closer and captured her shoulders. Gently he rubbed them, reassuring her, connecting them to one another, letting her know he was serious. "Now, Petal. Be my good girl." He left no room for argument, and he saw a responding flicker of compliance in her beautiful green eyes.

"Uh…"

"As you know, my preferred response is yes, Sir."

"Always?" Her lips parted. "I thought that was just last night."

"I'm a Dominant with you, Sasha." Before now, he'd sometimes been a switch—meaning he'd bottom for the right person who needed a release as much as he did. A sound thrashing could get him out of his head, and the taste of pain sharpened his senses—maybe why he enjoyed his punching bag, too, and being in the field. But his sweet Sasha had restored order to his universe. "When we're intimate, I expect certain things from you."

She took in a small, trembling breath.

"It was natural enough for you yesterday. You want this as much as I do. Stop thinking."

For a moment, she squeezed her eyes shut.

"Unless you'd rather we hang out on the couch, maybe watch TV?" At that, his lips did twitch. She hadn't moved at all, hadn't tried to get away. His Petal was as hot for him as he was for her. "Or you're welcome to shower and go to bed."

"That's not…" She shook her head. "No. That's not what I want."

"In that case, please do as I say." He released his grip but didn't step back. "Remove your clothes."

"Yes…"

He waited.

"Sir."

His cock hardened at the breathless respect in her voice. So fucking perfect.

With slow, tentative movements, she began to undress. Her jacket slid off first, followed by her shirt, revealing the smooth curves of her shoulders and the swell of her breasts encased in black lace. Gregorio watched, his breath growing shallow as each layer fell away.

When she stood before him in nothing but her bra and panties, he motioned for her to continue. She bit her lip, sending a jolt straight to his groin.

What had he been thinking? This was pure, fucking torture.

Her gaze on him, she complied, unhooking her bra and letting it drop to the floor. Her breasts spilled free, so beautifully full and tempting. In the coolness of the night air, her nipples hardened under his gaze.

"Beautiful, Sasha. So damn beautiful."

As if gaining courage from his approval, she slid her panties down her legs, then stepped out of them.

A small triangle of neatly trimmed hair tempted him. "I should keep you naked and available to me."

His cock strained even harder against his jeans, but he forced himself to fold his arms and maintain his composure while drinking in the sight of her.

"Now we'll have a lesson in patience."

"A lesson?" She frowned. "Patience? That's something I'm not good at."

"Walk to my chair and lean over the front of it." He inclined his head. "Grip the arms. Feet wide. And wait for my attention."

While she positioned herself, Gregorio strode to the fireplace, his movements measured and controlled. He knelt to arrange the logs and kindling. Then he struck a match and set the fire ablaze. The flames crackled to life, casting dancing shadows across the room.

Standing, he turned back to her.

His Petal looked gorgeous, her back arched, her ass on display. "That's right." Her long hair cascaded down her back and brushed her shoulders.

"Remain where you are." He went to the bathroom to grab a tube of lubricant. Then he returned, approaching her, still fully clothed, his boots echoing off the floor. Every action was purposeful, meant to make her aware of her submission, his mastery over her.

"I'm going to inspect you."

"Uhm…" She glanced over her shoulder. "What does that mean?"

"It's a BDSM thing. And what I mean is that you're going to remain exactly as I want you. You're not going to protest anything I do to you."

She tightened her buttocks, betraying her nerves. "But…"

He waited.

"I still have a safe word?"

"Always, my Petal. Always." He stroked her spine, and in response, her body became more supple. "That's it. Trust."

"Not so easy for me."

"Give it a try. Face forward."

Following his order, she swayed from side to side. Surrender, if not invitation.

After placing the lube nearby, he began his inspection at her shoulders, running his fingers along her smooth skin, then once more tracing the line of her spine.

She shivered beneath his touch, and his cock throbbed painfully in response. Did she feel she was the one suffering here? The truth was, he was in agony. Every part of him ached to yank his zipper down and force his cock inside her until she screamed his name and confessed that she belonged to him.

Calling on every bit of his Dominant control, he slid his hands down to her hips. He held her tight for a moment, fighting the instinct to drag her back against him.

Instead, he continued his exploration, moving to cup her ass. He lingered there, spreading her cheeks slightly. Then, very intentionally, he brushed his thumb against her tight hole.

"Gregorio!" She gasped, digging her fingers deeper into the chair.

He grinned. "Stay in position."

"But—"

"Patience," he reminded, delivering a quick smack to her right buttock.

"What the fuck?" She swung her head around, eyes flashing. But not from anger. More like curiosity and hunger.

He fisted a hand into her hair, and instantly her breathing increased. "I believe you were told what to do." He smoothed the injured spot. "Now use your safe word or behave." One eyebrow raised, he waited.

"You're being awful."

"On the contrary. I'm being more than generous by giving you a chance to apologize for your defiance."

She locked her jaw.

Oh, Little Petal. I'm going to enjoy this.

Gregorio slid two fingers inside her pussy, making her suck in a breath.

Still, she didn't move away.

Ruthlessly he fucked her, until his fingers were drenched. Then he pulled them out and pressed them against her mouth. "Open."

Staring at him, she remained still, even as he wiped her essence over her lips.

"Gregorio!"

Seizing the opportunity, he slipped his fingers inside her mouth and pressed down on her tongue. "Suck them. Lick them."

When she didn't immediately obey, he spanked her left buttock.

Her tiny flinch gave him the opening he needed and he fucked her mouth with his fingers. Tears swam in her eyes, and he captured one of her breasts and stroked her nipple. The change in her was instant. Closing her eyes, she turned herself over to him. "That's it, Sasha. That's it."

Hell and forever. She was the sexiest woman he'd ever been with. She might not know she was submissive, but he'd recognized the signs the night in the janitor's closet.

Maybe that was one of the reasons he'd walked away.

She was perfect for him. Absolutely perfect.

In a gentle motion, he pulled his fingers from her mouth. "Would you like to apologize so I can continue my inspection?" He gave her a second to think. "Or would you prefer that we continue this struggle before you capitulate?" He trailed his knuckles down the column of her throat. "Your call, Petal."

"Gregorio…" Her eyes were glazed.

"Up to you. You decide which way this will play out." No matter what she chose, he intended to finish what he'd started.

"I, uhm…"

He reined in the impatience gnawing on his insides. She was his woman and his body wanted her now.

"I'll behave."

"You'll be my good girl?"

"Yes." After getting back into position, she whispered, "Yes, Sir."

"Lord, woman. You make me happy."

Because she wasn't expecting it, he dipped between her legs again, grazing her pussy lips with his fingers. She was wet, proving their little power struggle turned her on. Or was it her ultimate surrender that excited her?

He trailed his touch down the insides of her thighs, then back up the outsides. He cupped her ass cheeks and lifted them a little, bending to taste her skin.

Moaning, she jerked her hips backward, asking for more.

"Back where you were," he said softly.

With a tiny murmur of protest, she did as he asked.

Getting her to be his perfect sub was easier than he'd imagined.

"Good. Now keep still as I continue my inspection."

"Yes, Sir."

Fucking hell. He growled, a low sound of satisfaction and need.

He slipped a finger inside her, and she clenched around him. He added another finger, pumping slowly, and he used a third to circle her clit.

Sasha moaned, her hips rocking in sync with his motions.

With his free hand, Gregorio reached under her to cup her breast, rolling her nipple between his fingers. He pinched lightly, and she gasped, her pussy tightening around his fingers. Her breath came in quick, desperate pants.

"I'm not quite done with you yet." He released her breast and brought that hand around to cup her mound. Then he pumped some lube onto his thumb. He coated the outside of the hole, then he pressed forward, sinking deep inside her ass. "Every hole belongs to me." He'd thought it before, but this was the first time he'd said it to her.

While squeezing her, he fucked her front and her rear, driving her until she lost control.

Then her body froze. *"Oh!"*

Abruptly, he withdrew his hand, leaving her empty and wanting.

Protesting, she whimpered, but she didn't move.

He'd been with subs with a lot of experience who didn't behave as perfectly as she did. "What is it you want, Petal?"

"You," she pleaded. "I have to have you inside me. I need to come."

Clenching her buttocks, she seemed to struggle to fight off a climax.

"As long as you stay right where you are."

"That's..." She took a deep breath and forced it out. "You don't ask for much."

"I warned you it was an exercise in patience." He grinned. "Not supposed to be easy, Petal." *But I do plan for it to be thrilling as hell.* Her wait would make the eventual release all the sweeter.

He left her only for a moment, to wash his hands and to retrieve a condom.

Returning, he unbuckled his belt. The hiss from the leather sliding through the loops echoed through the room, and she gave a sexy little shudder.

After unzipping his jeans to free his cock, he rolled on the condom.

Once he moved behind her, he gripped her hips. "Are you ready for me, Sasha?" Her glistening pussy and swollen labia told him all he needed to know.

"Do it. Please."

He exercised his own restraint, stroking in, claiming her a little bit at a time. She tried to wiggle back, but he issued a stern warning. "My pace, Petal."

Though she squirmed, she didn't utter any words.

Finally, he was balls-deep inside her, and he stilled.

"Ohh." Her internal muscles clamped around him. "Gregorio!"

He bit back a groan. The sensation of her tight heat enveloping him was almost more than he could bear. He began to move, each stroke deliberate, measured, designed to drive her to the edge of madness. He held her hips, controlling the pace, refusing to let her rush him.

With each thrust, Sasha's grip on the chair arms tightened, her knuckles turning white. Her feminine moans filled the room and echoed in his ears, a sound he'd never forget.

Leaning forward a little, Gregorio slid one hand around to her front, finding her clit and circling it with his fingers. She cried out, thrusting back against him, trying to urge him deeper.

"Not yet, Petal," he murmured, his voice rough with desire. "You come when I tell you to."

"But…I can't wait."

"You don't have a choice."

Her body shook as he continued pleasure her, relentlessly tormenting her clit, fucking her with a frenzied urgency.

Then there was a tightening inside him, a primal instinct to claim, to protect. This was beyond anything he'd shared with any other woman—something he would never have believed possible.

Gritting his teeth, determined to bring her off first, Gregorio fought off his orgasm.

He gently increased the pressure on her clit, rubbing in tight, quick circles, while he used his other hand to hold her in place as he drove into her.

"Dear God." Her words were broken, barely audible.

This was exactly what he wanted, what he'd thought of since that night he'd had his first taste of her…her as needy for him as he was for her.

"Now you may come, Petal. Anytime you want." He timed his motions on her clit, pushing her closer and closer to the edge.

"Ah!" She threw back her head.

"That's it." His voice was gruff and demanding. "Come for me like a good little submissive."

Crying out, she let go. Her supple body undulated as the waves of pleasure crashed into her.

Sasha's knees began to buckle.

He reacted so he could use both hands to support her, holding her upright. And the change in angle was enough to send him over the edge.

His cock pulsed, and he grunted as he came, filling the condom, wishing like hell there was no barrier between them.

As the last of the orgasm ripped through him, he slowed his thrusts, holding her lightly, giving his support as they both regained control. Their breaths synched, as if they were one. He never wanted to let her go.

Carefully, he pulled out and swept her up into his arms. After placing her weightless, trembling body on the couch, he draped a blanket over her.

Blinking slowly, she met his eyes.

Even though neither spoke, the emotional weight of the world seemed to hang between them.

They'd shared something special. And probably there were no words to describe it.

After tucking a strand of her wayward hair behind her ear, he headed to the bathroom to dispose of the condom.

With a warm washcloth, he returned to her, bathed her swollen pussy. Then he sat next to her and gathered her into his arms.

Without a protest, she curled into him, her head on his shoulder, her hair spilling down his chest, and for a moment of peace, the world around them didn't exist. Her tiny, contented sigh vibrated against him, and something fierce and possessive surged through him. She fit perfectly against him. Like she belonged here. Like she'd *always* belonged here.

"You doing okay?"

With a soft yawn, she pushed herself away from his body and looked up at him, her eyes soft and vulnerable. "I'm fine."

"Yeah?" he asked. Sasha had to be feeling what he was. Didn't she?

"That was…" Smiling, she laid her head back down. "Wow."

Masculine pride shot through him.

He'd pleased his woman.

Was there any better feeling?

"Wow?" he repeated. "Not too much?" He'd pushed her a little harder than he'd originally planned, but once he'd seen the way she reacted to him, his baser urges had taken over. The sight of tiny red marks against her creamy skin drove him mad.

"Honestly? It was perfect."

"Oh?"

"In fact, I'm..." She swallowed deeply. "Curious about some of the things I saw at the Den."

Are you? "Go on."

She kept herself hidden from him. Hiding her vulnerability?

"I might be ready to—"

"To?" he prompted.

When she didn't respond, he gently captured her chin and tipped her head back so he could meet her eyes. "What is it you want, Sasha?"

Chapter Thirteen

"Do you want me to take you to the Den?"

How did he seem to know her better than she knew herself?

As much as she wanted it, she couldn't force herself to admit the truth.

Every touch, every whisper, every *"yes, Sir,"* was dragging her deeper into emotional danger, leading her closer and closer to potential heartbreak.

Fear arrowed down her spine.

She was falling for Gregorio.

Sasha gave herself a mental shake. The idea of having a real future with Gregorio was a ridiculous impossibility.

She couldn't even begin to imagine the reaction from her sister or her parents. He'd been such an important part of their lives since he'd saved them all.

He'd arrived to pick up her sister for a date and unwittingly walked in during the holdup. Sasha had been huddled in the back room with her mother and

Adriana, shaking with fear, crying, while her father had a pistol pointed at his forehead.

With brutal calm, Gregorio had taken down one robber and disarmed the other.

That was the night she'd developed a severe case of hero worship for him.

Afterward, her sister had accepted his marriage proposal, and he'd been joyfully welcomed as a member of the DiLuce family.

Years later, their divorce had devastated everyone.

That fateful night had also shaped who she was as a human being. She'd hated feeling helpless. When she was safely in bed, she'd vowed she'd never be a victim again. Every decision from then on had supported that resolution. She'd taken self-defense classes, learned to shoot, joined Hawkeye—like Gregorio—and gone through their tactical training classes. Now, twice a month, she taught other women and children how to protect themselves.

"Tell me, Petal."

He refused to let her hide. Even from herself. "Gregorio..."

No matter how foolish or reckless, she wanted more.

The small taste of BDSM that he'd given her wasn't even close to enough.

Her whole life, she'd been searching for something like this.

Ordinary sex was ho-hum. She'd always wondered what the big deal was. The connection was okay, but until Gregorio, she hadn't understood.

He'd brought her to life.

And she craved the edge of danger that he was offering.

After this case was over, she had no idea if she'd see him again, and she'd rather have the memories, even if they were woven with regrets.

"I'm waiting for you to say the words, Petal," he prompted. "Be brave."

Damn the consequences.

As scared as she'd been lately, she wanted—desperately—to feel alive. Up here, there was so much security, she was totally safe, able to let go and indulge.

He hadn't pushed at all, and she appreciated that.

With a steadying breath, digging deep for courage, she finally looked at him. "I want to go to the Den."

A slow, sultry smile crossed his face, taking years off his age. The shadows that haunted his eyes vanished. Maybe not forever, but for the moment. "Do you?"

Drawing a steadying breath, she told him the truth. "Yes."

"That's my girl."

She could live and die on his approval.

"And what do you want to experience?"

"Anything." Another spanking like the one he'd given her, the orders, his gruffness, his shocking demands. What else was out there that she'd never experienced?

"Did you want to be on my leash?"

Her stomach plunged. He'd asked that before—jokingly, she'd thought. Had he been serious?

"Naked for me? Chained to the wall?"

Like the woman she'd seen last night.

"While I shove my cock down your throat?" Adding emphasis to his question, he cupped the back of her neck. "Is that it?"

Yes. A thousand times, yes. "That sounds horrible."

"Does it?" he mused.

Then the terrible Dom leaned in a little closer, giving no quarter.

"So why do I smell your arousal?"

God help her.

"Or did you want to be leaned over the school desk for a spanking like the one we watched together?"

"I told you I'm not a pain slut." *So why am I tingling all over?*

"Mmm."

Ferociously, she scowled. "What the hell does that mean?"

"Just noting what you're saying."

She huffed out a breath. "I'm serious about this, Gregorio."

"Of course you are."

Maybe his words were meant to reassure her. But they didn't.

"Have we done anything you hated?"

She exhaled a shaky breath. Of course they hadn't. "Not so far," she hedged.

"Do you always have your safe word?"

His voice contained urgency, compelling her to answer. "Yes."

"And are you curious about what you're missing?" He traced her bottom lip with his thumbnail. "Do you hunger for something that you can't name?"

Slowly, she nodded.

"Good. Then let's get you dressed."

And he meant *let's*, as in he took care of her.

After easing her from his lap, he helped her into her clothing, even crouching to tie her shoes. When she protested, he waved her off.

"You deserve to be treated like a princess."

His sexy, growled words shot her pulse into overdrive.

And then he asked her to return the favor.

Offering his shirt to him felt a little awkward. Then she handed him his jeans and he stepped into them.

He pulled them up, then purposefully glanced at the floor in front of him. "On your knees."

Her tummy turned inside out.

"If I have to repeat myself, things won't go well for you."

His voice was filled with warning. And still, a wicked part of her hesitated. What were the consequences for disobedience? And why did she yearn to find out?

"You're going to do what I want, aren't you, Petal?"

The purr in his voice, the confidence… Maybe if he was just stern, she'd push him. But suddenly she wanted his approval more than she wanted to find out about the threatened consequences.

He offered his hand, and she took it, accepting his assistance as she lowered herself to the floorboards.

"I'd keep you there if I could."

Head tipped back, she met his gaze. "Would you?"

"But nude." He swept his gaze over her. "I never get tired of looking at you."

"I never get tired of looking at you, either." After licking her lower lip, she added, "Sir."

"Fuck, Petal." He fisted a hand into her hair.

She'd never liked having her hair pulled, until now. *Until him.*

At the moment it seemed as though this moment was the reason she had grown her hair so long.

"And the zipper."

With a deep swallow, she reached for the metal tab and captured it between her thumb and forefinger.

"Not that way, Petal." He ensnared her wrist in his strong grip and moved her hand aside. "Use your teeth."

Sasha gasped. But she didn't ask if he meant it because she knew he did.

With every passing moment, his cock grew thicker, and she couldn't look away.

"Keep your hands behind your back, Petal. If you can't remember to do so, I will tie them for you."

"But—" The task he'd given her was somewhere between difficult and impossible.

"Don't you have something to say?" he prompted.

Miserably, she looked up at him. "Yes, Sir."

Then, seeming to take pity on her—at least somewhat—he fastened the buttons at his waistband.

"Now get on with it, girl."

Since she didn't personally know anyone who was involved in that kind of lifestyle, all this was new to her. Was that kind of relationship really like this? And if it was... She was more than just curious. She was intrigued.

When she was with Gregorio, he demanded a level of intimacy that she hadn't known existed. He pushed her out of her comfort zone, and the further she went, the more she wanted to explore.

He released her wrist, and she clasped her hands at the base of her spine.

"This could only be better if you were naked and I could torment your pouty little nipples."

Arousal flooded her, making breathing a challenge.

"I'm waiting, Petal."

She had to lower herself even more to capture the little metal tab between her teeth. With as big as his shaft was, doing what he said was almost impossible.

"You really don't want to nick any of my skin, or there will be hell to pay."

And since she would definitely suffer if she didn't get to have him inside her again soon, this was a warning she decided to heed.

She spent at least thirty seconds—and maybe as long as a minute—painstakingly pulling up the zipper, one metal tooth at a time.

When she was done, she sat back on her heels.

"Such a good Petal."

Somewhere along the line, without her being aware of it, he had loosened his grip on her hair, and now he tightened it again, tugging back slightly so that she was looking up at him.

"The position you are in right now is called kneeling back. It can be a very relaxed position for a submissive."

A submissive.

Is that what you think I am? Or was she just exploring a whole new dynamic with Gregorio?

"Kneeling up, like how you began, is perfect for times when you're waiting or when I want you to pay attention." His voice changed, dropping, becoming more sensual. "But when I want you helpless, spread wide with your pussy open and available to me, kneeling back is my personal preference."

Her clit throbbed, even though she was fully clothed. No one had ever spoken to her this way.

"You can expect in future that I will request this of you more often."

In the future.

Her heart leaped.

Was he really considering that possibility? Or were these just sex words?

He crouched in front of her, and with his free hand, he cradled the side of her head. "You were made for this. *For me.*" He paused, never severing the connection of their gazes. "Admit it."

Words lodged in her throat. Because the idea scared her, she couldn't agree. But nor could she lie.

"Now my belt." He released her long enough to grab it, and he held it in front of her. "Put it on me."

They were only going to walk a short distance to the Den, so he truly didn't need it. *Unless...*

She remembered the woman in the private room and the way her Top had used the leather on her rear.

Sasha swallowed hard.

Was Gregorio planning to do similar things to her?

Would she let him?

Painstakingly, she threaded the accessory through the loops, then secured the buckle. For a reckless moment, she pictured the metal, clenched in his palm, as he spanked her with the leather.

She glanced away, scared he might read her thoughts.

"Now my socks."

Was he serious about that?

The way his eyes narrowed told her he meant exactly what he said. "Yes, Sir," she whispered.

He released her hair, and she lowered her arms to her sides and started to stand.

Instantly, he clamped his hands on her shoulders and forced her back to her knees. "Did I give you permission to do that?"

Eyebrows drawing together furiously, she demanded, "Are you serious? You want me to crawl?"

"Believe me, my Petal, you will know anytime I'm teasing you. When I give orders like this, I fully mean for you to comply with them."

Self-conscious in ways she had never been, she did what he wanted, grateful she was fully dressed. Otherwise this would be lewd.

She was aware of his gaze on her, approving and encouraging.

When they reached the Den, she knew he was going to make her do this and much, much more.

Once she'd helped him into his socks and boots, she automatically knelt back.

"Perfect choice, my Petal. You're a quick study."

The way he mixed approval with unyielding demand made her senses swim, keeping her on a straightedge of desire.

"There's a duffel bag in my closet. On the floor. Far right side."

Why was he telling her that?

"Fetch it for me."

Automatically, she started to rise, then she stopped herself.

He smiled when she looked to him for direction.

"I'm a simple man. I want to see your hips sway."

"Meaning…"

"Crawl."

She was afraid of that.

"During a scene, assume that's my preference."

Unsure what he meant, she frowned. "A scene?"

"In this case, I mean when BDSM is part of what we're doing. I'm not a twenty-four-seven Dominant."

So others were.

"Though if you want to play more often, I'm certainly open to negotiation." He flashed a grin that made her emotions turn somersaults.

"I think I'm good with this." In fact, she was struggling to keep up with his never-ending requests.

"The duffel bag?" he prompted. "Has a Hawkeye logo on it."

Since she had a similar one at home, it should be easy enough to find.

Aware of his heated gaze on her, she made her way to the bedroom. Part of her rebelled at following his orders. After all, she was a competent private investigator who ran her own business. And yet there was something amazingly naughty—and fulfilling—about turning over control and surrendering herself to his sexy demands.

Sasha found his bag exactly where he said it would be. Not a surprise. Everything he owned was precisely organized. At her house, she knew where things were, but she was much messier than he was. She told herself it was because she was creative. But now she wondered.

Making her way back to the living room on all fours, was a challenge, and she settled for shoving the heavy load several steps in front of her, then catching up and repeating her process.

Gregorio had remained exactly where he was, arms folded across his chest. In her imagination, he was the absolute picture of masculine control.

"Well done."

She met his gaze, and her heart did funny little things when he smiled. At this point, his approval was becoming more important to her than the air she breathed.

"Now, put it on the coffee table and unpack what's inside."

Curious, she tipped her head to the side.

"Line everything up in a way that makes sense to you."

The zipper sounded unnaturally loud in the silent cabin.

When she had it open, she froze.

"Keep going."

Because of her recent visit to the adult toy shop in Denver, she recognized most of the items.

Her hand shaking, she pulled out several pairs of nipple clamps and lined them in a neat row. Next was a blindfold, followed by a vibrator, and a massive dildo.

As she continued, her senses swam.

Along with a package of wipes, there were cuffs and a leather paddle, along with one that was thick and clear. He also had a wicked-looking forked implement that she assumed was also for spanking.

Finally, there was an odd U-shaped piece of silicone. She guessed that it was a vibrator of some type.

"There's one more thing."

She ran her hand around the inside until she found a tree-shaped piece of metal with tiny purple crystals on the end. Her mouth dried. "A butt plug?"

"A very small one," he confirmed.

"Small?" she echoed in disbelief.

He shrugged. "Good place to start training you for taking my dick up your ass."

Fire blasted through her. "Are you serious?"

"I've told you that all your holes belong to me."

Her pussy throbbed, as much from fear as anticipation. By the time she finally knelt back, her legs were trembling.

"See anything that appeals to you?"

Plenty that terrifies me.

"Choose at least three things."

Fighting off her attack of the nerves, she surveyed the items. *None of the above.*

"If you stall, I'll choose them for you. But I'll select five. So if you're hoping for some sort of mercy, get on with it."

With his implacable tone of voice, she knew he meant every word.

Still, she hesitated.

"Okay, then." He nodded tightly, as if resolved.

Her pulse stopped as he crossed to the coffee table.

"We'll start with this." He picked up the ridiculously sized dildo.

"Oh, God. No way."

He simply grinned and put it back in the bag. "Since I'm feeling generous, I'll give you exactly one second to choose the next thing."

"Fine." She snatched up a pair of soft cuffs and dropped them on top of his toy.

"See? Not so bad, is it?"

Except now it meant he'd tie her in place, with no hope of escape.

"One last thing, Petal."

Trying to think, she hesitated. "Give me a moment? Please?"

"Don't overthink."

With a tiny frown, she considered the clamps. She'd never experienced anything like them, but she'd enjoyed the way he'd played with her nipples earlier. He'd used more pressure than she'd been accustomed to, and the sensations had been surreal.

Quickly, she scanned the rest of the options.

The paddles looked interesting. But the memory of seeing that Top spank his woman with a leather belt still lingered, teasing her.

Maybe if she didn't choose any of the impact toys, he wouldn't spank her hard.

"Time's up."

Frantic, she snatched up the blindfold.

Maybe she wouldn't be able to see what he was doing, and that would allow her to get out of her head. Or maybe it would make things worse.

"Excellent choices," he approved as he dropped in the wipes, then closed his bag and swung it over his shoulder. "I'm looking forward to using all of these on your beautiful body." He came closer, filling her vision with his strong thighs and the sight of his hard cock pressing against his jeans. "I want to get you to the Den." He offered his hand. "Ready to push your boundaries, Petal?"

Chapter Fourteen

Am I really doing this?

Being here at the Den with no one else around unnerved her more than just a little. Yet, would she have had the courage to ask him to play with her in front of a club full of people? Most likely not.

He turned the lights to a low, inviting setting, then turned the sound system up loud. Music thumped from the speakers and vibrated through her, ratcheting her anxiety one notch higher.

In the living room, he turned to her. Gently, he cupped her shoulders and rubbed with slow, reassuring motions. "Your safe word always applies, Petal. We will not do anything that you don't consent to."

She nodded. Because of their history, her trust in him was absolute. He meant everything he said. And the awful truth was…she had no idea how much longer they had together. Days? Hours?

If she were honest with herself, she'd admit that thought scared her more than anything they might do together. She hated the idea of living with regret, wondering what might have happened if she hadn't been able to shove her fears aside and seize the opportunity that he offered.

"Yes." She nodded. "I want this."

His slow, approving smile sent heat tumbling through her.

"In that case, strip for me. Show me what's mine for the taking."

Her fingers were nerveless as she removed her jacket.

Avoiding his gaze, she dropped it onto a nearby chair. He gave her a silent commanding nod, telling her to continue.

Taking a breath to steady her nerves, she crouched to untie her tennis shoes, then toed them off before removing her socks.

Even though she was not short, losing the inch or so of height made her feel slightly more vulnerable.

"Raise your arms."

His voice was ribboned with impatience, and he drew her sweatshirt off and tossed it on top of her jacket.

"Oh. Did you want me to move a little faster, Sir? Am I being too slow?" She tried—and failed—to hide her smile. His impatience was uncharacteristic, letting her know how much she affected him.

His lightning-fast reactions caught her off guard.

In an instant, he was seated in the chair, and she was across his lap, her rear in the air. Fighting for breath, wondering what had just happened, she scrambled to place her fingers on the floor for stability.

Without warning, he brought his hand down on her buttocks. "Sir!" Because she was wearing jeans, she didn't feel the sting as much as if he'd landed on bare skin. "Gregorio!"

Frantically, she kicked and squirmed, and he clamped her legs between his stronger ones.

"I think that'll teach you, my little Petal." He helped her up, turning her to face him. "What do you think?"

"Yes, Sir," she said obediently because he expected it, not because she meant it. She'd definitely learned something… To push him even harder. She adored seeing the crack in his iron control and knowing that she did it to him.

"Now, shall we continue?"

Pretending to be contrite, she kept her voice low and respectful as she responded, "Of course, Sir. Anything you say, Gregorio."

He narrowed his eyes slightly, as if questioning her response.

"In that case…" With his hands on her waist, he helped her to her feet.

But he remained where he was, sitting with an ankle propped on top of his opposite knee.

Heaven help her.

He was in charge and looking dangerously handsome. She could scarcely think when he looked at her through his deep, intense eyes.

"I'm waiting, little Petal." Warning wound its way through his soft words. "Finish undressing."

Emboldened by his earlier reaction to her, she took her sweet time unfastening the top button of her jeans and pulling the zipper down.

Then, her gaze on him, she wiggled exaggeratedly, slowly drawing down the jeans. Once they were around her ankles, she bent to pick them up. Then she tossed them in his direction.

He snagged them out of mid-air.

Wondering who this bold version of herself was, she turned her back to him and swayed from side to side as she lowered her panties. "Is my rear red, Sir?" She reached back to rub the skin. "I mean, it feels a little sore from your spanking. So I'm sure my skin has to be pink, at least."

He growled, and she grinned triumphantly.

So that it appeared she was being the perfect submissive that he thought her to be, she unhooked her bra. Then, with the piece of lingerie dangling from a finger, she pivoted back to face him. "It must be cold in here, Gregorio." She cupped her breasts and ran her palms over her nipples.

"Jesus."

"Can you see how hard they are?"

In a flash, he was on his feet, devouring the distance between them. Restraining his strength, he clamped his hands around her upper arms. "Want to push me, my Petal?"

Oh, yes.

His eyes blazed with passion, and a pulse ticked in his temple.

God, she needed this—him, what they shared.

He kissed her hard, deep, leaving her breathless, her knees weak as he fucked her mouth with his tongue, possessing, claiming.

This passion between them was the piece that had always been missing in her life.

"You'll be the fucking death of me, Sasha," he said when he dragged himself away from her.

Good. She didn't want to go down alone.

"I can't get enough of you."

She'd never get enough of him.

He swept her off the floor and carried her to the kitchen island and placed her on the cold stone.

With a shocked gasp, she attempted to escape, but he forced her down onto her back.

"Time for you to learn another lesson."

He captured her ankles and placed her feet flat on the surface. Then he used his elbows to force her knees apart. "Keep your pussy exposed. It's mine, and you'll do as I say."

She shivered, and not just from the cold.

No matter how much control she thought she had, it was nothing more than an illusion. She only had the power that he granted her.

Chastened, she squirmed just a little, trying to get comfortable. But not even for a second was she tempted to use her safe word.

"Stay where you are." He leaned over her. "I'll be back in less than thirty seconds."

She read the promise in his eyes, and she nodded.

His footfalls were heavy on the wooden floor.

Being here, alone, exposed, nervous about what he had planned, her mind spiraled, and she struggled to bring her breathing under control. She hadn't experienced anything like this. Never even imagined that this kind of experience even existed. In such a short amount of time, he'd shown her the world.

"Keep your knees apart," he called across the distance.

How had he known that she'd moved? Maybe it was a guess, or maybe he just knew her.

Moments later, she noticed the ceiling cameras. *Of course.* She had nowhere to run, nowhere to hide. Even if she could, she wouldn't want to.

A few moments later, he was back, holding things she couldn't quite make out, beyond a small bottle and strips of thin leather.

He placed the items above her head, where she couldn't see them. Curiosity drove her mad. He dropped his bag on one of the stools, then pulled out the gigantic dildo that he had selected earlier.

Frantically, she shook her head. "No, no, no."

With annoying masculine superiority, he grinned. "There are ways to punish bratty subs that have nothing to do with spanking, which I think you might like a little too much."

So she didn't admit to exactly that, she clamped her mouth shut. Having his hands on her was a dream come true.

He cleaned the toy.

Once it was dry, he started to pump dollops of lubricant on top.

Horrified and helpless, she watched as the gel made its way down the silicone. "You can't seriously be planning to put that in me."

"Absolutely I am."

She struggled to gulp back her knot of fear in her throat. "There's no way that's possible?"

"It is. And you're going to cooperate." He paused and raised an eyebrow, as if unconcerned how she responded. "Unless you prefer I also insert a butt plug in your ass."

Instinctively, she drew her knees together.

Reacting ridiculously fast, he forced them back apart. "I'm waiting for your answer, little Petal. Up to you entirely. You can relax and let me fuck you with this, or you can fight me, and I'll shove a butt plug in you so quickly that you won't be able to breathe." He grinned in a way that told her he'd enjoy that. "And then I'll fuck you with this."

She swallowed hard.

"Before you ask if I'm serious, you know I would do exactly that."

For a moment, the word *halt* flitted through her mind, but she let it go. "There's no way it will fit."

He quirked an eyebrow. "I think you had that same fear about my cock going inside you."

"The two can't even be compared."

"My darling Petal..." He feathered strands of hair back from her face. "I gave you plenty of opportunity to pick all of tonight's implements. Did I not?"

She hated when he was right.

"You hesitated, and there's a price to pay for that. Still, you're lucky I didn't choose five on your behalf."

"You do have a mean streak, Sir."

He seemed totally unconcerned. "Do I?"

In a way, his inflexibility was comforting, even though she'd never admit that to him. She always had the ability to call a stop to any of this at any point. But the fact he didn't offer any quarter meant she was free to turn over control to him.

Ever since that night at her parents' restaurant, she'd been on guard, always waiting, watching for threats. The ability to trust someone else, if only for an hour, was the greatest kind of freedom.

"Will you be able to keep your knees apart for me, or would you like to use a spreader bar?"

Even though she wasn't exactly sure what that was, she definitely didn't like the sound of it.

"Keep in mind, if you choose that option, there will be a price to pay. In BDSM, mercy has a price."

"Mercy?" she sputtered, wide-eyed with disbelief.

"When you're fighting against yourself, your instincts, wanting to protect yourself from what you know is coming, you'll understand what I mean."

His expression was filled with foreboding.

"Which will it be?"

Maybe, if she were smart, she'd choose a spreader bar. "I'll keep them apart."

"Brave girl."

Perhaps she should reconsider while she had the chance. But wondering what payment he'd demand if she chose the bar made her keep her mouth shut.

"Put your arms by your sides."

Narrowing her eyes, wondering what the hell he had in mind, she did as he said.

Quickly, he cuffed her knees and thighs. Then he clipped each hand to a knee.

She was wide open for him, and the way he'd secured her severely limited her ability to get away.

When he'd packed his bag in the cabin, she'd assumed they would use all of the items once they reached the dungeon. But they hadn't even made it that far. Mostly because she'd been bratty—not that she would change a single thing or apologize, even if given the opportunity.

"I might put you back in this position anytime I'm cooking," he observed.

After tonight, she would never look at a kitchen island the same way again.

"Definitely my new favorite."

She wrinkled her nose. "That's one of us."

He grinned.

Beneath his gaze, her pussy throbbed. Her brain might scream in protest, but her knees opened a little more, in silent invitation.

His expression turning serious, he moved in closer. But surprising her, he didn't try to insert the toy.

Instead, he told her to open her mouth.

A little apprehensively, she did what he said, and he stuck two fingers inside.

"Get them wet."

Her eyes wide, gaze fastened on his inscrutable features, she complied.

"Wetter."

A few seconds later, he nodded his satisfaction and drew the dampness to her pussy.

"You want this."

Even though she shook her head, the truth was obvious to both of them. She was ready for him. When he parted her labia, her clit was already swollen and throbbing.

"How did I ever wait so long for a taste of you?"

After slowly circling the bundle of nerves, making her lift her hips from the island, he slid both fingers inside her.

Arching her back, she moaned.

"You're so hungry for me, Sasha."

She didn't, couldn't, deny his words.

With deliberate strokes, he fucked her with his fingers. Then he changed his angle to find her G-spot.

"Oh, Gregorio!"

He knew exactly how to arouse her and keep her on the edge.

An orgasm built, and she met his thrusts, craving the completion he kept just out of reach.

"You're almost there." Gently, he withdrew, and she cried out in frustration.

"This isn't..." Just in time, she clamped her mouth shut.

A knowing smile teased his lips. "This isn't fair?" he guessed. "This exercise is to prove a point. One of us is the Dominant. The other is not. This isn't meant to be fair."

She curved her fingers into fists and dug her fingernails into her palms. "I got it," she promised. "Now can—"

"When we're in a scene, your orgasms belong to me. I decide when you come, if you come, how many times you come." He caught her chin so she had no choice but to look at him. "Got that, as well?"

"Yes." Belatedly, she added, *"Sir."*

"We can keep up your lessons as long as you like."

"I'll behave." *If I can. Maybe.*

His motions slow and intentional, he placed the tip of the oversize toy at her entrance. In anticipation of the fullness, she tightened all her muscles.

"Relaxing will help."

She couldn't help her self-protective reactions.

He inserted the dildo a fraction of an inch before pulling back and licking her.

"Oh!" She lifted her hips.

"That's right, Sasha. Give up the struggle and turn yourself over to me. You can trust me. I won't give you more than you can bear, not ever."

So far, that had been true.

Gregorio took his time, sliding the toy in, pulling it back to tease her and suck her, then repeating the process.

Surprising her, her body began to accept the intrusion.

As he reached the halfway point, taking it became more difficult.

He paused, allowing her to adjust to the size. She panted, her body tensing as she tried to accommodate the thick silicone. To his credit, he didn't rush her. "Exhale. Try to relax."

I wish I could.

Giving her a small break, he cupped her breasts and kneaded them gently. He stroked her nipples, then used his thumb and forefinger to roll them until they became hardened peaks. At the distraction, she drew her shoulder blades together, offering him more.

"So pretty." His tone held a note of appreciation.

After releasing her, he leaned down to capture one of her nipples in his mouth, sucking and biting gently. She moaned, the dual stimulation making her forget her discomfort. How could she ever be with anyone but him?

He continued to lavish attention on her breasts, all the while keeping the dildo steady, not advancing it farther until her body relaxed.

"Gregorio!" She was so ready for this. "Yes..."

"Open your knees wider."

As she complied, he pushed the toy deeper, stretching her wider. The sensations were overwhelming. Too, too much. She groaned, and her body heated.

"That's it." He pulled the dildo back slightly, then slid it forward again, starting a slow, torturous rhythm.

Her breath caught on a tiny sob, but her hips moved in time with his strokes. Tension built in her, and she murmured his name over and over as if it were a mantra.

"Not yet."

"But…" Her pleas were useless, she knew. When he was in Dominant mode, nothing swayed him. He was going to draw this out, push her to the edge and keep her there for longer than she would have believed possible.

With his free hand, he captured the nipple that he hadn't yet tormented.

She wasn't sure how much more she could endure.

He pinched the tip between his fingers, hard enough to make her whimper, then he soothed the terrible sting with gentle rubs.

Alternating between pleasure and pain, he kept her off balance, making sure she could focus on nothing other than him and what he was doing to her body.

"Please," she whispered, her body shaking. Sasha was far beyond pride. She was willing to plead for what he made her need. "Please, Sir. Gregorio… *Please.*"

He smiled, as if he loved nothing more than the sound of suffering. "Not quite yet, Petal. You can accept more."

She couldn't. *"No."* Tears stung her eyes. Not from pain, but from the anguish of not being allowed to orgasm.

He increased the pace with the dildo, fucking her harder now, but still not letting her come. At the same time, he leaned down, capturing an already tortured nipple in his mouth, nipping a little harder this time. She cried out in sensual protest, her body convulsing, but he didn't stop.

Even though he was demanding she not climax, the urge clawed at her. She wasn't sure how long she could hold it back. "Oh, Sir…"

How was it possible she'd changed from a woman who didn't care one way or another about sex to one willing to sell her soul to get rid of this angst inside her?

"You've almost earned it." His voice was soft and soothing, and his reassurances didn't help at all.

Somewhere in the back of her mind, she remembered this was about teaching her a lesson. Miserably, she realized she'd learned it.

She wouldn't be a brat anymore.

Her breaths were now coming in short, desperate gasps.

The tears she could no longer blink back slipped from the corners of her eyes to trail down her temples.

With the pad of his forefinger, he captured one, and he brushed it across her lips. "These are for me."

"Yes," she admitted in a broken whisper. He'd caused them, and only he could take them away.

"I love them. You should cry for me all the time, Petal."

If it pleased him, she would.

"And I'd give you the world in return."

For a moment, she believed him.

"Now, Petal."

His roughened words were all she needed.

With a final cry, she fractured, writhing as waves of pleasure crashed over her. Her hips bucked against the toy, and she rode out her orgasm, sobbing his name.

Eventually, her Dominant slowed his movements, gently bringing her back down from the dizzying high.

Long seconds later, when she finally stilled, he carefully drew the dildo out.

Shocking her, she whimpered at the loss, but he shushed her softly, placing a kiss on her inner thigh.

"You did so well, little sub, my Petal."

She would never get tired of hearing his adoration.

"So beautifully." Then he licked her pussy, using his mouth and tongue to clean up her orgasm.

She'd never been with anyone this thoughtful, this erotic.

"Gregorio..."

He kissed her, and she tasted her satisfaction on him.

She closed her eyes, wanting this evening to last forever.

"Don't think I'm done with you, Sasha. We haven't even started yet."

Stunned, she blinked her eyes open.

"I'm giving you a few minutes to relax and recover. Before."

"Before?" she asked, confused. "Before what?"

"This..."

Chapter Fifteen

Gregorio picked up one of the leather straps he'd brought into the room earlier.

"What is it?" She frowned a little.

"A collar," he explained.

Her mouth dried.

"So that I can attach you to my leash."

Heaven above. This couldn't be possible. When he'd mentioned a collar and leash earlier, she'd hoped he was joking.

"Lift your head for me and ask me to put it on."

She clamped her lips together and glared. With one of his wickedly evil grins, he leaned in, putting his face mere inches from hers, filling her vision with his determination.

"You've already had a taste of what happens when you push me, little Petal. Are you sure you want to defy me?"

Unless she used a safe word, that thing was going around her neck. Why did it scare her so much? In all ways, she had already become his. What was another symbol?

But it was a meaningful one.

At the adult store, she had seen all kinds of different choices, from plain collars like this one to decorative silk to rigid steel that locked in place. This was made from some type of leather, and it was meant to be sturdy, rather than silky and feminine. Maybe she should thank her lucky stars that it wasn't metal, heavy and unyielding.

"I'm waiting."

As best as she could with her wrists still secured to the outside of her knees, she did as he said.

Within seconds, he had it clicked into place, and her breathing sped up. It was symbolic, she reassured herself. Nothing more.

But she knew better.

He'd put it on for a reason—as a mark of his ownership.

He traced her throat above it and below it, then he outlined her collarbone. "I may never let you take it off."

Her insides plummeted.

He couldn't mean that.

This was for tonight only, she reassured herself. She wouldn't even go to sleep with it on.

He threaded his pinky through the attached D ring and tugged on it lightly.

"Jesus, Petal. Fuck me into next week."

His words turned her molten.

"I knew you'd look sexy as hell in my collar, but I had no idea."

His eyes were filled with emotion, approval, possession.

For a moment, their gazes were locked on each other's, and she stopped breathing.

He opened his mouth as if to say something, but then he shook his head, and the opportunity passed.

Slowly, he trailed his thumb and forefinger down the column of her throat. *"Mine."*

"Yes," she whispered, wanting nothing more than for his statement to be true...if only for this moment.

He stepped back, and she glanced at his crotch

His hard-on was so big and thick that she wondered if his cockhead would peek above his waistband.

Gregorio had taken such exquisite care with her, given her amazing orgasms, and right now, she realized he hadn't taken one of his own. Did he have iron control?

For a moment, he turned away, and when he faced her again, he was holding another strip of leather, this one longer with an end fastened into a type of handle.

A leash.

She opened her mouth to protest, but nothing emerged. Womanly assertion urged her to protest, but feminine submission made her keep her mouth shut.

But only for him.

There would never be another man who she would allow to do this to her.

A minute ago, he'd asserted that she was his, and every part of her responded to that impossibility.

After fastening it in place, he wrapped the lead around his wrist so there was nowhere she could go, no running, no escaping, no hiding, unless he let her go.

"I want you to remain in this position," he instructed her.

Holding the leash taut, he unclipped each of her wrists and rubbed sensation back into her skin.

"Move slowly, otherwise you may cramp up."

Even though she intellectually understood what he was saying, once her knees were free, she had to fight the urge to clamp them together and lower her legs to hide herself.

"Do as I say," he reminded her, as if he'd read her mind.

With his back to her, he gently smacked her pussy.

Gasping, she bucked, lifting her hips and crying out at the delicious pain that rocketed through her.

"If you don't behave, more of that is coming."

The sting receded almost right away, leaving her breathless with need. Even though she had been stuffed full of the silicone cock, she was ready for him to claim her in whatever ways he wanted.

"I enjoyed your reaction. Let's do it again. Shall we?"

She braced herself for the spank that never came.

Instead, he gently kissed her. Not knowing what to expect kept her completely off balance, swimming in pheromones.

He trailed his fingers up the inside of her thighs to her apex, where he teased her pussy.

"That's it. Always keep yourself relaxed."

She blew out a breath.

"Most often I won't spank you there, but if I do, it's because I want to drive you wild or because you deserved it." He met her gaze and lifted an eyebrow. "Or simply because I wanted to."

After rubbing sensation back into her lower body, he helped her to move slowly, then to sit up.

When she was steady, he lifted her from the counter and stood her in front of him.

Automatically, she kept her gaze low.

"Goddamn, you are a fast fucking study."

Not for the first time, she wondered who she was becoming.

Gregorio—*her Sir*—threaded his fingers into her hair and pulled her head back.

"So fucking perfect for me."

"And you, Sir, are perfect for *me.*"

"Sasha." A pulse throbbed in his temple. "Sasha. My Sasha."

Every womanly part of her throbbed with need.

"Are you ready?"

Her eyebrows drawn together in question, she looked at him.

"To go to the dungeon."

Her heart missed its next few beats.

Without waiting for her response, he went on, "Sometimes I prefer that you walk behind me. Especially if we're playing publicly. But since the sight of your ass turns me on so much, I want you to lead the way."

Swallowing this sudden lump of trepidation in her throat, she made her way to the top of the stairs.

"After you, Petal," he said when she hesitated.

Even though he didn't release the leash, he gave her plenty of slack.

Fighting her sudden nerves, she curled her hand around the banister.

With every step she descended, the music became louder, more resonant, thumping through her, heightening her senses.

Like upstairs, he'd kept the lighting low and intimate.

The last time she'd been here, the place had been a beehive of activity. Yet it seemed smaller, more intimate with just the two of them here.

Every single thing that existed in the Den was a possibility for her tonight, and she wished she had some idea of what he had in mind for her.

He exerted just enough pressure to tug her to a gentle stop.

The blood drained from her face when she realized where she was—in front of the sturdy metal ring attached to the wall where the submissive had been kneeling for her Dominant.

"This will work for us."

She'd been afraid of that.

"Get yourself in my favorite position, my Petal."

Nerves nearly paralyzing her, she eased herself onto the floor.

"That's it."

Without him coaching her, she knelt back, her thighs parted. If there were other people around, she absolutely could not do this—especially since she was nude.

"Knees a little wider, if you can manage it."

Closing her eyes against a ridiculous flood of embarrassment, she did.

With a small thunk, he dropped his bag to the floor next to her.

"I've been thinking about this."

Have you, Sir?

Motions quick and efficient, he secured her to the wall.

She waited for fear that never came.

"Nice."

At his feet, his to command, was where she wanted to be.

"Fuck…" He dragged a hand into his hair, the closest she'd ever seen him come to losing control. "If you had any idea what you do to me…"

Tell me, she ached to say.

Maybe it was for the best that she couldn't force out the words.

"Free my cock, sub."

She was vibrantly aware of the way he stood over her, fully dressed while she was naked and helpless, reinforcing their sexual dynamic.

To comply with his orders, she had to adjust herself a little.

His belt buckle was warm from his body, and she released it, then unbuttoned and unzipped his jeans. With a whoosh, the pants fell to the floor, and his cock sprang free, already hard, pointing toward her.

"Fellate me."

Wondering how she would take all of him, she closed a hand around his shaft.

With an iron grip, he captured her wrist. "Hands behind your back."

No way could he mean that.

"And kneel back."

He wanted her helpless, at his mercy?

"You're thinking too much."

For a moment, she squeezed her eyes shut.

"Get out of your head. Focus on your Dom's request—on pleasing me."

Because she didn't move fast enough, he captured her shoulders and guided her to where he wanted her.

"Why is my dick not already in your mouth?"

"Yes, Sir," she replied helplessly, miserably.

Instead of making a mental list of all the reasons this wasn't possible, she allowed his instructions to roll around in her mind.

"Sasha..."

At the warning note in his voice, she licked a drop of pre-cum from his slit.

"Nice. But that's not what I asked."

She looked up to find him gazing at her with a mixture of determination and appreciation.

"Open your mouth and take my cock like a good little submissive."

He was asking the impossible.

Without another word, he captured her nipples and quickly pinched them.

The shock distracted her, and she opened her mouth wider in protest. He took the opportunity to press his cockhead inside.

"Let me in."

Having no option other than obedience, she closed her eyes and turned herself over to the experience.

Gregorio captured the back of her head, holding her imprisoned as he fucked her mouth, going deeper and deeper, making her choke and gasp.

"That's it. Be my good girl." His voice was soothing as he brushed the shell of one of her ears with this thumbpad. "Take me."

He was holding her tenderly, offering constant praise, and she was no longer fighting for air. Without her knowing how, she was in sync with him. There was nothing but Gregorio, their need for each other, and profound sense of satisfaction in her.

As he continued, she felt the change in him. His cock became thicker, harder, and his breathing became shallower.

Suddenly, he fisted her hair and tugged back her head.

As he withdrew his cock, he left her breathless and confused.

"Sir?" She tipped her head to one side.

"Not yet."

"But..."

"Denial is good for the soul."

She wasn't convinced about that.

But his actions were decisive as he pulled up his jeans and stuffed his damp cock back into place.

How he didn't catch himself on the zipper, she had no idea.

He crouched in front of her and swiped his fingertips across her lips to dry them.

"Thank you for that, my Petal."

Only for you. She'd never been this wild and free with anyone else. "Thank you, Sir."

Her words were sincere, and it shocked her how much she meant them.

"No matter the fantasy, you make the reality better."

No other man had been this openly approving of her. His words emboldened her, made her want to be even more pleasing.

He released her from the ring in the wall. "Now I want you to make your way down the hallway."

When she started to rise, he pushed her back down.

"You want me to crawl?"

"Of course." A ridiculously proud smile sauntered across his mouth. "Did you expect anything different from me? Watching your hips sway, hoping for a glance at your pussy..."

Her temporary Dominant was all man.

Self-consciously, she lowered herself to all fours. Doubtfully, she looked down the long hallway.

He gave her right buttock a swift pinch.

Glaring, she glanced over her shoulder.

"Quit hesitating."

His *"or else"* hung unspoken in the air between them.

He held the leash lightly, giving no real direction. Slowly, awkwardly, she crawled past the room where they'd watched the Dom and sub together.

So he didn't intend to reenact that same scene.

"Keep going. Last door on the right."

When she reached it, she started to stand, but he tugged on her leash. "I didn't give permission for you to get up."

He reached above her to open the door. "Now you may enter."

The room was dominated by a wooden, X type of structure.

"It's a St. Andrew's cross," he explained to her.

In the middle of the room, she knelt back, waiting for him to tell her what to do.

"Right choice, Sasha." His voice was husky. "You're a natural." After crouching to unclip her leash, he continued, "Go to the cross, then stand and face it. Spread your arms and legs."

The cross was tilted slightly, making her lean forward a little, meaning gravity would help hold her in place.

Within minutes, he had her wrists and ankles attached to the structure.

"We can't forget to put this on you."

He came to stand in front of her, holding the blindfold she'd haphazardly grabbed earlier. Now she wished she had picked something else.

After putting it in place, he adjusted the slide at the back so it was secure. Then he tipped her head back to double-check the fit, ensuring she couldn't see anything.

"You've never looked more beautiful."

Because of the acoustics and the music in the room, she couldn't quite make out where his voice was coming from.

Was he still in front of her? Or had he moved somewhere else?

Not knowing exactly where he was left her a little disoriented.

"Have you ever been spanked with an implement?"

"No," she said. He scooped her hair to one side. So he was behind her. "In fact, until you, I never had a spanking at all."

"The way it should be." Pride rang through his voice. "You watched a scene, and you looked at some of my toys. Did anything in particular intrigue you?"

She kept quiet.

"Something you're reluctant to say?"

She should have known he'd continue to push.

"You told me you wanted to come over here. I think you can admit what you're hoping for."

Maybe it was a good thing she couldn't see him because that gave her the courage to confess her secret. "I'd like to try your belt."

"Oh, Petal. Would you, indeed?"

His voice sent little ricochets of pleasure up her spine. She loved his reaction to her, as if she meant as much to him as he meant to her.

"For now, I want to start you out with something a little less intense."

Like what?

"I'm going to use a short, suede flogger."

She'd seen some of those at the adult store, next to other longer, slightly terrifying ones with thick, black strands.

"This is one of my favorites. Pale pink, to match the marks I'm going to leave on your skin."

Goose bumps shot up her arms.

His footsteps echoed off the floor, then soft leather whispered across her shoulders. The falls of the flogger, she presumed. They had little weight, yet their touch electrified her, making her skin tingle with anticipation.

"Feel this, Sasha." He trailed the flogger down one arm, and the broad leather straps dipped into the crook of her elbow. Then he drew them back up and repeated the motion on her other arm.

Her breath caught in her throat as he traced a path across her collarbone and down between her breasts. She leaned forward, seeking more contact, but he moved away, leaving her wanting.

His voice came from a different angle now, closer to her ear, like earlier. "You're dependent on my voice, aren't you, pet? It anchors you in your dark, unexplored world."

Her heart pounded in rhythm with the thumping music that filled the room.

His breath was warm on her neck, and when he spoke, he kept his words low, seducing her. "Every stroke, every touch, makes you more aware that you're mine, doesn't it?"

He moved again.

Leather strips suddenly danced down her spine. Gasping, she leaned forward, trying to get away.

"You're sensitive there. Good to know."

Without any warning, the first thuddy stroke landed across her buttocks. It was more of a firm tap than a sting, and the sensation didn't hurt as much as she expected.

She slowly exhaled the tension she'd been holding.

His second stroke was slightly harder, making her moan a little.

"Keep breathing, Sasha," he reminded her gently, landing another stroke. "The more relaxed you are, the more enjoyable this will be."

She wasn't sure enjoyable was the right word.

"In and out. Slowly. Measured."

She focused on doing as he said, matching the rhythm of the flogger's falls.

Each of his strokes made her skin warmer, and that heat radiated through her whole body.

"That's it. Find your pace."

On and on he went, and she squirmed as the sensations began to overwhelm her. But his restraints held her in place, forcing her to accept whatever he chose to give.

"Your body is turning the most beautiful shade."

He moved the implement lower, landing the leather strands on her upper thighs.

She yelped and tried to close her legs, but the cross kept her spread open.

Then, shockingly, her pussy began to throb.

He teased her inner thighs with lighter strokes, making her whimper and writhe. Then, without warning, he swung the flogger directly between her legs, the falls smacking against her pussy lips.

She cried out, more from shock than pain. The sensation was indescribable, raw and intense.

"How was that?"

Maybe because he'd spanked her there earlier, her flesh was more sensitive than ever.

"You liked it, didn't you?"

Much as she wanted to, she couldn't deny what he'd said.

She was on fire, every nerve ending alive and yearning for more.

"Sasha?"

"*Yes,*" she admitted on a whisper.

"That's my girl." He gave her more, alternating between harder strokes on her buttocks and softer, teasing ones on her breasts, her pussy, her thighs.

Suddenly, he cupped her sex and slid his fingers through her damp folds.

"You're soaked, Petal."

Helplessly she jerked forward, seeking more.

He played with her clit, pinching and rolling it gently between his fingers, then smacking it lightly.

Combined with what he'd done to her earlier, he was overwhelming her, pushing her closer and closer to the edge.

But he wasn't done tormenting her yet.

He moved around to her front, the flogger now dancing across her breasts. The falls caught her nipples, making them harden into tight peaks. Each stroke sent jolts of pleasure-pain directly to her core. She panted, her breath coming in ragged gasps, her body shivering with need.

"Please," she begged, not even sure what she was asking for.

"Please what, Petal?" His voice was demanding, yet tender. "Tell me what you need."

"You," she cried out. "I need you."

He responded with a low groan, coming in closer to press his body against hers. His cock was hard, straining against his jeans as he ground into her.

"I love the way you respond to me."

He claimed her mouth, kissing her deeply, passionately, while his hands roamed over her body. Since he'd plunged her world into darkness, all of her other senses were on overload.

Gregorio cupped her breasts and lightly pinched her nipples. When she wordlessly sought more, he slid his hands behind her to squeeze her ass, pulling her more tightly against him. She moaned into his mouth, surrendering to his touch, his taste.

Abruptly, he broke the kiss, leaving her gasping. His voice was rough, hungry. "You're doing so well, Sasha."

So why had he stopped?

Suddenly, he moved away, and something clattered against metal.

Anticipation coiled within her. She was already so close, every inch of her skin tingling, her pussy aching for release.

Stunning her, the flogger struck her buttocks again, harder this time, striking her with a thuddy impact.

She groaned, trying to push into the cross, but the angle made that impossible.

"Is this what you need?" He landed a series of alternating strokes that built in intensity, each one sending shockwaves through her.

"Feel it, Sasha," he commanded, his voice hoarse. "Feel the way your body responds to me. My touches. My commands."

"I do." So much so that she was flying… The warmth of her skin, the throbbing of her pussy, the painful tightness of her nipples.

The music vibrated around her, and he synched the falls of the flogger to it.

Then… She was lost, drifting on a sea of sensation, anchored to the world only by Gregorio's voice, by his presence.

He moved around her, trailing the leather strands over her heated flesh. When he flogged her breasts, she cried out, the tingling sharp and intense.

Before she fully registered it, pleasure bloomed, and it was as dark as it was wicked.

A true Master, he followed the more painful strikes with gentle strokes, teasing her nipples.

"My God. Please, Gregorio," she begged again, her voice barely a whimper. She was so close, hovering on the precipice of something massive, something she desperately needed. "I'm coming apart."

"Please what, Sasha?" he asked, his voice tight with control. "What do you need?"

With a growl, he dropped the flogger and pressed against her, his hand delving between her thighs. His fingers found her clit, circling it with firm, precise movements. She bucked frantically, arching her body in silent plea.

"Give me the words."

"I want to come."

"Yeah. You earned it." With his hand, he fucked her. "Come for me, Petal," he whispered in her ear, his voice low and commanding. "Let go." He found her G-spot. "Show me how much you love this."

The raw emotion in his voice was too much.

She shattered, her orgasm ripping through her with such force that she screamed and pulled against the restraints.

He wrapped his arms around her, holding her through it, pressing a soft kiss to her neck and another to her shoulder. He whispered praises, endearments, his voice anchoring her overwhelmed body.

As she slowly came down from the sensual high, she was teary-eyed. Not from pain or upset, but from the sheer intensity of her emotions. She'd never felt this connected to anyone, this cherished, this taken care of.

"Shh, Petal," he murmured. "I've got you. You're safe. You're mine."

Without her being aware of it, he unfastened her and swept her from the floor. Swiftly, he carried her across the room. Then he sat with her, cradling her body against his.

"Keep your eyes closed for a minute," he instructed as he removed the blindfold and gently wiped away her tears.

Finally, after remaining where she was for long minutes, her breathing returned to normal, and a chill traced down her back.

He held her tighter, offering his body's warmth.

"That was…" Her eyes were still closed, and she didn't have the energy to lift her head. "Yeah." She wasn't sure words existed to explain what she'd been through.

But she absolutely wanted to do it again. When she was physically capable of it.

For minutes, she drifted, letting her thoughts rise and fall, not caring about anything but the moment and him.

All too soon, reality returned, and she allowed her eyes to open.

She became aware of his cock, hard and throbbing, pressing against her buttock. "You still haven't come."

"Denial makes the completion better."

"But..."

"But?" he prompted, capturing her chin and leaning forward a little so he could see her better. The angle made his earring wink in the overhead light.

"Too much is a bad thing, isn't it?"

A smile flirted with his beautiful lips "What are you saying?"

"The more I get, the more I want."

"Is that a fact?"

Before him, it hadn't been.

"Are you sure you're up for it?"

"I am." No matter what happened in their case, it would end. He'd go back to his life, and she'd return to hers. While she could, she wanted every moment, because all too soon, they'd become memories.

"Then I may have an idea."

"Do you?" she asked.

"Or maybe two."

Oh?

"Come with me, Sasha." He slid her from his lap and helped her to stand. "You can walk."

Small mercy.

"A thank-you would be appropriate."

God, yes. Manners. "Thank you, Sir."

Holding her hand, he guided her into the next room. A leather contraption hung from the ceiling.

Her heart stopped.

Wide-eyed, she turned to him. "You're not really serious about this."

Are you?

Chapter Sixteen

"Very much so," Gregorio said, his jaw set in a firm line.

As she stared at the leather contraption hanging from the ceiling, Gregorio gave her hand a reassuring squeeze.

"What is it?"

"It's a type of sex swing, Petal."

Sasha wrinkled her nose. "Are you sure? That's not at all what it looks like to me."

"It's versatile," he agreed. "The pieces can be rearranged in a couple of different ways."

Wondering how the thing actually worked, she frowned, taking in the sturdy, thick pieces of leather. They lay flat, and there were leather stirrups hanging from it.

"Another first for you?"

"Since I've never seen anything like it, that would be a yes."

"I think you'll enjoy it."

She wasn't so sure about that. "How scared should I be?"

"Not at all." He leaned in closer to her, filling her vision, stealing her breath. Then he flashed a wicked smile. "Or maybe slightly."

At the small, implied threat, she shuddered. "Not reassuring, Sir."

"Wasn't meant to be." With that, he went to the wall to adjust a pully, lowering the apparatus until it was about the same height as her waist. "You'll be facedown."

Which meant she'd bend over, not much different than when he'd taken her over the chair in the cabin.

But now that she didn't have to figure out how to climb into it, she was slightly less terrified.

He returned to her and took her shoulders. His eyes were locked on hers, and their depths were filled with intentions that made her shiver. "Since I intend to fuck you hard, you need to undress me."

"Of course," she whispered. Why had she suddenly lost her voice? "Sir."

"I'd happily keep you here and shut out the rest of the world."

She wanted nothing more. Forget the danger. The outside world. The impossibilities.

Slowly, her hands shaking, Sasha grasped the hem of his T-shirt and began pulling it up. He raised his arms to help her, and she tossed the shirt onto a nearby chair. As always, she couldn't help but take in his muscular biceps and chiseled abs. But her gaze caught on his bandage. No matter how much they wanted to lose themselves in this, in each other, there was no forgetting who either of them really were.

"I'm a little impatient, Petal."

"Sorry, Sir." Giving herself a mental shake, she crouched to pull off his boots and socks and tucked them beneath the nearby chair, out of the way.

Then she knelt up to loosen his belt buckle. Still, at some point, she'd love to feel it on her ass.

"Careful," he warned as she started to pull down the zipper.

"Protecting your cock would be in my best interest, Sir," she teased.

"So it would." He grinned back.

Magic sparked between them, a lighthearted intimacy that ripped down even more of the emotional walls they'd each erected to keep people out.

As she continued, her knuckles brushed against his hard length.

"Focus on your assignment. Nothing more."

His eyes were fire and his voice held a soft threat.

Maybe she should be grateful he didn't intend for her to repeat the blowjob she'd given him when they'd first entered the dungeon.

Hooking her fingers into the waistband of his jeans, she lowered them. When they reached the floor, he kicked them the rest of the way off.

He took a condom from a side pocket in his bag and tossed it onto the counter. Then he returned to her. "Ready?"

To have you inside me, yes. But as for the swing, she wasn't so sure, and she gave the contraption a sidelong glance.

"It's perfectly safe. I would never let anything happen to you, Petal."

That much, she believed.

"Would you like to use a safe word?" he asked.

"No," she replied, shaking her head. She trusted him implicitly, even if she was skeptical that she'd enjoy the experience.

"In that case..." He guided her to where he wanted her. "Lean forward." He placed a hand in the middle of her back and exerted just enough pressure to enforce his order.

Forcing down a sudden attack of apprehension, she did as he said.

The leather was cool against her skin, supporting her lower body and head, but leaving her breasts hanging down, unsupported.

"Goddamn, Petal. You look so fucking hot."

Beneath the swing, he cupped her breasts to warm them and gently tease her nipples. "This gives me such perfect access to you."

Now that she was in place, her fear began to recede. And all of a sudden, she saw the appeal. The swing conformed to the shape of her body, and she was much more comfortable than she would have been if he'd placed her over a table or desk.

"Are you doing okay?"

Better than expected. She nodded.

Gregorio ensured she was safe, with her arms by her side. "I'm going to raise you up a little bit."

Butterflies danced inside her tummy. Having her feet on the floor was one thing, but being completely at his mercy was another.

"Sasha?"

She appreciated that he was giving her a chance to use her safe word. "I'm okay," she assured him, even as she closed her eyes so she didn't have to watch what he was doing.

Moments later, the swing shifted, and she was lifted up onto her tiptoes.

Instantly, she opened her eyes, needing to orient herself.

"So sexy." His breath was on her inner thighs as he spread her legs and placed each one into a stirrup. "You're totally safe. I promise."

She wished her nerves would get that message.

One more time, he raised the swing.

Now she was totally suspended, her legs and breasts hanging down. He'd left her helpless, completely at his will. The sensation overwhelmed her. But along with that was a thrill unlike anything she'd ever experienced. Once more, he'd taken her to the edge and upended her world.

After him, there would be no going back.

"You know I can do anything to you."

His voice rocketed desire through her. "Yes."

"Your pussy, your ass, your breasts…" He circled her, and because she had no way to use her muscles, she could barely lift her head to look at him.

He lifted her breasts then released them again, making her sway.

Then he gently pushed the swing sideways.

Adrenaline catapulted through her. Shocking her, she became even more turned on.

She'd die if he didn't touch her.

Seeming to know that, he moved behind her. Then, starting with her shoulders, he skimmed his rough hands over her body, moving across her shoulders, down her back, continuing to her thighs and calves.

"Oh, Gregorio."

"That's it." He rubbed her ass, slowly at first, then a little faster and harder.

Even though she knew what was coming, the sudden, quick smack on her ass caught her off guard, making her yelp.

Instantly, he rubbed the spot he'd just spanked. "Red is my favorite color on you."

The warmth that blossomed in her was her favorite feeling.

After stepping away for a few seconds, he was back, playing with her pussy, fingering her, ensuring she was wet and ready for him.

She tried to push back, attempting to take him, but the swing made it difficult for her to move, giving him total control over her body.

Desperate for him, she whimpered. How could he keep denying her like this?

Once more, Gregorio left her for a few seconds. As best as she could, Sasha craned her neck, trying to track his movements. Even over the music, a distinctive click of a bottle opening reached her, and heart rate took off.

Knowing what was coming, she tightened her ass cheeks against his intrusion.

"That won't save you." His voice was rich with amusement.

Amusement at my expense.

Within seconds, he was behind her, and the heat of his naked body radiated against hers. Then he squirted the lube onto her tightest hole. The cool gel chilled her a little. "Gregorio…"

"You're going to let me in, aren't you, Petal?"

They both knew his words were a command and not a question. "We can do this the hard way or the easy way. But my fingers are going in your ass."

She sucked in a shallow breath, unsure that this would ever be easy for her.

"Your choice, Petal."

With a fingertip, he circled her anal whorl, spreading the lube, easing it a little inside.

Slowly, he pressed a finger inside, breaching her. She moaned, feeling a tiny nip of pain blossom into pleasure.

Then deliciously he moved his free hand to her pussy to play with her clit, making her writhe as she gasped.

Relentlessly, he inserted a second finger in her ass, filling her, fucking her as he worked deeper inside.

Her breaths came in short, ragged bursts. The dual sensations were overwhelming, consuming her entirely. She was adrift in a sea of pleasure, anchored only by his touch, his voice.

"Gregorio," she whispered desperately.

"That's it, Petal. Say my name." His statement was a demanding growl against her ear. "Let me know you're mine." He continued to stroke her clit, his fingers slick with her arousal, while his other hand worked her from behind, stretching her, preparing her.

"Oh God, I can't." She needed more, needed him.

"Can't what? Can't endure me filling your ass? Playing with your cunt?" His voice was rough, demanding.

"It's too much."

"Not nearly enough," he countered.

"I want your cock, Sir."

His gruff, appreciative curse was filled with pure male satisfaction. "As you wish, Petal."

Her Dominant slid a third finger into her rear and spread them apart. She'd never experienced anything this mind-blowingly overwhelming.

"You're going to take my cock, too, Petal. I want you completely full of me."

With his fingers still stretching her impossibly wide, he pressed his sheathed cockhead against her pussy, hard and insistent.

He placed a hand on her shoulder to hold her and the swing steady, then began to enter her slowly, inch by inch.

Because of the way he'd fucked her with the toy earlier, she was so wet, so ready. She needed this, him. *"Sir!"* Her entreaty was as much a demand as a plea.

"We'll go at my speed, little Petal."

Closing her eyes, she sighed. Of course the unyielding Dominant insisted on keeping control.

Finally, he was in all the way, and he stilled for a few moments.

Being suspended and dominated at the same time was almost too much for her.

"Better than I imagined," he told her, removing his fingers and cleaning them with a wipe before gripping her hips. Holding her steady, he began to thrust, setting a tempo that matched the beat of the music filling the room.

Each of his movements sent a wave of pleasure through her, building on the residual pleasure from her earlier orgasm. Another climax began to unfurl and the tension in her body increased with each of his powerful thrusts.

He leaned forward to cradle one of her breasts, tweaking her nipple.

"Gregorio!" Thrashing as best as she could, she tried to get enough stimulation in order to orgasm. But he was too clever for that.

"You'll wait until I say, Petal." His voice was hoarse with desire.

She hated his command as much as she loved it.

He continued to thrust, his balls slapping against her, the sound of their breathing and her moans filling the room.

His cock swelled inside her, and every feminine instinct responded.

"Now. Now, Petal."

Finally.

With a hard, deep thrust, he sent her spinning into the abyss where she shattered completely.

Screaming his name, she came, her body clamping around his cock. The stunning force of her orgasm left her breathless.

"Fuck. Yes." His words were a guttural moan.

Gregorio dug his fingertips into her hip bones, and with a moan of pleasure, shuddering, he emptied himself into her.

Together, they rode out the pleasure.

All of her remaining energy drained from her, and he eased his grip.

For a moment, neither moved.

"My Petal." He withdrew from her, then he kissed her shoulder blade. "You couldn't be any more perfect."

He held onto her for a long time, until her breathing returned to a more normal pace, then he slowly lowered the swing so that her feet reached the floor.

Suddenly, she didn't want the experience to be over.

"I want you in my arms." He lifted each of her feet in turn to release her from the stirrups, then he used his strength to help her up.

Her knees wobbled. If he wasn't holding her, she wasn't sure she could actually stand.

Feathering aside her hair so he could stroke her nape, Gregorio held her close.

"Thank you, Sir," she whispered, looking up at him. The experience was something she'd never forget.

The intrusive thought made emotion lodge in her throat.

"Yeah."

He carried her to the chair and sat, holding her tight.

The tiny dots of perspiration on her body began to dry, chilling her, so she snuggled in closer.

Determined to enjoy the moment, rather than focusing on the future, she relaxed, allowing her breathing to sync with his.

"You'll be the death of me, Petal."

Her heart soaring, Sasha smiled, grateful he couldn't see her.

"But I'll die a happy man."

That the man she had considered her hero felt this way about her, thrilled her.

After a few minutes, she softly admitted, "That was incredible."

"Was it?"

The idea that she might never have known this kind of connection and pleasure left her reeling.

"It's new for me."

His admission caught her off guard. "You've played with plenty of subs." And no doubt plenty who weren't.

"But never experienced it like this."

Maybe because she couldn't see him, she pushed ahead, maybe a bit recklessly. "Really?"

His answering growl was deep and rumbly. "You should know better than anyone that I always say what I mean."

Even though he said no more, he didn't change the subject.

Around them, the haunting, primal music created a moody atmosphere that gave her courage.

Her mouth was dry, and still she forced out the words that she had to know the answer to, "Does that include with my sister?"

He cursed. "Little Petal…" With a hand fisted in her hair, he tugged back her head so that she was looking up at him. Then he leaned in a little closer.

His eyes dark, unblinking, he captured her gaze.

"I've never had a romantic relationship where BDSM was involved."

Not ever?

"What happened with Adriana has nothing to do with us."

Hoping he would go on, she remained quiet.

"Since Adriana, I haven't gotten involved with anyone. I play with Tops and submissives here and other clubs around the world."

"Was it something you wanted?" When he didn't answer, she clarified. "I mean BDSM. In your relationship with Adriana?"

Beneath her, his cock hardened again.

"I'll let you answer that question for yourself."

Now that she'd had a taste, she knew she would want this physical and emotional connection as part of her life, forever. "How did you manage?"

"To?"

"Live without this?"

"Necessity." His voice was matter of fact, as if that was the obvious answer. "BDSM is all about consent, and if my partner does not consent, then it doesn't happen."

She couldn't imagine a man so Dominant, so virile, would make that choice, and it made her admire him even more.

"If you don't have any more questions, I want to get you back to the cabin."

With his thumb, he outlined her mouth, making her taste the essence of her pussy.

"I'm ready to make love to you—long and slow—for the rest of the night."

"If you insist, Sir." She sassed him with a quick, cheeky grin.

"Oh, I do, little Petal."

He adjusted their positions so that she was sitting on the chair and he was standing.

Too relaxed to move, she watched him wash his hands. Then he returned with a warm cloth to bathe her swollen pussy and tormented asshole.

He placed his T-shirt over her head and threaded her arms through the holes. "Even though I love the look of your nipples all hard and swollen, the Dominant in me insists you be warm."

"That's part of this whole thing?" she asked, curiosity taking over.

He raised an eyebrow "Caretaking?"

She nodded.

"Very much so. Nothing is more important to a Dominant than his submissive's well-being. He would crawl through cut glass for her, because he cares."

"Or because he's self-serving and wants to make sure her body is available to him?"

He answered with a devilish smile. "Maybe a little of both."

Before she could respond, he tipped back her chin.

"Have no doubt how important you are to me, how important your safety is, your comfort, your pleasure. *You.*"

No one had ever said anything that meaningful to her before.

Gregorio made her feel cherished, important.

He repacked his bag, dropping the lube in alongside her leash, then he hooked a finger through the D ring of her collar, like he had earlier. "I'd like you to keep this on. For now."

He was giving her a choice?

Earlier, when he'd placed it around her neck, she hadn't been sure she liked it, but now she couldn't imagine taking it off. "Yes, Gregorio."

The appreciation in his eyes made her doubly glad she'd agreed.

"Ready?" He offered a hand to help her up.

This time, he didn't ask her to crawl. Instead, he placed his fingers at the base of her spine as they left the room.

Upstairs, he helped her to dress, and she offered him back his T-shirt, even though she didn't want to give it up. It smelled of him, and the outdoorsy scent comforted her.

"Give me a couple of minutes." He dropped a quick kiss on her forehead. "I need to sanitize our playrooms."

"Do you want me to help?"

"Not at all."

While he returned to the dungeon, she wandered to the patio doors. She didn't see much beyond her own reflection.

Her hair was mussed, and her sweatshirt was bunched around her waist. Her lips were slightly swollen. But her eyes… Wide, expectant, happy.

Happy.

When was the last time she'd felt that way?

Generally she was too busy with cases and running the business to think about much of anything beyond work.

And being with Gregorio had changed all that.

The atmospheric music continued, keeping her aroused. Or maybe it had more to do with the memory of what they'd shared and the anticipation of what was still to come. Regardless, she was in a deeply surrendered place.

A few minutes later, the music shut off, making the dark mountain silence press in around her.

He rejoined her.

Even though they'd just been together, he swept his gaze approvingly over her. "You're even sexier than you were earlier."

Maybe because of his openness, she was softer, less fearful of letting him see her vulnerability or the way she was falling for him.

"I want to get you home."

At the door, he locked the house, reset the alarm, and turned off the lights.

Hand in hand, he guided her down the path, back to his cozy cabin.

Once they were secured inside, with the lights on a romantic setting, he turned up the heater, then he folded his arms as he stood over her. "You've had clothes on for far too long."

"Oh?"

"Don't try me."

The way he raised his eyebrows turned her insides liquid.

"Take them off."

Braver than she'd been before, she curled her hands around the bottom of her sweatshirt and began to lift the material.

"Naked," he snapped. "Now. I have no tolerance for a strip tease."

"Yes, Sir," she agreed, while still taking her time.

Suddenly, her phone vibrated, and the device skittered across the counter.

Part of her wanted to ignore it, but a stronger part of her knew she couldn't. It was late, and no one would be reaching out unless it was important.

Gregorio tipped his head to one side, encouraging her. "Check it."

Smoothing her top back into place, she crossed the room to look at the screen.

He came back. That man. That man. He. He said –

With a frown, she looked at Gregorio.

Taking in her frown, he asked, "Mrs. Santos?"

"Yes. But her messages are cryptic."

Moments later, a second text followed.

If I tell Felix he was here, he'll –

Chapter Seventeen

He'll... What?

Frustrated, Sasha dialed Mrs. Santos' number.

Gregorio's jaw clenched, eyes darkening to obsidian as he picked up his own phone, ready to act.

Terror was in each hesitating word of the messages, and it was frustrating not to be able to leap into action and problem solve.

Was Mrs. Santos even safe?

Each ring felt like a countdown. By the third one, she knew the woman wasn't going to answer. Then, inevitably, the woman's voicemail picked up.

Battling impatience, Sasha listened to the prerecorded greeting.

Leaving a message was probably futile, but she had to try. "Mrs. Santos, it's Sasha. Call me the moment you get this."

Frustrated, she ended the call and blew out a breath.

Impossible to believe that minutes ago nothing had existed but her and Gregorio, and now...

Finally, her phone chimed again.

That man. Forced himself into the house.

"Goddamn it."

Over her shoulder, Gregorio read the message. "I'll call Inamorata."

"Thank you." Hawkeye had agents in every part of the country, ready to act at a moment's notice. And since they were based out of Denver, getting someone to the Santos' home quickly wouldn't be difficult for them.

Tried… Get in Felix office.

Immediately she fired off a text of her own.

Are you safe?

The fact the woman hadn't answered the phone terrified Sasha.

Forcing back her frustration, she strode into the bedroom for her coat. "We need to get back in Felix's office," she said as she returned to the living room and double-checked that her gun was in her purse.

Gregorio had already armed himself and pulled on a tactical jacket. From experience, she knew the jacket would be filled with tools and supplies they might need.

More than ever, she appreciated him.

"Let's roll," he said, striding to the alarm panel.

Gregorio had just opened the cabin's door when her phone vibrated again.

I don't know what to…

After relaying the message, Sasha started to type her own reply. Gregorio took her upper arm, keeping her safe and steady as he led her toward his waiting SUV.

Do you have somewhere safe to go?

Gregorio helped her inside the compartment and buckled her into place while she hit the Send button.

The reply came back almost instantly.

No. And I need to be here for Felix.

Even though she understood the woman's loyalty to her husband, Mrs. Santos had no idea what she—or her husband—was up against.

At the end of this, people might end up dead.

"So is Felix still home?" Sasha asked Gregorio as he turned onto the main road and opened up the accelerator. "Or did he leave again?"

The back and forth text messaging was driving her mad, increasing her tension. They were too far away to be of much help.

Not convinced it would do any good, Sasha nevertheless dialed the woman's number again. She had to do something. Anything.

This time, Brenda answered.

"Are you safe?" she asked, immediately cutting off the woman's greeting.

"That horrible man…" She choked on a sob. "He's gone."

Thank God for that. Closing her eyes, she sighed. "Is Mr. Santos there with you?" she asked for clarification.

"No. He was only home for a little while. Said he forgot something. He went into his office."

The ledger?

"Then he left again."

"He didn't say where he was going?"

"I asked." For a few seconds, Brenda couldn't speak, before finally managing, "He wouldn't tell me. Just kept saying everything would be okay."

Determined to keep her client safe, Sasha redirected the conversation. "I know I already asked you this, but is there anywhere you can go? Don't you have a sister?"

"I won't put anyone else in danger."

Though she understood the sentiment, Sasha's only concern was for her client. "In that case, I'm going to make arrangements to get you to safety."

"I'm not leaving." Stubborn determination filled Brenda's voice.

"Listen to me... Please." She forced measured calm into her words. "Mr. Santos will do better if he knows you're safe."

For a moment, the older woman was silent.

Pressing her advantage, Sasha added, "Whatever is going on, your husband doesn't need to worry about you right now."

"I'm not sure."

At least she wasn't saying no. "How do you think he'd feel if he knew that man had been in your house? And if he comes back, do you really want to be there?" Sasha hated using scare tactics, but nothing was more important than Brenda's safety.

Without waiting for a response, Sasha changed her tone, making it more imploring as she asked, "Please, will you pack a bag? And then leave the house as quickly as you can? Just start driving away from the house while I find somewhere for you to go where you'll be safe."

"I—"

"Please, Mrs. Santos. This is important."

"But what about my husband?"

"We'll protect your husband, as well." She offered a quick prayer that she'd be able to do that.

In the background, Sasha heard the woman's footsteps, as if she was pacing.

"I want to talk to Felix."

"I understand that. I promise you'll be able to stay in contact with him."

Another sound reached her, like a door opening, maybe. A closet, she hoped, meaning the woman was packing.

"Where should I go?"

"I'll call you back with instructions."

"The airport," Gregorio said immediately.

In the dark compartment of the SUV, she turned in his direction.

"Long-term parking," he added.

Solid plan. Nodding, she repeated his instructions to her client.

"*No.*" Panic made her voice shake. "I won't leave the state."

"You're not actually getting on a plane." At least she assumed not.

Gregorio nodded his agreement.

The airport would have good security, and a place to leave her car where it wouldn't be easily found.

"I also want you to check your mirrors constantly. If you're being followed, call me right away."

"You're scaring me, Sasha."

"I don't want you to be scared. I want you aware." She waited for a second. "Do you understand?"

"Yes. But I don't like it."

"You're doing great." Before ending the call, she thought to ask, "Have you talked to Felix since that man visited?"

"I tried, but he didn't answer. Then I called you."

"If he gets in touch with you, please don't tell him where you're going."

"We don't keep secrets from each other."

Keeping secrets was how Mrs. Santos had ended up in this situation. Since pointing that out wouldn't be helpful, Sasha kept the thought to herself. Instead, she said, "Are you packing?"

"Yes."

"Let me know immediately if anything happens."

"Okay, Sasha."

"Be sure to answer when I call you back in a few minutes."

Mrs. Santos said nothing to that, but a moment later, she started to cry. "I want this to be over."

So do I. "I meant it when I said you're doing great. Your husband will be proud of you."

Without saying goodbye, Mrs. Santos hung up.

Instantly, Gregorio pushed a button on his steering wheel and the sound of a ringing phone filled the SUV.

Before the second tone, Inamorata's crisp voice echoed around them.

"Got a situation," Gregorio said.

"I'm listening."

Within seconds, he'd brought Hawkeye's second in command up to date. "I want surveillance in place at the Santos house. And Mrs. Santos needs to be moved to a safehouse."

"Roger that." In the background was the efficient clicking of computer keys. Moments later, she added, "Code word—snowblind."

Sasha nodded. How she wished she had an Inamorata on her team. Over the years, she'd learned a lot from the woman famous for her no-nonsense pencil skirts and kickass demeanor. No one fucked with Inamorata.

"Sasha and I are en route to the Santos residence. I'll ping you when we're entering."

No doubt the place was being watched, and an ambush was always a possibility. So they'd definitely need the backup.

More than ever, she was grateful she'd come to Gregorio. The man was competent and calm.

For a moment, a memory teased her mind, but she deliberately shoved it away. She had to be focused on the case and nothing else.

At least they were in this together.

Her sister hadn't understood Gregorio or what he did for a living. Sitting home, waiting, wondering couldn't have been easy.

In some ways, it seemed that maybe their relationship had never had a chance.

Adriana was planning to marry her fourth husband in the next few months. Sasha had supported her through all of her divorces and new romances, but she honestly didn't understand her older sister. It seemed that she was always searching for something that she never found.

"What's on your mind?"

They passed through the main part of Winter Park, headed toward Berthoud Pass. "Nothing important," she assured him.

When he touched her knee, she added, "Okay. Maybe I'm worried about Mrs. Santos."

"That all?"

How was he so damn perceptive? "Yes."

Since she wasn't sure how long she'd have cell phone reception for, she called her client again.

When Mrs. Santos picked up, Sasha heard background noise, as if she was driving. "You'll be meeting some people in the airport parking lot. I'll be giving your phone number to them. Anyone you're meeting with or talking to must use the word *snowblind*. Do you understand?"

"Snowblind?" she repeated.

"You got it. Any questions?"

"I feel like I'm in a nightmare, but I can't wake up."

In a way, she was. But the harsher reality was that she'd been living it for months, maybe years, since the first moment her husband had become entangled with Argentum. "Snowblind," Sasha reminded her. "Anyone who calls, anyone you meet."

"Where are they taking me?"

"A nearby safehouse. You'll have agents with you, plenty of food, water, TV."

"I want to tell Felix," she pushed.

"Not yet," Sasha insisted. "I'm sorry. We don't know where he is and if that information can be coerced from him. He'd want you to be safe," she reminded her again. No matter how many times Sasha had to repeat herself, she would.

If the situation were reversed, no one would be able to stop her from calling Gregorio.

There was silence for so long that she wondered if the call had dropped.

"I hate this."

Agreeing wouldn't help, and neither would assurances that she understood. Instead, Sasha settled for, "I'm sorry. Remember, I'm here if you need to talk or if anything happens."

"I know I should say thank you."

"No. Definitely not yet. I've just turned your life inside out," Sasha empathized. "It's completely normal to be confused and upset. I'd be worried about you if you weren't."

"Really?"

"One hundred percent."

"I'm falling apart, Sasha." She sniffed hard, as if battling her overwhelming feelings. In the background, the GPS gave directions. "I need to go."

Before Sasha even had a chance to respond, a beep indicated the call had ended.

As she dropped her phone into her purse, Sasha closed her eyes and exhaled.

"You're doing great, too," Gregorio told her.

The last of Winter Park's light had faded into the distance, and low-hanging clouds meant there was no moonlight, so she couldn't read his expression. "I appreciate you saying that."

"But?" he prompted.

How well he knew her. Or maybe he'd heard the wistful note in her voice. "I know she's scared, and I wish we had already solved this case."

"You're being a little hard on yourself. We've only known about Argentum for a few hours."

Had it only been that long? It seemed like forever.

"God knows how long Felix has been involved."

That he was right didn't help. "Maybe I should have moved her this afternoon. As soon as we found out."

"Would she have gone?"

"Maybe not." After all, Felix had returned home. And with Sasha's reassurances that he wasn't having an affair, Mrs. Santos might have ended her contract with Pathways.

"We can't make decisions for our clients. The only thing we can do is follow the investigation and make the most logical choices. Until a day or two ago, this seemed to be a straightforward case of spousal infidelity."

The reminder didn't help. And she'd be on edge until Mrs. Santos was in Hawkeye's capable hands.

The drive to Denver seemed to take forever, maybe because this was the second time today that they'd done it, and the clock was inching toward midnight.

Inamorata called back to update the arrangements for the meeting between Hawkeye and Mrs. Santos. "We've got it from here."

"I'll let my client know," Sasha replied. "Thank you."

Gregorio glanced at his GPS. "Arrival at the Santos residence in nineteen minutes."

Each mile steadied her focus. She knew what she had to do.

"Roger that."

Inamorata was gone, and Sasha reached out to Brenda one last time. "I'm here for you," she swore after giving her the final details. "And I need the code to turn off the alarm at your house."

"Why?" her voice was sharp.

"We want to look through your husband's office one more time."

"I don't know that it will do you any good." Still, she gave the code, along with one to the keypad on the back door. "The Hawkeye people are calling on the other line."

"Call me if you need anything, and I'll keep you up to date."

Without saying goodbye, she was gone.

Both Sasha and Gregorio fell silent as they neared the Santos' subdivision. Game face, as she'd called it when she was going through tactical training. Nothing mattered but the mission.

About a quarter of a mile away, Gregorio pulled over. "We'll go on foot."

Anyone watching the house would be watching for a vehicle to approach.

"Good thing I got some recent practice at scaling a fence," she said wryly.

In the ambient light, she saw his answering grin.

She hadn't been on an actual mission since leaving Hawkeye, and she'd never worked with Gregorio before.

Still, her training had been intense, and she was praying her reactions would be second nature.

Voice clipped, not wasting a breath on an extra syllable, Gregorio informed Inamorata that they were ready to approach the Santos house.

She acknowledged the communication.

Before and after exiting the vehicle, Sasha and Gregorio both surveyed their surroundings.

Gregorio tapped her arm in silent signal.

Go. Now.

Out of the view of security cameras, they made their way over the iron fence protecting the neighborhood.

He dropped down first, landing silently and turned to offer his help. She wasn't too proud to accept.

As they neared the Santos property, they paused, taking in the Hawkeye surveillance team.

Seeing nothing out of the ordinary, they scaled the same fence they'd climbed a few hours ago, landing in Brenda's backyard.

Gregorio took the lead as they hugged the shadows, staying out of sight until they reached the door. As she entered the code to release the lock, he stood guard. Once they were inside, she disarmed the security system.

Using only flashlights, they crept through the home, toward Felix's office.

Sasha's pulse thumped in her ears.

Part of her had missed this adrenaline rush. But she preferred the pace of the life she lived now.

By silent accord, she moved to the desk where she'd found the ledger while Gregorio wasted no time striding back to the bookcase.

Within seconds, she realized the ledger was gone.

Disappointed, but not surprised, she exhaled.

Obviously that had been the reason Felix returned home.

Gregorio glanced over her shoulder and she shook her head. Since she'd hit a dead end, she joined him, moving books, and checking behind them.

A few seconds later, he pulled out his cell phone, unlocked it, and handed it to her. Quickly, she scrolled to the most recent message.

You're a dead man.

And then an older one.

You fucked with the wrong people.

Gregorio stood and looked over her shoulder.

One last chance to prove your loyalty.

That one was received yesterday.

So the threats had been escalating over the last two days.

She zipped the device in her jacket, and Gregorio continued searching.

Just then, her cell phone vibrated. In case it was Mrs. Santos, she pulled it out and glanced at the screen.

Ashley.

She scowled.

What did her office manager want at almost two a.m.?

Dread chilling her, she answered with a whisper, "Ashley?"

"Sasha! Thank God!"

Aware of Gregorio's intense gaze locked on her, she started to say something, only to have Ashley rush on.

"They know you're there."

Everything inside her went still. "Who does?"

"Oh, God, Sasha! They're going to kill you." She sobbed. "I'm so sorry. So, so sorry. This is all my fault."

"Ashley, what did you—"

Chapter Eighteen

A soul-wrenching scream tore across the phone line, followed by a blood-chilling pop.

Then a sickening thud.

And haunting, echoing silence.

Breathless, unable to move or think, she stood there.

"Petal?" Gregorio plucked the phone from her nerveless fingers and pushed the End button before handing it back to her.

"She was trying to warn me about…" She wrapped her arms around herself. "Jesus. They just fucking killed her."

Around them, the air shifted, taking on an ominous quality that made the hairs on her nape rise. Her instincts, honed by years of training, shrieked with danger.

Gregorio went rigid, on high alert, reminding her of a predator catching the first hint of prey—or threat. When his dark eyes locked on hers, she saw her own awareness reflected there, that bone-deep certainty that something was terribly wrong.

"Let's roll." His voice was clipped, and he switched off his flashlight.

Instantly, she did the same.

Then—

A gunshot shattered the night.

The sound cracked through the silence like thunder, and Sasha jerked in response as her flight or fight instinct flooded her system.

The shot wasn't close enough to pose immediate danger. Hawkeye, engaging the enemy?

Gregorio tapped her shoulder twice. "Back door."

The screech of tires cut through the darkness outside—rubber burning against asphalt—followed immediately by the thunderous boom of a shotgun blast that shook the house.

Even though every instinct urged her to run, they stealthily made their way in the dark, leaving the office, hurrying down the hallway and back into the kitchen.

The back door exploded inward with a deafening crack, wood splintering as a black-clad figure surged through, weapon already raised.

Gregorio's reaction was instantaneous. He grabbed Sasha, practically lifting her off her feet as he shoved her behind him. In the same fluid motion, he drew his weapon. His shot was fast and lethally precise, slamming into the intruder's chest before the man could squeeze his trigger.

Another blast rocked the house—this time from the front entrance. The door didn't just break open—it flew completely off its hinges, crashing against the entryway wall with enough force to crack the plaster.

"Shit."

Argentum wasn't just coming for them. They were coming with overwhelming force.

Gunfire erupted from both sides—deafening, brutal, relentless. The sounds bounced off the walls, creating a disorienting explosion of devastation.

Bullets tore through the drywall, kicking up clouds of plaster dust and raining debris over them. Gregorio was already moving, his grip on her wrist like iron as he yanked her toward the far side of the room.

The realization hit her with crystal clarity—they were being herded.

"We're cut off." Her voice barely carried over the chaos, but she knew Gregorio heard her.

His gaze swept the room with tactical precision, dark eyes taking in and discarding options with ruthless efficiency.

"Up the stairs."

From the landing, they headed through the first door—into a bathroom.

He studied the far wall, and she followed his line of sight.

The window.

They had seconds. Maybe less.

A second-story exit was as stupid as it was dangerous, but what choice did they have?

Gregorio released her wrist just long enough to fire twice down the stairs, forcing their would-be assassins to take cover. Then he spun, weapon transitioning smoothly to target the window.

His first bullet struck the glass, creating a spiderweb of fractures.

The second shot blew it out completely, sharp fragments raining down like lethal diamonds.

"Go!"

Sasha didn't hesitate. She threw herself at the opening, twisting mid-air as she crashed through what remained of the frame. The drop was farther than she'd anticipated, and she hit the ground hard, the impact jarring through her knees and up her spine. *"Fuck."*

She forced herself to her feet.

Gregorio was right behind her—

A single shot rang out, distinct from the rest of the chaos.

Sasha whipped around in time to see Gregorio's body jerk violently mid-leap.

Her stomach plummeted to her feet.

His landing was wrong—all his usual control absent as his body folded, crashing to the ground with brutal force.

"Gregorio!"

Terror clawing at her, Sasha scrambled to him, hands shaking as she grabbed at his jacket, desperately searching for the wound. When her fingers came away wet and sticky, her heart nearly stopped.

Darkness bloomed across his side, the fabric of his shirt growing steadily darker as blood seeped through.

Not his chest. Not immediately fatal. But still bad. Too bad.

His teeth clenched, jaw flexing as he sucked in a sharp breath. He was conscious, still moving, but she could see the strain in his features, the way his usual fluid strength had deserted him.

Another gunshot cracked through the night. Closer this time.

Sasha's head snapped up, tactical awareness flooding back. "We gotta go, Gregorio."

Figures were moving toward them, shadows outlined against the harsh glow of headlights. Their actions were coordinated, professional—the kind of efficiency that came from extensive training.

They were being hunted by experts. Definitely Argentum.

"Go." Gregorio's voice was rough with pain but still carried that note of command.

"No fucking way am I leaving you."

"Goddamn it, Sasha. Fucking go. I mean it."

Stubbornly, she shook her head. *You never leave your partner.* "Get off your ass and give me some help."

"I'm warning you."

"Yeah?" she demanded. "Fucking take it out on me later, when we make it out of here."

Her pulse slamming against her ribs, she crouched to curl her arm under him, hauling him upright with strength born of desperation.

No time for panic. No room for fear.

Another shot rang out, missing them by inches, and her ears rang, shattering her hearing.

A counter shot came from near the fence.

Hawkeye.

Thank God.

Backup had bought them a short reprieve, thirty seconds, if they were lucky.

Gregorio stumbled forward, but he was too heavy, his usually powerful body refusing to fully cooperate. Blood continued to seep between her fingers where she tried to support him.

Too much blood. Far too much.

She blinked back tears.

She didn't have time to think, only to act.

A vehicle roared up the street—headlights cutting through the darkness, tires screaming as they fought for purchase against the pavement.

A door flew open with enough force to rock the entire vehicle.

A familiar voice cut through the chaos—sharp, authoritative. "Get in!"

Sasha didn't hesitate, didn't question the salvation being offered.

She heaved Gregorio toward the SUV, raw terror lending her strength she shouldn't have possessed. Gregorio barely managed to drag himself inside before Sasha threw herself in after him, her body instinctively curling around his as if she could shield him from further harm.

The door slammed shut behind them with brutal finality.

The moment the SUV accelerated away, bullets ripped through the night.

Sasha barely had time to process their escape before Gregorio's weight slumped more heavily against her.

Her hands, slick with his blood, pressed desperately into his side, trying to stem the flow.

His eyes met hers—slightly dazed but still alert, still aware. Still fighting.

"Sasha…" His voice was rough, carrying something too raw, too broken. As if he needed to tell her something vital while he still could.

"Shh. Save your breath." Fighting against the tears, she pressed harder against the wound, as if she could keep him anchored to this world through sheer force of will. "I've got you."

She wasn't sure if she meant it as a promise—or a desperate prayer to whatever gods might be listening.

The security gate swung open and the SUV roared forward, clipping the metal but not slowing down as a bullet shattered the rear window in a shower of safety glass.

When they hit an open road, the driver's eyes met hers in the rearview mirror.

"Stryker." She exhaled in relief. The best, among the best.

"Cut it a little close there, DiLuce."

"Yeah," she responded as lightly as she could.

Gregorio's eyes rolled back in his head.

"How bad?"

Unable to answer, struggling to keep it together, she clamped her lips together before managing, "Drive faster."

The vehicle fishtailed as he threw the vehicle around the next corner, the accelerator all the way to the floor.

He keyed a radio and spoke quietly.

She'd been in enough of these situations to know Inamorata had a hospital on standby, and that everything that could be done would be done.

Blood soaked everywhere, and she frantically shrugged out of her jacket, bunching the material against his wound.

"Stay with me." Her voice cracked as she pressed a kiss to his forehead. "Don't you dare leave me."

Their rescuer took another corner at breakneck speed, tires screaming in protest. The SUV's backend swung wide, and she braced herself against the door to keep from crushing Gregorio.

Stryker didn't apologize, nor did she expect him to. "Red light ahead," she warned.

Stryker didn't slow. "Hang on."

Horns blared as they shot through the intersection. A delivery truck swerved, barely missing them.

"We've got a tail." Stryker's voice was steady as he wrenched the wheel, cutting down a side street.

No. No. No.

"You have a gun?"

"Yeah." Since the car wasn't close enough for her to engage, she pressed harder on Gregorio's wound. His skin was growing clammy, his breathing shallow and uneven.

"Come on, come on." She wasn't sure if she was talking to Gregorio or willing the vehicle to go faster. "Open your eyes for me."

His lashes fluttered.

"That's it." Desperately, she smoothed a hand across his forehead, needing to touch him, to keep him with her.

Beneath a streetlight, his diamond earring winked, and she struggled against the lump in her throat. "Don't you dare leave me."

Another hard turn. Then another.

Frantically she steadied him. "Stay with me, Gregorio. Fight, damn it."

She lost track of where they were, how fast they were going.

"Almost there." Stryker's voice was grim as he keyed the radio again.

Thankfully, the scream of sirens cut across the night air, and two police cars fell in behind them.

"Friendlies," Stryker assured her.

Nodding, Sasha focused on the weak rise and fall of Gregorio's chest beneath her hands.

Seconds stretched into eternities.

Then—finally—the hospital's lights pierced the darkness ahead.

Rather than pulling up to the ER entrance, Stryker whipped the SUV around to a side door where a small group waited. Even in the darkness, she recognized Hawkeye's commanding presence.

Before the vehicle completely stopped, her door was wrenched open.

"How long's he been out?" Hawkeye demanded as medical personnel swarmed around them.

"Three minutes." Her voice sounded foreign to her own ears. *Too damn long*. "Maybe four."

The hospital staff loaded him onto a gurney with practiced efficiency.

"BP's dropping—"

"At least one GSW—"

"Starting an IV—"

The clinical terms blurred together as she scrambled out after him. Her legs barely held her as she ran alongside the gurney into the hospital, her blood-covered hand finding his.

"Gregorio…" She couldn't lose him. Not now. Not like this. "I need you."

His fingers twitched in hers, but his eyes remained closed.

They crashed through a set of double doors, the gurney's wheels squealing against the floor as they rounded a corner.

"Ma'am." A nurse blocked her path. "You can't go any farther."

"But—"

"They'll take good care of him." Another set of hands caught her shoulders. "Let them work."

She tried to follow as they wheeled Gregorio toward the operating room, but the walls were tilting, and her legs wouldn't cooperate.

"Wait—" Her voice was hoarse and weak, but it didn't matter. No one was listening. The doctors were shouting over each other, and the gurney kept moving.

Her vision blurred as she stumbled, barely catching herself on the doorway. The world narrowed to Gregorio's bloodied chest, the too-pale shade of his skin.

This can't be it.

With the last of her strength, she reached out and grabbed his wrist, fingers pressing against his cooling skin.

"Ma'am! You need to let go."

"Gregorio…" She wasn't even sure what she meant to say. *Come back to me. Don't leave me. I'm not ready to lose you.* The words tangled on her tongue, but the ache in her chest said them all. *I can't live without you.*

The gurney jolted as they turned a corner, and she lost her grip.

The world spun around her.

Then black sucked her under…

Chapter Nineteen

Pain lanced through Sasha, sharp and immediate, clawing through her ribs like an iron band tightening around her lungs. Her ankle throbbed with each heartbeat, her skin burned as if she'd been dragged across concrete, and something was constricting her wrist.

Forcing her eyes open a fraction, she made out the IV tubing snaking away from her arm.

What the hell?

She curled her fingers into the stiff, unfamiliar sheets that carried the distinct scent of industrial bleach. The steady *beep… beep… beep* of a heart monitor threaded through her senses, dragging her fully into awareness.

The overhead fluorescent light was too bright, too sterile, burning behind her eyelids even when she squeezed them shut again. The air around her reeked of antiseptic, barely masking the metallic sting of dried blood—her blood, Gregorio's blood…

Gregorio.

The name jolted through her consciousness like a lightning bolt, obliterating everything else. Her eyes flew open despite the stabbing pain it caused.

This wasn't the SUV. This wasn't the Santos house.

Hospital.

The realization snapped her into place with crystal clarity, and a new wave of panic surged through her.

She had to find him.

Sasha forced herself fully awake, but the movement rocketed a dull, nauseating ache through her skull. She gritted her teeth against it, pushing up on her elbows—

"Whoa there, tiger." A warm, steady hand pressed against her shoulder, catching her before she could fully collapse from the sharp, breath-stealing pain that lanced through her ribs.

The edges of her vision went white, and she gasped.

Every part of her—her ankle, ribs, hands—screamed in protest.

"Yeah, that's definitely a no." The voice was familiar, tinged with both amusement and concern.

Through the haze of pain, she focused on the man beside her. Stryker. His usual cocky grin was replaced by concern as he carefully eased her back against the pillows. In his free hand, he held out a paper cup of coffee like a peace offering.

"You almost hit the floor pretty spectacularly back there, tiger." Though his mouth quirked up at one corner, his eyes were serious as they swept over her face with quiet assessment.

Hit the floor?

Was he serious? Since she couldn't remember anything after she was prevented from following Gregorio, maybe he was serious.

"You passed completely out. Not exactly your most graceful moment."

Sasha swallowed, her throat desert-dry and scratchy. "I don't faint," she protested weakly.

Stryker's eyebrows shot up, and genuine warmth crept into his expression. "No? Then I suppose I imagined having to catch you before you cracked your head open?" His voice held a gentle teasing note that took away some of her fear. "And I definitely didn't have to carry you in here while you were doing a very convincing impression of Sleeping Beauty."

She tried to glare at him, but suspected it came across as more of a weak grimace.

He just extended the coffee cup closer to her face, the rich aroma cutting through the antiseptic hospital smell. "Here. I had them make it exactly how you like it—strong enough to strip paint and sweet enough to rot teeth."

She hesitated, then took the coffee with trembling fingers. The warmth seeped through her cold hands, grounding her in the moment. But the brief comfort vanished as memory crashed back with brutal force.

"Gregorio." His name came out as a desperate whisper. She snapped her head toward Stryker so fast the room spun. "Where is he?"

Stryker's playful expression sobered instantly, the change making him look dangerous for a fleeting moment before his features softened with compassion. "Still in surgery."

The words hit her like a physical blow. Her stomach plunged, and the coffee nearly slipped from her grip.

"The docs say he lost a lot of blood," Stryker continued, his voice steady and calm, as if he could transfer some of that steadiness to her through sheer force of will. He reached out to stabilize the coffee cup in her shaking hands. "But he's strong. Too damn stubborn to give up without a fight."

He nodded at the IV in her arm, then at her ankle, still propped on a pillow and wrapped so tightly it looked mummified. "You, on the other hand, don't go ripping those IVs out just yet. Doctor's orders." He tipped his head to one side. "And mine. I'll tell you everything I can, but you need to stay put."

Sasha pressed her lips together, fighting back the sharp, irrational spike of helplessness that threatened to overwhelm her. She was supposed to be by Gregorio's side, not lying here useless while he fought for his life.

"What about my office manager?"

He scowled. "Office manager?"

"Ashley Lakin." Quickly, she brought him up to speed, telling him about the odd things that had happened at the office and her home, the way Ashley had been overly concerned about Sasha's whereabouts this weekend, and the phone call that came seconds before all hell broke loose at the Santos home.

"She was trying to warn you?"

The thundering in her head became a hammer. She would never have believed that Ashley was capable of betraying her. But even then—

She choked on a sob. "And I'm convinced that was a gunshot that cut her off."

"We'll check it out."

No matter what, Ashley hadn't deserved to be executed.

The door swung open, the sound sharp against the backdrop of steady beeping from her monitors.

Hawkeye walked in, his presence filling the small room with quiet authority. His expression was carefully neutral, but she caught the flash of concern in his eyes as he took in her condition.

Sasha straightened despite the protest from her ribs, squaring her shoulders. To hell with being treated like an invalid. "Debrief me."

Hawkeye turned a chair backward and dragged it next to the bed then took a seat facing her.

Sasha hated this. The feeling of being sidelined, being handled like she might shatter. She'd been on countless missions. She was a professional who'd seen worse.

But her heart had never been invested before.

She forced herself to breathe through the frustration, counting each inhale and exhale while she waited for Hawkeye to speak.

"FBI's officially involved," he said finally, watching her reaction closely. "We turned over the photos you took at the house."

"And the burner phone?"

"Burner phone?"

"Yeah. It's with my personal one inside my jacket."

Stryker inclined his head toward a small closet.

"Mind if I get it?" Hawkeye asked.

"Please do."

Her belongings were in a large, opaque plastic bag, and he dug through her jacket until he found the two devices. "The bigger one," she said.

He pocketed the phone. "Good job, DiLuce."

If she lost Gregorio, none of this would have been worth it.

"Org Crime is on the case. I'll see they get it soon."

Meaning after Hawkeye conducted their own forensics. Probably for the best. Bureaucracy moved slow, allowing Argentum time to plan and react. Hawkeye was able to act much quicker. "What else do we know?"

"Mrs. Santos is safe," he assured her. "She's still at the safehouse. Her husband hasn't contacted her."

Sasha squeezed her eyes shut. "And the Hawkeye agents at the Santos property?"

"One injury on our side. Two dead on theirs."

Thanks to Gregorio.

If she lost him, she'd never recover.

She cut off that train of thought. He was going to make it, if only through the sheer force of her will.

"The rest of the Argentum thugs?" she pressed, proud that her voice remained steady.

Hawkeye's expression tightened, and Stryker shifted, his easy charm replaced by coiled tension.

"Gone." Hawkeye's response was clipped and succinct.

Sasha gripped the coffee cup harder, the heat now burning against her palms. She shouldn't be surprised. Argentum didn't generally leave loose ends. "And no leads on Felix Santos?" She was guessing not, if he hadn't contacted his wife.

Hawkeye and Stryker exchanged glances.

"None," Hawkeye said finally.

"If we don't get to Santos first—"

"There's no we in this equation," Stryker cut her off, his voice gentle but brooking no argument. "You need rest."

"You don't understand. My office manager might have been killed over this. And Gregorio..." Not to mention the injured Hawkeye agent who'd been on surveillance.

Frustration and fear crystallized into determination. She swung her legs over the edge of the bed, ignoring the way the room tilted. "I need to—"

Stryker moved faster than she would have thought possible. His gripped her shoulders with surprising gentleness despite the absolute authority in his hold. The warmth of his touch seeped through the thin hospital gown, steadying her even as she tried to shake him off.

"You," he said, his voice dropping to a dangerous level, "are running on adrenaline and determination. And considering you collapsed less than an hour ago, you're not going anywhere."

Sasha set her jaw, meeting his gaze with stubborn defiance.

But Stryker didn't back down, his hands remaining steady on her shoulders until some of the fight drained from her. Only then did his grip ease, though he stayed close enough to catch her if she tried anything foolish.

"Call your parents," he said, his voice gentling. The sudden shift from command to compassion caught her off guard. "They deserve to know what's happening." A shadow of understanding crossed his features. "And they'd want to be here. For both of you."

She swallowed hard and looked away, unable to hold his knowing gaze. Stryker knew both of them from their time at Hawkeye, and he'd heard every word she said to Gregorio in the SUV.

Still, the thought of calling home made her chest tight. Stryker was right—her parents needed to know. But calling them meant her sister would hear about it too. And they'd find out about Gregorio. "It's complicated."

"Avoiding it won't make things easier."

Her fingers clenched in the thin hospital blanket, and she twisted the fabric until her knuckles went white. "Fine."

Stryker nodded, satisfaction flickering in his eyes. "Good." The corner of his mouth quirked up. "Because you'll need clothes anyway. That hospital gown isn't exactly your best look."

Before she could summon a suitably scathing response, the door swung open again. Inamorata entered, her movements efficient and purposeful.

"We got a hit on Santos' location." Ever efficient, she spared no greetings, no preambles.

Sasha jerked upright, every nerve suddenly on high alert. Stryker's hand returned to her shoulder, steadying rather than restraining this time.

"Traffic camera caught him near Salt Lake City."

Finally.

"Feds will be picking him up. He'll be safer in custody than he will be out there alone."

"When that happens, I will want to update Mrs. Santos," Sasha said. "Get her back home when it's safe." Hopefully he'd cooperate with the investigation and testify against Argentum. In a perfect world, the couple would be approved for acceptance into the witness protection program.

The door opened again, and a nurse entered.

"You wanted an update."

"Yes," she said before anyone else could speak.

The nurse offered a small, careful smile that revealed nothing.

"Mr. Conti is out of surgery."

Sasha's lungs locked. The words seemed to echo in the suddenly too-small room. Her fingers curled deeper in the blanket, heart hammering so loud it drowned out the steady beeping of the monitors. She swallowed against the tightness in her throat.

"And…?" Her question was a desperate whisper.

The nurse hesitated, and Sasha's world teetered on the edge of a knife.

Stryker's hand tightened almost imperceptibly on her shoulder, offering silent support as they waited for the news that would either save or shatter her.

"He's—"

Chapter Twenty

The pause stretched.

Too long.

Oh God. *No.*

Her heart stopped.

She saw it in the nurse's eyes—the hesitation, the cautious way she shifted her weight from one foot to the other.

He wasn't out of the woods.

Say it. For God's sake, just say it.

Desperately, she clenched her fists to stop her hands from shaking. Behind her, Stryker's grip on her shoulder tightened fractionally, grounding her.

Finally, the nurse exhaled.

"He made it through the operation," she said gently. "But he lost a lot of blood. We had to perform an emergency transfusion."

Sasha nodded automatically, processing facts like she was collecting pieces of evidence. Around her, the tension in the room shifted a little. Hawkeye's stance loosened slightly, and Inamorata exhaled sharply.

"Thank fuck," Stryker said.

Gregorio had made it.

"He's alive." Her words were barely audible, and tears burned her eyes, clinging to her eyelashes.

But there was more, had to be with the way the nurse kept watching her.

The way the air in the room felt too still.

"What aren't you telling me?" Sasha's voice was steady, but clipped, a blade's edge away from breaking.

The nurse shifted again.

"There was some organ stress," she admitted carefully. "He coded once on the table, but the team got him back quickly."

Coded.

The word sank its teeth into her. Stryker muttered something under his breath—a curse, maybe a prayer.

Her stomach turned, but she didn't flinch. Didn't let it show.

"Oh, God."

Stryker placed his hand on her shoulder again, and Hawkeye moved closer to the bed, a little protectively, as if trying to shield her from the news.

Inamorata tipped her head to one side, and it might have been the first time Sasha ever saw the woman's usual efficiency replaced by quiet concern.

The nurse hesitated. "His vitals are stable for now, but he's heavily sedated. We won't know the full picture until he wakes up."

Sasha let out a slow, measured breath.

So that was it.

They'd patched him back together, but they couldn't guarantee a damn thing.

Her mind supplied worst-case scenarios faster than she could stop them.

Internal bleeding. Organ failure. Infection.

Her gut twisted.

He'd coded. He'd flatlined, his body shutting down, and she hadn't been there.

She'd been out cold, completely useless, while Gregorio fought for his life on an operating table.

The nurse must have seen the shift in her expression because her voice softened. "We just need to give him some time."

Time.

That was the problem, wasn't it?

Time meant waiting. Waiting meant thinking. Thinking meant drowning in the knowledge that she was the one who'd pulled him into this.

This wasn't supposed to happen.

She was the one who'd gotten him involved.

And now he was in the ICU, tubes and machines keeping him stable, because she hadn't been careful enough.

"He's the toughest son of a bitch I know," Stryker said quietly, reassuringly.

She thought of the wound he still had on his abs, one that had never made him flinch though it must have been horrifically painful.

Blinking against the burn behind her eyes, Sasha asked, "When can I see him?"

The nurse hesitated. "The ICU has strict visitation—"

"I don't care," Sasha cut in, her voice sharp, the panic slipping through before she could pull it back. "I need to see him."

"We'll make it happen," Hawkeye interjected quietly, his tone leaving no room for argument.

The nurse softened, but didn't bend.

"They need to stabilize him first," she explained. "Probably a few hours, maybe more. If all looks good, you might be able to sit with him for a bit."

Hours.

She hated the way the word settled in her heart, like lead.

But pushing wouldn't help. She knew that.

Slowly, she unclenched her fists, forcing herself to nod, to breathe.

"I'll let you know as soon as it's possible," the nurse added.

Sasha gave a small nod. "Thank you."

The nurse lingered another moment, as if debating whether to say something else, then gave her a small, tight smile before leaving.

Moments later, Inamorata followed her from the room.

When they were alone, silence rushed back in behind her.

Sasha sagged against the pillows, staring up at the ceiling.

Stryker finally released his grip.

"We'll ensure he has the best care on the planet," Hawkeye promised.

"He's hanging in there," Stryker said.

That wasn't enough.

She had to get out of this bed and out of here.

Inamorata opened the door a little, and she and Hawkeye excused themselves. There really wasn't any sense in them hanging around.

"You still need to call your parents," Stryker reminded her. "You need the support."

Was that what she was going to get?

She sighed over the pounding headache.

"Anyone else?"

"Damien. From the Den. He'd want to know about Gregorio."

"Do you have his contact information?"

She shook her head, then regretted the movement.

"I'll take care of it. Anyone else?"

Even though she and Gregorio had shared something hot and combustible, she didn't know much about his ordinary life. His parents had been killed in a car bomb explosion when he was a child. To her knowledge, he didn't keep in touch with any of the foster parents whose homes he'd been shuffled between. As far as close friends, she had no idea. "I'm not sure," she admitted. "Maybe Damien knows."

"On it."

She tried to get out of the bed to find her phone, but the room wobbled beneath her.

"Stop pushing it, tiger." Stryker captured her upper arms and helped her to sit back down. "Where you going?"

In frustration, she squeezed her eyes shut. "I need my cell phone."

"You got it."

After grabbing the device, he brought it to her.

"Thank you."

"You might need this." He pulled out her gun from his waistband.

"How…?" She blinked.

"Figured you wouldn't want any questions from the hospital staff."

And she definitely didn't want it to be confiscated. "I owe you one."

"Way more than that." He flashed her the smile that had ensnared at least a dozen women in the few years that she'd known him.

He tucked it into her plastic bag of belongings and closed the closet door.

A few moments later, Inamorata was back, along with two men in suits.

FBI, according to their credentials.

Since she was no longer employed by Hawkeye, Inamorata owed her nothing. But the woman stayed, regardless, off to the side, her presence reassuring.

"Just a few questions, ma'am, if you don't mind."

Did it matter if she wasn't up to it?

Sasha answered dozens of questions, most of them repeats, phrased in slightly different ways.

She had very little information about the case, just information she'd found in the ledger and the burner phone. "And I understand the phone has been turned over to you?"

"Affirmative," the older man replied.

Then they asked about Ashley, and she repeated exactly what she'd told Stryker and added, "I have no idea if she's involved, or why she would be."

"Anything else you can think of?"

She rubbed the bridge of her nose, as if that could force back the never-ending pounding in her head. "You may want to talk to Brenda Santos when you can. She can get you a description of the man who threatened her. I believe he was at the house on at least two occasions."

"We have agents en route."

"Do you have Felix in custody?"

"Afraid I can't say one way or the other."

"So it's a one-way street. You get information, but you don't give any?"

"Thanks for your time, ma'am. If you think of anything else…" He pulled out a business card from inside his suitcoat and offered it to her.

When she didn't accept, he dropped it on the table next to her bed.

The two men left, and once the door was closed behind them, Inamorata said, "They picked him up less than ten minutes ago."

Sasha nodded in appreciation.

How Inamorata knew stuff, she had no idea.

"Get some rest," the woman said. "I'll stay on top of things here. As soon as I can get you in to see Gregorio, I will."

"I…"

Inamorata raised one of her very carefully sculpted eyebrows. No matter the time of day or night, she was impeccably put together.

Sasha settled for, "Thank you."

"You might not say that when you see our invoice."

She winced. Since she'd dragged Gregorio into this, the bill was definitely hers.

"I'll have accounting hold it until you're out of the hospital."

"Generous."

At the door, Inamorata paused and looked back. "Per Stryker, we sent a team to Ashley Lakin's house."

She braced herself.

"There's no sign of her or a struggle."

Sasha frowned.

"We'll keep checking." She shrugged. "And so will the feds."

Finally, she was alone, and the beeping and emptiness overwhelmed her.

Dropping her head onto the pillow, she allowed the tears to come, until she was exhausted.

She closed her eyes, willing all of this to go away.

A nurse came in to check on her, and Sasha asked how quickly she could leave.

"Right now, it would be against doctor's orders. I wouldn't try it until you can stand on your own, unless you want to get around in a wheelchair."

And she wouldn't get far without actual clothes.

Which brought her back to her parents and calls she didn't want to make.

Knowing she couldn't stall forever, she picked up her phone.

* * * *

Sasha heard her parents arrive before she saw them—less than forty-five minutes after she'd told them what hospital she was in.

There was a sharp click of hurried footsteps on the floor and a murmur of voices just beyond the door.

Then the door swung open, and her mother was the first one through, a blur of familiar warmth and frantic hands, arms already reaching for her before words even formed.

"Oh, Sasha! Honey—thank God!"

Rosa DiLuce's words were wrapped in emotion that she couldn't hide.

Her mother gathered her close, her hug warm and desperate at the same time.

Then she pulled back, but kept hold of Sasha's shoulders, as if she needed to reassure herself that

Sasha was really okay. As Rosa swept her gaze over her daughter, tears swam in her eyes.

"I'm okay, Mom," she promised, but that didn't matter.

As if needing to see for herself, her mother brushed hair back from Sasha's face and studied her carefully.

In the doorway, she saw her father.

The weight of his worry made his shoulders roll forward, and she experienced another wave of regret.

Unlike her mother, he didn't rush in, but he took in everything—the IV in her arm, the hospital gown she hated, the ugly bruise blooming along her forearm.

"Che diavolo è successo?" His voice was low, gruff with the kind of emotion he didn't show easily as he softly demanded to know what had happened. "You should have called us sooner."

For their sakes, Sasha forced a small, tired grin. "I've been a little busy."

"Madonna santa!" Her mother scowled. "Don't joke about this."

"I'm sorry." Instantly, she was contrite.

In their situation, she'd be scared, too. And, really, she should have known better.

This was how things seemed to go in their family.

Her mother led with emotion, and her father was always more reserved, stoic, keeping his voice even, never overreacting, pretending he had everything under control.

She landed somewhere in the middle, balancing between the two, keeping it together because she didn't know how to do anything else. Her older sister was much more like her mother—dramatic, always going to the worst-case scenario.

Had it always been this way? Or had that been a result of that night that changed all of their lives?

The moment her father's focus shifted, she knew it.

His gaze landed on her wrapped ankle, then lifted to meet her eyes. "Sprained?"

She nodded. "And some bruised ribs. I'm fine."

"You're in a hospital bed, Sasha."

"Would've walked it off, but they frowned on that."

His mouth pressed into a tight line, but it wasn't from amusement.

Her mother sighed, brushing a hand lightly over Sasha's forehead before her fingers trailed down her arm, landing just above the IV tape. "They said you weren't shot," she murmured, "but… You were in the middle of it, weren't you? That story on the news this morning… The shooting."

Sasha exhaled, closing her eyes for a beat. "Yes. I was there, Mom."

"At least two dead."

"I'm afraid so."

Before they could ask any more questions, Adriana rushed in, still wearing her pajamas with whimsical coffee cups on the pant legs.

"God, Sash! You've done it this time." She rushed over, her bunny slippers making no sound on the floor. "What happened?" she asked, standing way back from their parents, as if afraid that whatever was happening to Sasha might be contagious.

"What do the doctors say?" her mother asked.

"That I can go home today." If she hadn't passed out, she wouldn't be in here to begin with.

"So what happened?" Adriana demanded.

In response, Sasha offered only vague details. "I was working on a case where the wife thought her husband was cheating—"

"Don't they all?" Adriana interrupted.

Rosa scowled at her oldest daughter. *"Shh."*

Unconcerned, Adriana shrugged. "Two out of three of mine have."

Which brought them back to…

There was no choice but to drop the news like a bombshell in the silence. Once more holding onto the bedsheets, she said, "Gregorio was working the case with me."

Silence ricocheted around them as her parents and sister exchanged glances.

On some level maybe she'd been a coward, hoping she'd never have to have this conversation with them. But now there was no choice.

"Gregorio?" her mother asked, perching on the side of the bed while Adriana dropped into a chair. Her father folded his arms.

Adriana narrowed her gaze. "How did he get involved?"

Wishing her stomach wasn't flip-flopping, she looked at her sister. "I called him."

"Because?"

"I had a stalker. And I was scared," she admitted.

"A stalker?" their mother demanded.

Thank God for the interruption.

"So you needed my ex-husband to protect you?" Adriana asked.

Her heart was pounding in her ears. "I didn't know who else I could trust." She left the words hanging. Her answer was clear, even though she hadn't overtly said it. *Yes.* Gregorio had been the only person she'd trusted to take care of her.

And she'd make the same decision again.

Mr. DiLuce looked between his two children, then he settled on Sasha once more. "And where is Gregorio now?"

Taking a steadying breath, she told them, "Recovering from surgery."

In Italian, their mother swore and crossed herself. "Surgery?"

For now, she wasn't mentioning the fact he'd been shot.

"How is he?" Adriana asked.

"Beyond stable, I don't know." A knot of emotion threatening to choke her, she swallowed hard and added, "I haven't been able to see him yet."

Her eyes narrowing even further, Adriana snapped, "Is that how it is?"

They'd never been able to keep secrets from each other. "Adriana—"

"Don't, Sash. Just fucking don't, okay?" She stood and flounced to the door.

"I..." Because she didn't know what to say, she trailed off. "I'm sorry. So sorry."

She threw a look over her shoulder. "Are you? Are you really? Sorry for hurting me? Or for fucking my ex-husband?"

As if slapped, Sasha recoiled.

"Adriana!" their father scolded.

Maybe she shouldn't have gone to Gregorio, but at the time, that had been her best—maybe only—option. And once she'd seen him at the Den, she'd been confident she'd made the right decision.

Then heart had gotten involved, and she'd been lost.

But now…? She'd never want to cause this kind of hurt.

"I'm sure your sister—"

"Mother!" Adriana interrupted. "Will you listen to yourself? Sasha knew exactly what she was doing."

Falling in love.

Her heart constricted, and she couldn't breathe.

Love?

Was that what this was?

Ever since she'd been young, she'd adored him, and that feeling had turned into hero worship.

But love?

Until now, until Gregorio, she hadn't even understood what the word meant.

She'd give her life for his.

And he'd risked his to save her.

Saying nothing else, Adriana left, grabbing the knob to slam the door.

The sound echoed from the ceilings.

Then, the noise faded, leaving only the constant sounds of beeping.

Her parents looked at each other as the silence descended.

Finally, her mother touched her hand. "Sasha…"

"I…" Sasha shook her head. "I'm sorry," she said again. But even if she repeated it a thousand times, things wouldn't get better. "Honestly, I never meant for any of this to happen." Furiously, she blinked so the tears didn't fall. "Go ahead and leave. Adriana needs you."

"So do you," her mother said.

Once more, her parents exchanged glances, and a moment later, her father walked out of the room.

Feeling even more miserable, she allowed a tear to fall. "You have to believe—"

"Shh," Rosa soothed, reaching for a tissue to dab Sasha's cheeks. "You've spent your life making other people happy. Maybe it's time that you thought about Sasha."

Stunned, she stared at her mom. "You can't mean that. This is a disaster."

"After what we've been through…"

That night.

"You were stronger than you ever should have had to be. You took care of us. Then you became our warrior child." Rosa smiled, part with pride, part with regret. "Adriana didn't want to go out with Gregorio that night. Did you know that?"

"What?" Furiously, trying to remember, she thought through the layers of her memory. "No."

"She'd fallen in love with someone else." Rosa scoffed. "Was planning to go out with the other boy…Luigi, I think it was."

The name didn't sound familiar.

"We told her she had to do the right thing and tell Gregorio first." She shrugged. "Then…"

He'd become their savior. Adrianna had sobbed in his arms, and he'd gently cared for her.

"She never really loved him. But that night, when he proposed, she was swept up in the romance of the moment."

The news left her speechless.

"I kept telling her she didn't need to marry him, but she loved being the center of attention in the news stories. Their picture was everywhere." She sighed. "Everything was fine until she got tired of his job and being alone. Being ignored." Her mother sighed, as if debating whether or not to go on. "She met someone else. For once she did the right thing and asked for a divorce."

Sasha sank deeper into her pillow. "I had no idea."

"No reason you should have. You were at school, focused on your guns and self-defense." She spoke to herself in Italian for a moment. "You should never have had to go through that experience."

"It wasn't fair to any of us."

"You were so young. Only a child."

"Doesn't make it any easier for you," she insisted. "To be scared for your family…"

Her mother's eyes filled with emotion. "I was so frightened. And you were so brave."

She didn't remember it that way at all. All she could recall was the terror, the sight of the gun barrel waving in her daddy's face, the man screaming, so hysterical she couldn't make out the words.

"Do I like this situation?" Rosa picked up one of Sasha's hands. "No. But we love you. And we love Gregorio. Always hated that he wasn't still part of the family."

"Adriana will never forgive me." *Nor would I, if the situation were reversed.*

"She's getting married soon. I'm sure she'll enjoy the drama of the story."

"How her little sister betrayed her and stole her man?"

A smile ghosted across Rosa's lips. "Quite thrilling, isn't it?"

"Maybe." But it wasn't at all true. The pair had been divorced for years. Enough time for Adriana to marry and divorce another two times.

"You need to spend your energy getting well."

And out of this hospital bed.

"God will sort everything else out."

She wished she had a fraction of her mother's unshakable faith.

The door opened again, and she looked up, expecting to see her father or sister. Instead, the nurse from earlier was there.

Her face was set in a serious line, sending Sasha's tummy topsy-turvy.

"Would you like to see Mr. Conti?"

Chapter Twenty-One

"Yes."

Heart racing, Sasha threw back the blanket.

Nothing and no one could keep her away.

Her mother stood, and Sasha pushed herself off the bed, only to have her knees wobble and the world tilt beneath her once more.

She hated being so weak, especially now that she knew Gregorio was conscious.

Before she collapsed entirely, her mother helped her back onto the edge of the mattress.

Frantically, Rosa looked to the nurse.

"I'll get you a wheelchair."

"I can walk—"

"If you want to see Mr. Conti, that's not going to be an option, Ms. DiLuce."

"But—"

"Honey, if you hurt yourself even more, you'll be no good to anyone," her mother said.

In frustration, she raked her hair back. She wanted, needed, to get to Gregorio's side—where she belonged—as soon as possible.

"Can you at least help me into some real clothes?" she asked her mom. She'd feel better if she wasn't in a hospital gown.

"Will the staff be okay with that?"

She shrugged. Did it really matter? "I'll be checking myself out of here really soon."

Rosa pursed her lips. "Not if you can't stand up."

Forcing back a sigh, she nodded.

After squeezing her hand, Rosa crossed the room to pick up the bag she'd brought along.

Her mother turned her back while Sasha struggled into her underwear and bra, then she helped her with the cozy fleece sweatshirt.

Getting the sweatpants over her bandaged ankle was a challenge, making her glad she hadn't asked for a pair of jeans. No way would she have been able to get into those.

"I don't suppose you have a brush with you?" Sasha asked. Her mother carried a purse the size of a small piece of luggage. Whatever anyone needed, she always seemed to have.

Rosa smiled. "I promise you, he's not going to care what you look like."

"But I do."

"Of course you do." Without another word, Rosa pulled out a brush.

On the first pull through her hair, the bristles caught on a tangle. Sasha grimaced. Every damn part of her hurt, and the pain seemed to be getting worse instead of better.

Rationally, she knew it was because she'd had an adrenaline dump, but that didn't help her frustration.

"Let me help you, honey." Her mother's warm hand curled around her shoulder.

She didn't remember her mother brushing her hair since the night of the robbery. Until now, she hadn't realized what a dividing line that was. Between being a kid and becoming a grownup.

Since she couldn't go anywhere until the nurse returned, she nodded. "Thank you."

A few minutes later, she was settled in the wheelchair, an IV pole attached to the side. The nurse draped a blanket over her legs, and her mother stroked her hair one last time.

"I'll be here when you get back."

"Thank you." She looked at her mother's pale, drawn features. This had really taken an unfair toll on her. "I'm sorry." She extended her hand. "I mean it. For everything." Getting hurt, the Gregorio situation, hurting her sister.

Her mother offered a small smile. "As long as you're okay, everything else will be fine."

Will it?

Sasha sighed. The last time she'd been in a hospital had been the night of the robbery. Back then, she'd been too young, too scared to do anything but watch as others took control. But now…

In the hallway, there was no sign of her dad or sister.

God, if she could change things…

The journey to the ICU was endless. The elevator swooshing to a stop shot pain into her ribs, and every turn made her grimace.

As they approached the unit, the antiseptic smell grew stronger, more clinical. More frightening.

In the waiting area, Hawkeye stood near Damien and a woman she didn't recognize.

Damien swept his gaze over her, his expression unreadable. "Looks like the two of you had a hell of a weekend."

"Unfortunately." Then, summoning courage, she met his gaze. "I'm sorry I dragged your friend into this."

At that he lifted a shoulder. "I'm not sure there was anything you could have done to keep him away."

At his understanding words, she summoned a half-smile. "Thank you." She'd feel guilty about this for the rest of her life.

"I'm Catrina," the woman standing next to him said.

"My apologies." Damien's gaze took in both of them. "Sasha, this is my fiancée."

She had long, black hair, past her waist. Like it had been that night at the Den, Damien's hair was fastened back with a strip of leather. Together, the pair were striking.

Where Damien had been empathetic, Catrina was somewhat standoffish. "Gregorio is one of my closest friends."

Was there a note of warning in her voice?

If so, she didn't blame the woman.

"He can never resist a damsel in distress."

Her first guess had been right. Catrina cared for Gregorio and didn't want to see him hurt.

She was thankfully saved from replying by the nurse saying, "Are you ready?"

"We won't keep you," Damien said.

"He's been through a lot, and he's still groggy," the nurse warned as they approached his room. "Try not to excite him."

The ICU room was stark, sterile, dominated by beeping machines and hanging IV bags.

Despite the warning and her bracing herself, nothing could have prepared her for being wheeled into the room.

The fluorescent lights cast harsh shadows across Gregorio's face, making him look ghostly pale against the white sheets. Bandages covered his torso, stark and clinical. Tubes and wires snaked from his arms, monitoring every breath, every heartbeat.

This couldn't be Gregorio—her protector, her warrior, her hero—the man who had always seemed larger than life.

Now he looked almost fragile, and she choked back a sob.

The nurse wheeled her closer.

His earring was missing. The small detail scared her as much as the machines and bandages. As if it had been yesterday, she remembered the first time she'd seen the earring catch the light, how it had made him seem dangerous and thrilling to her much-younger self. Now its absence felt like a reminder of how close she'd come to losing him forever.

For a moment, fighting for control over her runaway emotions, she squeezed her eyes shut.

Even though they'd entered almost silently, his eyes fluttered open, dark and intense despite the medication. His gaze found her immediately, as if drawn by an invisible thread. "Petal?"

Relief flooded her, leaving her weak. "I'm here."

"I need you next to me."

The nurse maneuvered the chair so it was as close to the bed as possible. "Five minutes," she warned.

Grateful for every second, Sasha nodded.

"Get over here, Petal." His voice was rough, but the command in it was unmistakable—so Gregorio that joy lodged in her throat, making her shake.

Somehow, she managed to come a couple of inches closer to his bedside.

He reached out to cup her face, and she leaned into his touch, savoring the sensations.

For hours, she'd been so scared that they'd never again share anything like this.

"You look like hell," he murmured.

A watery laugh escaped her. "Told you it had been an awful long time since I'd scaled walls. Even longer since I've been shot at."

The same probably wasn't true for him.

"Sasha—"

After locking the wheelchair for stability, she forced herself upright, and she held onto the bedrails for support.

His expression pained, stark, he threaded a hand into her hair, and he pulled her down to him.

"*Gregorio!* You can't!"

"Quiet, Petal. We don't need an audience."

His kiss was desperate, claiming, his mouth hot and demanding against hers. She melted into him, careful of his injuries but unable to resist the magnetic pull between them.

His touch was achingly familiar—the same calloused fingers that had wiped away her tears years ago, that had pushed her to safety mere hours before.

Beneath her palm, his heart thudded, strong and steady. *Alive.* The reality of almost losing him crashed over her again, leaving her weak.

"You shouldn't have taken that bullet." She'd never forgive herself.

"Don't you understand? I'd die for you, Sasha."

Tears burned her eyes. "Gregorio—"

Cutting her off, he pulled her against him again. "I'd do it all over again." Hand cupped against her neck, he claimed her mouth with searing passion, and the monitors shrieked in protest as his heart rate spiked.

"Mr. Conti!" The nurse's voice was sharp with disapproval as she rushed into the room.

But his arms stayed locked around Sasha, holding her close despite the pain it must have caused him. Even now, he was trying to protect her, shelter her.

"You scared the hell out of me," she whispered.

"Likewise." His thumb brushed away a tear she hadn't realized had fallen.

"No more playing hero without me."

"That goes both ways."

He gave a half-smile that simultaneously reassured her but reminded her how long of a path was ahead of them. "We'll negotiate the terms later."

The monitors continued their angry protest, and the nurse warned her that she needed to leave.

But in that moment, wrapped in Gregorio's arms with his heart beating strong and steady beneath her palm, nothing else mattered.

He smoothed back hair from her forehead.

"Oh, Petal. What the hell am I going to do with you?"

The words echoed their first night together, but now they carried the weight of everything they'd been through—the near miss, every moment of protection, every toe-curling touch and command, every time she'd tried to deny what was between them. "I don't know, Gregorio." Her love overwhelmed her, making her voice crack. "What *are* you going to do with me?"

"I fucking wish I could keep you forever."

She blinked. *"What?"*

Of the millions of things she'd thought he might say, that was not on the list.

"I wish I could be the kind of man who deserved you."

The monitors screeched.

"Are you…?" Her heart shattering, she pushed herself away.

What was he saying?

"Time's up." The nurse interrupted them.

"Gregorio." Frantically, she shook her head. "No. Please. *No…*"

Chapter Twenty-Two

Over her sobs and protests, the nurse wheeled Sasha from the room.

This time, she barely felt the movement.

Her world had suddenly narrowed to the searing pain in her chest that had nothing to do with her injuries.

Hot tears spilled down her cheeks, but she didn't bother wiping them away.

"I wish I could be the kind of man who deserved you."

His words echoed through her mind, devastating her all over again. After everything they'd been through—the gunfight, nearly losing him, her sister's anger—his words and the aching coldness in his tone was what broke her.

As she was pushed through the waiting area, she caught Hawkeye's sharp intake of breath at her appearance. Damien stepped forward, concern etching his features, but she couldn't meet his gaze. Couldn't bear to see the pity there.

"Sasha…" Hawkeye started.

She shook her head sharply, the movement sending fresh pain through her ribs. The physical hurt was nothing compared to the way her heart was shattering.

"Please, keep moving," she begged the nurse.

The wheels squeaked against the floor as the nurse guided her toward the elevator. The sound seemed to mock her—an echoing, painful reminder that she was being taken away from Gregorio, the one person she needed most.

The man who'd just pushed her away.

The man she loved.

Stupid, she thought bitterly. *So stupid to think we could overcome everything standing between us. Stupid to think he cared for me as much as I care for him.*

Back in her room, her mother took one look at her face and rushed forward to crouch in front of her wheelchair. "Oh, honey…"

The sympathy in Rosa's voice unraveled the last threads of Sasha's control. A sob tore from her throat as she fell forward into her mother's arms.

Her father was back, and he moved closer, his usual stoicism replaced by fierce concern. "What happened? Is Gregorio…?"

"He's pushing me away." The words came out broken. "Says he doesn't deserve me."

Her mother's arms tightened. "That foolish, noble man."

"He's trying to protect everyone." Her father's voice was gruff with understanding. "Your sister. You."

"I don't need protection." Sasha swiped angrily at her tears. "I need *him.*"

The simple truth of those words hung in the air between them.

Her mother smoothed back her hair, the gesture achingly gentle. "Then fight for him."

Sasha blinked up at her in surprise.

"What?" Rosa's lips curved. "You think I don't know what it's like to love a stubborn man?" She cast a meaningful look at Sasha's father, who shifted from foot to foot. "Sometimes they need sense knocked into their thick skulls."

"But Adriana…"

"Your sister will survive." Her mother's voice was firm. "You know she's in the middle of wedding preparations. But you…" She cupped Sasha's face. "I've never seen you look at anyone the way you look at him. The way you've always looked at him."

"I love him," Sasha whispered. Saying the words out loud made them more real, more powerful. "I think I always have."

Her father cleared his throat. "Then don't let him push you away because he thinks it's the right thing to do." He met her gaze steadily. "Sometimes the right thing…" He cleared his throat again. "It isn't what's noble. It's what's true."

Fresh tears spilled down her cheeks, but this time they weren't entirely from pain.

Her mother grabbed a tissue from the nightstand and pressed it into Sasha's hand. "Now, shall we see about getting you out of this hospital? You have a stubborn man to knock some sense into."

For the first time since Gregorio's devastating words, Sasha felt hope flutter in her chest. She wasn't giving up. Not on him. Not on them.

Not ever.

But even as the thought formed, determination sparked through her grief. She hadn't survived a gunfight, hadn't faced down Argentum's killers, hadn't risked everything just to let Gregorio's misplaced nobility tear them apart.

Her mother was right.

If he thought she would just accept this, he didn't know her at all.

* * * *

What the fuck have I done?

The look on her face…

Jesus Christ.

The rhythmic beeping of the monitors mocked him as he stared at the empty doorway where Sasha had disappeared.

Trying to force away the haunting memory of her stricken features, he squeezed his eyes shut, but the image was burned into his memory—her devastation, the tears she couldn't hide, the way her shoulders had rolled forward as if he'd physically struck her.

Better this way, he told himself, even as every instinct screamed at him to call her back.

He'd rather she hate him now than watch her destroy her relationship with her family. Than see her caught in the crossfire of his dangerous life. Than attend her funeral because someone from his past decided to use her to get to him.

His side burned, the pain medication doing little to dull the agony. But the physical pain was nothing compared to watching her being wheeled away.

Petal.

She'd come to him for protection, and he'd failed her. Nearly gotten her killed. The memory of her throwing herself between him and danger made his chest constrict. The sound of gunfire still ricocheted in his ears, along with the desperate sound of her voice begging him to stay with her.

The monitors shouted their alarm as his heart rate spiked again.

A nurse rushed in. "Mr. Conti, you need to calm down."

How could he do that when he'd just destroyed the person who mattered the most to him?

From the moment he'd walked away after their exchange in the janitor's closet, he'd known that he needed to deny his attraction to Sasha.

A relationship between them was an impossibility.

He was her sister's ex-husband. A man who lived in shadows, who killed without remorse. Who'd never be able to give her the normal life she deserved.

But knowing that didn't stop him from aching for her. Didn't erase the memory of her surrender in his arms, the way she trusted him completely, the spark in her eyes when she challenged him. Didn't stop the debilitating devastation from crashing through him.

The door opened again, and Damien strode in, his expression grim. *"Fuck."* He shook his head. "You're alive."

"Clearly."

"They called a code, and…" He dug a hand into his hair. "Scared the shit out me."

Except for the time Damien had lost his relationship with Catrina, Gregorio had never seen him this unsettled.

"When we saw the way Sasha was crying, we thought something had happened to you." He balled his hands into a fist. "Goddamn."

Gregorio closed his eyes, willing his friend to go away.

When he opened them again, Damien was still there, arms folded, a knowing expression in his eyes.

Beyond pissed, Gregorio waited for the incoming interrogation.

"So what the fuck just happened? Before she got in to see you, she was beside herself with joy. From what Hawkeye said, she stayed with the gurney until she was physically stopped. And then she collapsed. She'd have broken her head open if one of Hawkeye's guys hadn't caught her."

His fucking fault for that, too.

He should have been able to protect her better.

"I'm waiting."

Damien would know if he was lying. They'd been with each other through the hardest parts of their lives. This was no different. "She deserves someone better than me."

"What about what she wants? What you want?"

He knew what he wanted. Her beneath him, beside him. As his partner. Calling him Sir. On her knees.

Wearing his ring.

"You're making a mistake," Damien said softly.

"I'm protecting her."

"Are you?" Damien moved closer to the bed. "Because from where I'm standing, you're breaking both of your hearts for no good reason."

"She's my ex's little sister."

"And?"

He lifted his hand as much as he could before the pain made him drop it again. "Family. My job."

"And?" Damien persisted.

"Are you fucking listening to me?"

"Have you asked Sasha what she wants? She chose you. She came to you when she was in danger. She saved your damn life, according to Hawkeye. No one knows how she had the physical strength to do what she did."

Each word was like a knife between his ribs.

"She's strong as hell."

He couldn't argue with that.

"So tell me again how pushing her away is protecting her."

Gregorio clenched his jaw against the wave of emotion threatening to overwhelm him. "I can't be what she needs."

"No?" Damien asked. "Because it seems to me she needs exactly what you are—someone who'll fight for her, protect her, love her enough to let her make her own choices."

The impact of Damien's words hit him like a physical blow.

"Stop being a damn idiot and think about it," Damien said, moving toward the door. "Before you lose the best thing that's ever happened to you." He looked over his shoulder. "Stop sacrificing yourself before there's nothing left to give."

The door closed behind him with a soft click, leaving Gregorio alone with the beeping monitors and the crushing weight of his choices.

What the hell have I done?

Chapter Twenty-Three

Nadia knocked once before entering Sasha's office, a stack of mail balanced in her hands. Unlike Ashley, who would have breezed in humming under her breath, Nadia moved with quiet efficiency—competent but reserved.

"Just these for you today," she said, dropping a small stack in front of Sasha.

The envelope on top was from Hawkeye Security.

Sasha tightened her grip on her coffee mug—the one that had started this whole mess. The ceramic was cool against her palm now, the coffee long since forgotten as she'd lost herself in memories of Gregorio.

Three weeks of silence stretched between them. No calls. No texts. Not even a message passed through Hawkeye or Damien. Just emptiness in her life where his commanding presence should have been.

She wasn't even sure what she'd expected from him anymore. A goodbye, maybe. Some acknowledgment of what they'd been to each other in those intense days—the way he'd claimed her body and soul, the way she'd surrendered everything to him, the way he'd sworn she belonged to him. And the way he might have taken a bullet meant for her without hesitation.

And more...the way she'd fallen hopelessly, irretrievably in love with him.

"Do you need anything else?" Nadia asked, hovering by the desk. There was genuine concern in her eyes, even if she wasn't sure how to express it. She'd started right after Ashley's death, walking into an office heavy with grief and unspoken tension.

Sasha shook her head, forcing a small smile. "No, thanks."

"I'll be cleaning off my desk, then heading out for the night."

"Enjoy your evening." Since she'd arrived an hour before dawn, she should consider leaving, as well.

Nadia closed the door behind her with a soft click.

The Pathways office felt different now, more subdued. Ashley had filled the rooms with life—humming while she worked, trading playful barbs, knowing exactly when Sasha needed coffee or a sympathetic ear. Now there was just...space. Empty space where Ashley should have been, would never be again.

After Sasha had left the hospital, Hawkeye had updated her about the woman's betrayal and death.

According to her journal, someone at Argentum had gotten to her and threatened her boyfriend's life if she didn't provide information and put the tracker on Sasha's car. As a warning, they'd gone as far as to jump him after work one night, injuring him badly enough that an ambulance had to take him to the emergency room.

Despite that, Ashley had tried in her own way to warn Sasha, moving her coffee cup, letting her know that things weren't normal.

Her body, riddled with gunshot wounds, had been found the next day. Though Sasha hated that it had happened, she wasn't entirely sure she blamed Ashley for her choices. Sasha knew she would do anything to protect the people she loved. Even now, knowing how deep the betrayal ran, she wanted Ashley back.

Sighing, dragging herself back to the present, Sasha reached for the delivery from Hawkeye. She already knew what it contained—the astronomical bill that Inamorata had promised, for the services of the agents who'd saved their lives, the investigation assistance, surveillance, taking care of Brenda Santos, the use of the safehouse, running interference with authorities…

She'd been dreading this moment, wondering how she'd manage to keep her business afloat while paying it off.

Even though technically the invoice should be charged to the Santos account, she knew the couple didn't have the resources to pay—even if she could find them ever again. Their house had been abandoned, and they had both vanished as if they'd never existed. Which told her they had most likely been placed in witness protection. Because she'd been concerned, she'd found Brenda's sister and contacted her. The woman swore she knew nothing at all about her sibling's whereabouts.

Sasha would never know how things had been resolved. She hoped they were together and safe. If they helped to bring down Argentum, maybe the cost would have been worth it.

Then again, maybe not.

The paper crinkled as she tore it open.

With a breath, steadying herself for the blow, she glanced at the bottom line.

Zero.

Her heart missed a beat, then began to race. She smoothed the paper flat, certain she was missing something, some joke or mistake. But there it was in black and white—*Paid in full.*

And below that, a single name that made her chest constrict painfully. Gregorio Conti.

The edges of the paper blurred as tears threatened. *Of course.* Of course he would do this—settle accounts, tie up loose ends, make sure she was taken care of before disappearing completely. It was so perfectly, infuriatingly Gregorio that it made her want to scream.

"He loves you, Sasha," her mother had continued to insist, just last weekend when she'd dropped by the restaurant.

Sasha had been tired of her own company, tired of grieving, going through the motions of living. Mostly, she'd been exhausted from loneliness.

In the kitchen, while making tiramisu, Rosa had reached over and patted Sasha's hand. "I know he does. You have to trust that. And the nice Damien man."

Who'd told her to give Gregorio some space, let him realize how badly he'd fucked up.

Since Damien knew his friend probably better than anyone on the planet, she'd listened to him.

Had that been a mistake?

Her mother had said to fight for him, and that's what she'd vowed to do. This form of fighting just tore her heart to pieces. "I just wish I could believe it will all work out." Either that or she'd somehow have to find the courage to move on without him.

She mentally scoffed. As if she was capable of doing that while she was broken inside.

"Some men aren't sure what to do with a good woman. We can be terrifying." She'd smiled. "They run before they can get hurt. Or before they can hurt anyone else."

Armed with to-go boxes of lasagna and desserts, along with a generous serving of encouragement, Sasha had left the restaurant, clinging to a thread of hope that everyone was right. Gregorio needed time.

But every minute that passed seemed like an awful, drawn-out goodbye. A closure she hadn't asked for and didn't want.

A sharp knock jolted her from her spiraling thoughts.

"You have a visitor," Nadia said as she entered Sasha's office. Her eyebrows were furrowed in a deep frown as she looked back toward the reception area.

Sasha barely glanced up, still lost in the ache spreading through her chest. "Who?" A new client, maybe?

"He wouldn't say."

Instinctively, Sasha curled her fingers around the chair's armrests. And then—

The world stopped turning.

Gregorio filled the doorway like a storm rolling in from the mountains. He looked devastating—unshaven, his usual immaculate appearance replaced by exhaustion and a desperation in his gaze that was raw, almost feral.

The arms of his T-shirt didn't bulge like normal, and he'd tightened his belt another notch.

He was pale, gaunt.

But it was the cane that broke her heart—the visible reminder of how close she'd come to losing him forever. Of the sacrifice he'd made to keep her safe.

Their eyes met across the space between them, and the air crackled with everything left unsaid. She could see the struggle in his face, the war between duty and desire that had haunted him since that first explosive kiss in the janitor's closet at her friend's wedding.

He scrubbed a hand over his scalp—a gesture so unlike his usual control that it made her breath catch. His fingers trembled slightly.

Aware of Nadia watching them with uncertainty, Sasha summoned a half-smile. It was the best she could do. "Thank you. I've got it from here."

"Are you sure? I can stay."

"I'll be fine." When Nadia remained in place, Sasha reassured her. "Really."

After shooting Gregorio a warning scowl, she moved around him, leaving Sasha alone with the man who'd broken her heart.

"I'm an idiot," he said finally, his voice rough with emotion.

A wry, disbelieving breath escaped her. "Yeah," she murmured, the word carrying all the hurt and hope of the past weeks. *You are*. "I'd say that tracks."

With careful, measured steps, Gregorio moved into her office. The soft tap of his cane against her hardwood floors echoed like a metronome, marking each moment that brought him closer.

Even wounded, he carried himself with that predatory grace that had first captivated her, though she could see the cost in the tight line of his jaw, the way his knuckles whitened around the cane's handle.

"I tried to do the right thing," he said, his voice carrying that same raw edge that had been there in the hospital. "Stay away from you and leave you alone. To give you the chance at a normal life, without complications. Without me."

The words hit her like physical blows.

Fighting for control, she curled her hands into fists, her nails biting into her palms. "The right thing?" She was proud that her voice remained steady despite the tremor running through her. "According to who? Yourself? This is about my life, too, Gregorio. And you didn't even ask me what I wanted. What I needed."

His throat worked as he swallowed, and she saw the moment her words landed. The mighty Gregorio—warrior, protector, the man who'd faced down death without flinching—looked utterly lost.

"I thought..." He stopped, seemed to gather himself. "Damien told me to stop running. Told me to look in the damn mirror and see what I was really doing." His laugh was self-deprecating, bitter. "Said I was sacrificing myself to the point there'd be nothing left to give."

God bless Damien for being right. "And did you?" she pressed. "Look in that mirror?"

His lips formed a thin line as he nodded. The silence stretched between them, filled with the steady ticking of the clock on her wall, the distant hum of Denver traffic below. Above all that, Sasha heard the thunder of her own heartbeat, echoing through her ears.

Then, so quietly she almost missed it, he went on.

"I love you."

The words she'd longed to hear, dreamed of hearing, crashed through her defenses like a tidal wave. Her breath caught painfully in her throat as tears burned behind her eyes.

"I know the path forward won't be easy," he continued, taking another step closer. His voice gained strength, momentum, as if now that he'd started, he couldn't stop the flow of words. "I'm difficult—maybe impossible—to be in a relationship with. I was a terrible husband to your sister. I have baggage and scars and a thousand reasons why I don't deserve this. Don't deserve you."

He paused, and she saw the same intensity in his eyes that she'd seen at his cabin when he'd first claimed her. "But you deserve the choice. You deserve to decide for yourself instead of having me make that decision for you."

The lump in her throat nearly choked her. This was Gregorio stripped bare—no walls, no protective distance, just raw honesty that must have cost him dearly.

"If you'll have me," he said, his voice unsteady in a way she'd never heard before, "I'll do this right. I'll face your parents, along with the consequences of what we are to each other."

"They already know." The words came out barely above a whisper.

He went preternaturally still, like a predator scenting danger.

"They were at the hospital," she explained softly, remembering her mother's knowing looks, her father's quiet understanding.

Gregorio's dark eyes searched hers, looking for judgment or condemnation. Finding none, his shoulders loosened fractionally.

"Adriana isn't talking to me," she added after a pause, needing him to understand the full scope of what they faced. "But that's nothing new."

His jaw ticked—a tell she'd learned meant he was wrestling with something difficult.

And because he deserved to know… "She's getting married again."

"Is she?" The words hung between them, weighted with shared history and complicated family ties.

"You can't take all the responsibility for the failure of your marriage." Especially now after what she'd learned, that Adriana had been planning to break up with him before the robbery. She'd been infatuated with the idea of being with a savior, nothing more.

Another silence fell, but this one felt different. Charged. Like the air before a storm breaks.

He exhaled slowly. "If you want to try, you need to know that things won't be easy. I am who I am. I'll always have enemies. Always have missions that take me away. Always be the man who lives in shadows."

Sasha's chest ached with the truth of it. But she'd known who he was, watching him comfort her family after the robbery. Had fallen in love with every complex, dangerous, honorable piece of him.

"I've never asked for anything different," she whispered, letting him see the depth of her feelings in her eyes. "I want you. All of you. The warrior and the protector." Breathlessly, she added, "The Dominant. The man."

Something broke in his expression—like ice cracking on a frozen river.

Then he moved.

The cane clattered forgotten to the floor as he demolished the distance still between them. His hand cupped her face with devastating gentleness, even as his other arm wound around her waist with possessive strength, pulling her against the hard planes of his body.

"Petal," he breathed, the nickname carrying years of longing.

And then he kissed her.

It wasn't like their first time years ago in the janitor's closet—all heat and desperation. Or like their kisses at the Den—commanding and primal. This was something else entirely. This was coming home. This was surrender and claiming all at once, tender and fierce, as if he was pouring every unsaid word, every moment of separation, into the press of his lips against hers.

For the first time since that horrible night at the hospital when she'd almost lost him, Sasha let herself believe in forever.

Let herself hold on.

And finally, *finally*—she was exactly where she belonged.

When they eventually broke apart, Gregorio kept her close, as if he couldn't bear to let go. His dark eyes searched hers with an intensity that made her breath catch.

"There's something else," he said softly.

Before she could respond, he reached into his pocket. The movement made him wince—a flash of pain he couldn't quite hide—but his hand was steady as he withdrew a small black velvet box.

Sasha's heart stopped.

"I've had this for more than two weeks," he admitted, his voice rough with emotion. "I was trying to convince myself to do the right thing while the lesser part of me was determined to selfishly have you forever." He swallowed hard. "The moment I saw it, I knew it belonged to you."

Her eyes burned with tears as he shifted his weight, preparing to kneel.

"Gregorio, don't—your injuries—"

But he was already moving, gingerly lowering himself to one knee despite the cost she could see written in the tight line of his jaw. His warrior's pride wouldn't let him do this any other way.

"Petal." The nickname carried every moment between them—from that scared young woman filled with hero worship, to the stolen moments at Leah's wedding, to going through two life-changing events

together. "I've spent my whole life in shadows. But you…" His voice caught. "You make me want to step into the sun."

With trembling fingers, he opened the box. The ring was stunning in its simplicity—a single diamond that caught the light like his missing earring used to do, set in a band of white gold that twisted like infinity.

"I can't promise you an easy life," he continued. "But I can promise you all of me. Every scar, every mission, every dream I never let myself have before you. Will you marry me?"

Tears spilled down her cheeks as she sank to her knees in front of him, uncaring of anything but being on his level for this moment.

"Yes," she whispered. Then louder, "Yes!"

His hands shook slightly as he slipped the ring onto her finger. Then he pulled her close, kissing her with all the passion and tenderness that had made her fall in love with him.

They were both crying now, holding each other on the floor of her office, neither wanting to move.

"I love you," she breathed against his lips.

His answering smile was like the sun breaking through storm clouds. "And I love you, my Petal. Always have. Always will."

In that moment, all the complications—her sister, his dangerous life, the wounds, both physical and emotional, they still carried—none of it mattered.

They had found their way home.

Together…

Chapter Twenty-Four

Three months later

The crunch of tires on gravel brought Sasha's head up from her laptop. Through the wall of windows overlooking the Colorado mountains, she watched Gregorio's black SUV wind its way up their private drive, early morning sunlight glinting off the bulletproof glass.

Their compromise of a home—a high-security estate set on twenty private acres outside of Evergreen—had seemed excessive when they'd first found it. But now she understood why Gregorio had insisted on the security features and isolation. Here, he could relax his guard, at least marginally. And she had enough space to work from home most days, heading into the Denver office when cases demanded it or for meetings.

She'd formed an alliance with Hawkeye Security to handle some of their smaller cases. As a result, she'd hired another three investigators. Nadia was doing an excellent job managing all the day-to-day details, allowing Sasha to make sales calls, concentrating most of her efforts on growing the business.

The front door opened, and his presence filled the house. Even after months together, her pulse still quickened at the sound of his boots on the hardwood floors. Some things would never change.

"You're back early," she called out, not turning from her computer. The faster she finished this report, the sooner she could focus on him.

"Had Wolfe cover the rest of my shift." His voice was closer now, rough with exhaustion. "Damien's handling the expansion details."

Then his hands settled on her shoulders, strong and possessive. "You're working too hard, Petal."

She leaned back into his touch. "Says the man who just pulled a double at the Den."

"Mmm." He bent to press a kiss to her neck, right where it made her shiver. "But I'm not the one who spent yesterday chasing a bail jumper across three counties."

"I was perfectly safe. Stryker had my back."

His grip tightened fractionally. They'd had this discussion before—her insistence on keeping some fieldwork, his instinct to protect her. They were still finding the balance.

"Besides," she added, tilting her head to give him better access, "you've been busy with that Hawkeye mission in Vegas."

He made a noncommittal sound against her skin. They both knew there were parts of his work he couldn't talk about, even with her. But he'd cut back on the most dangerous assignments, splitting his time between the Den and Hawkeye's local operations. It wasn't perfect, but it was working.

"Shower with me?" he asked, though it wasn't really a question. His thumbs worked into the knots at the base of her neck, and she melted further into his touch.

"Let me just send this to the client—"

"It can wait." There was that edge of command in his voice that still made her stomach flip. "If my guess is right, you've been at it since dawn."

She started to protest, but he spun her chair around to face him. The sight of him—still in a black leather jacket, fresh scruff darkening his jaw—made the words die in her throat. His diamond earring caught the light as he studied her.

"Don't make me carry you, Petal." His eyes glittered with both amusement and warning. "Your ribs are healed enough that I won't feel guilty about throwing you over my shoulder."

Heat bloomed in her chest. They both knew he would do it, and they both knew she secretly loved it when he did.

"Fine." She lifted her chin in mock defiance. "But only because I was almost finished anyway."

His answering smile was pure sin. "Whatever you need to tell yourself." He pulled her to her feet, then paused, his expression softening as he caught sight of her ring. He still did that sometimes—looked at it like he couldn't quite believe she was his.

"I love you," she said quietly, because she could. Because they were past the point of holding back.

The fire in his eyes banked, turning molten. "Show me how much." He pulled her close, his touch just this side of rough. "Upstairs. Now."

As she followed him toward their bedroom, Sasha smiled to herself. They might have traded the drama for domesticity, but some things—the electricity between them, the way he commanded and she yielded, the bone-deep certainty that they belonged together—would never change.

And she wouldn't have it any other way.

Outside their bathroom window, a deer wandered past. In the near distance, evergreens reached for the sky, and their needle-covered branches swayed in the breeze.

This view was so different from the one she'd had at her Denver apartment—open, vast, and soothing. Would she ever get used to it?

Gregorio moved behind her and once more placed his hands on her shoulders. His touch was firm yet gentle, as it always was. "I've had a hard-on the entire drive home."

"Oh? See something interesting at the Den?"

Against her ear, he growled as he brought a hand firmly against her right ass cheek.

Yelping, she turned to face him.

"You know there's only one woman who gives me that reaction."

She loved his possessiveness and reassurances.

"I was thinking about being balls-deep in your pussy. That's why I came home."

His raw words always made her tremble with anticipation.

"I want you naked. Now."

When she reached for the hem of her long-sleeved shirt, he brushed her hands aside.

"I've been thinking about doing this."

Her future husband—her Dominant—stripped off her shirt. Then he made short work of her bra.

Finally, he crouched in front of her to pull down her leggings and panties.

He cupped her pussy and squeezed it a little, making her suck in a breath.

"This belongs to me."

"Yes," she whispered, tipping her head back. "Yes, Sir." There never had been another man for her. Never would be.

Before releasing her, he squeezed again, this time much harder.

Response rushed through her.

"I love the way you react to me."

Desperate for him, she reached for his black henley. "May I?"

"Make it quick." There was fire in his eyes, like there always was when she was naked and aroused.

Once she had taken it off and dropped it on top of her discarded clothing, she traced the lines of his chest, feeling the ridges of his muscles and the rough edges of his scars. Some were still healing. But he'd regained most of the muscle mass he'd lost after taking the bullet that would have ended her life.

She finished undressing him, savoring the sight of his hard, powerful body.

When he was naked, she sank to her knees. The position was one of her favorites—making her feel both vulnerable and in control.

Glancing up at him, she saw the desire making his eyes even darker.

Keeping her gaze on him, she grasped his hips, digging her fingers into his defined, firm muscles.

"Sasha," he warned.

"What, Sir?"

He fisted a hand into her hair and held her tight as she closed her mouth around his cockhead.

His taste was intoxicating. She loved the way he responded to her touch, the way his body tensed and his breath caught.

"Woman..."

She swirled her tongue around his shaft as she sucked, taking him deeper.

Gregorio let out a low groan, his hand tightening even more. "Just like that, Petal," he murmured, his voice gruff.

He grew harder in her mouth, and tension built in his body. She loved doing this to him, loved the way she could bring him to the brink with just her mouth and her hands.

"Enough," he said finally, his voice strained. He pulled her to her feet, his eyes blazing with need.

His cock was hard, throbbing, and his taste lingered in her mouth.

Motions abrupt and efficient, he led her to the shower, turning the spray to hot until the room was filled with steam.

Before they entered, he adjusted the temperature and set the spray to a jet setting.

The sensation of the water pounding against her skin was almost as intense as the feel of Gregorio's hands as they roamed over her body.

"I'll never get enough of you."

He turned her around, his hands lathering soap over her skin. He massaged her shoulders and her back, his touch as soothing as it was arousing.

"Do you like this, Petal?" he asked, his voice a low growl in her ear.

Did she really need to answer? "Yes, Sir," she whispered. "I love everything you do to me."

He smiled, his hands moving lower. "And what do you want me to do to you now?"

She leaned back against him, her body shivering with anticipation. "I want you to take me, Sir," she said, her voice filled with longing. "I want you to make me yours, again and again."

"Always," he promised, his voice filled with love and dominance. Slowly, he slid his hands to her hips, then he tightened his grip. "Always, Petal."

He spun her around to face him before lifting her up.

Her back hit the cool tiles as he pinned her against the wall. Instinctively, she wrapped her legs around his waist, opening herself up to him.

His cock, hard and eager, pressed against her entrance.

Not long after his proposal, she had gotten on birth control. There wasn't anything she liked more than the feeling of him being inside her without any barrier between them, then his hot seed spilling inside her.

"Are you ready for me?"

Without waiting for an answer, he slid a finger between her folds and ensured she was slick. "I have been, Sir," she told him. Since the moment she heard his car on the driveway.

In a single, powerful thrust, he was inside her, filling her completely. She gasped, digging her nails into his shoulders as her body adjusted to his size.

"God, you feel incredible," he growled, his voice hoarse with desire. He began to move, each thrust deep and demanding. "I couldn't stop thinking of you."

The water cascaded over them, making their bodies slick and slippery.

He ground his hips against hers with each thrust, ensuring she felt every inch of him.

Her breaths came in short, desperate gasps, matching the rhythm of his movements. "Gregorio!" She clung to him, her body shivering with pleasure as he fucked her hard and deep.

His grip on her tightened, his fingers digging into her flesh as he held her in place. The sensation of his body against hers, his cock filling her, was overwhelming. Deep inside, her orgasm built, the need intensifying with each of his strokes.

"Give it to me," he commanded, his voice sharp. "I want to feel you come all over my cock. Do it *now.*"

His order pushed her over the edge. With a cry, she climaxed hard, her body convulsing around him as waves of pleasure crashed through her. He didn't let up, continuing to thrust into her, drawing out her orgasm until she was a trembling, gasping mess.

"So fucking hot. So perfect."

Only then did he allow himself to find his own release.

With a deep, guttural groan, he came, his body shaking as he spilled himself inside her. The heat of his release flooded her, and his cock pulsed demandingly as he took his satisfaction.

They stayed like that for a moment, their bodies pressed together, their breaths ragged and uneven.

Slowly, he lowered her, holding her steady while she found her balance.

Beneath her palm, his heart pounded reassuringly.

"Jesus, Petal." After adjusting the water pressure so it was more of a gentle, rain-like spray, he captured her mouth, kissing her deeply.

When he finally pulled back, her mind was swimming in pheromones once more.

"That will do for starters," he told her.

She gulped. "Starters, Sir?"

"I think it's been far too long since you had a spanking, my Petal."

"Oh?" She laced a teasing note through the question.

"And I'm not going to dry you off first."

Sucking in a sharp breath, she looked up at him. "Isn't that supposed to sting more on wet skin?"

"It is indeed." With a wolf-like grin, he swept his gaze over her. "Problem?"

"No, Sir," she replied quickly. Despite the warm water, she shivered. "Of course not." If she complained, he'd give her a few extra strokes.

"That's my girl."

He was awful, showing no mercy.

"Since I'm so considerate, I'll give you a choice. What implement do you want to sear your ass? A leather paddle? My hand? Or my belt?"

She wrinkled her nose. *None of the above.*

His grin deepened. "In that case, I've made the choice for you. And when your rear is on fire, I'm finally going to fuck your ass. You're mine in every way, Sasha. In a few minutes, there'll be no doubt in your mind."

She shivered deliciously. There had never been anyone else for her.

And being his in every way possible suited her just fine.

"What do you have to say for yourself?"

With a sassy glance she asked, "What are you waiting for, Sir?"

Epilogue

The Den's 'Once Upon a Time' night was in full swing, and the main floor was filled with couples in elaborate fairytale costumes. Sasha laughed as Gregorio led her through the crowd, past princes, princesses, woodland creatures, and even a few dragons mingling near the fireplace.

"You could have warned me about the theme," she said, adjusting the simple black mask he'd given her when they arrived. "I would have dressed up."

His diamond earring caught the light as he grinned down at her. "And what would you have chosen, Petal?"

"I don't know." She worried her lower lip for a moment as she considered. "Maybe Morgana."

"From the Arthurian legends?"

"Not in the villain kind of way, but the powerful enchantress who commanded respect." She gave him a knowing look. "A woman who knew her own mind and wasn't afraid to claim what she wanted."

"The sorceress who could bring the most dangerous of men to their knees," he murmured, his voice roughening. "It suits you perfectly."

She grinned. The costume would have been fun and easy, as well.

"And you?" She reached up to touch his earring. "Never mind. You're already my pirate."

"Am I now?" His grin widened as he guided her toward the patio doors.

"Mmhmm. The diamond… The dangerous aura… The way you swept in and stole my heart." She traced the scar on his jaw. "And not to mention the nightly plundering."

"Argh." He raised one of his eyebrows. "Not my fault you have an amazing bootie, my sweet."

As she laughed at his ridiculousness, he swooped in for a kiss that promised more plundering in the night ahead.

The evening air held the first bite of autumn, but the firepits kept the chill at bay.

They walked to the bar. The woman mixing up drinks was wearing a puffy parka and goggles, and she had a snowboard leaning against a rack. Sasha wasn't sure how this fit the Once Upon a Time theme, but she was dressed warmer than anyone else, which made her smart.

As Sasha studied the menu, he ordered a soda water with a splash of cranberry.

When she ordered a Safe Word mocktail, Gregorio's eyes darkened with amusement.

"Still testing your limits, Petal?" His voice held that rough edge that made her shiver.

"As I recall, you're the one who taught me to push my boundaries, Sir." Moments later, drink in hand, she ran her finger around the spice-dusted rim, remembering that first night—how the heat had curled through her, how she'd wished for something stronger…for him.

"And have you ever needed to use it?" He lifted an eyebrow. "Your safe word?"

"Not with you." She took a slow sip, letting the contradictory sensations of smooth coconut cream and spicy cayenne play across her tongue. "Never with you."

His eyes blazed as he watched her lick the sugar and spice from her lips. "Good answer."

He moved them close to a firepit. Flames danced in the cool, late-fall breeze.

"To us," he said, clinking his glass against hers.

She smiled, remembering the first night she'd come here searching for his help. How far they'd come since then.

Her engagement ring caught the firelight, sending prisms dancing across their skin.

"Have you thought more about the date?" he asked, his voice carrying that note of gentle persistence she'd come to know well.

"Still trying to pin me down?"

"Always." His expression softened. "I've waited my whole life for you, Petal. I don't want to wait much longer to call you my wife."

When she didn't respond, he went on. "We've known each other forever."

And he'd consumed her for that long.

While her parents were okay with their relationship, her sister was another matter. Even though her wedding was upcoming, she still didn't want anything to do with Sasha.

Last Saturday, she and Gregorio had stopped into her parents' restaurant for dinner. And while the four of them had been in the kitchen chatting, Adriana had stopped in.

When she saw Gregorio, she'd gone for his jugular.

Patiently, he'd raised his hand and owned his part in the failure of the relationship. "Look, I was a shitty husband."

"And you're still a shitty human being," she'd countered.

Gasping, their mother had crossed herself and their dad had scolded her.

Gregorio had shaken his head, telling his future father-in-law that he had things under control. "I deserve it."

"Damn right you do," Adriana had fired back. Then she'd rounded on her father. "Quit defending this cheating pair."

"Adriana!" Sasha had protested. "That's uncalled for."

Eyes flashing anger, Adriana had glared at Sasha. "You've spent your whole life in my shadow, always settling for my hand-me-downs."

Before she'd been able to respond, Gregorio had stepped in front of her, in Adriana's line of fire. "I'll tolerate your disrespect, but I won't put up with you being rude to your parents or my future wife."

"Wife?" she'd scoffed. "You two are getting married? Fuck that." Then, she'd turned on Sasha once more. "I guess you'll never deserve better than my leftovers."

"You had one warning," he'd said, voice scarily soft as he took a step forward.

Automatically, Adriana had moved back. "What are you going to do?"

"Throw you out of here."

Adriana had gasped and Sasha blinked. *He planned to escort Adriana out of the restaurant?*

"You're welcome to come back as soon as we leave."

Chin tipped in defiance, Adriana had gasped. "Why I never!"

"Maybe someone should have taught you some manners before now. Rudeness is never okay. Like I said, come at me all you want. But never Sasha or your parents."

"Gregorio is right," her father had said.

Sasha had gaped at him. Not once in her life had her father said anything slightly harsh to his favorite child.

Her mother had blinked back tears.

Still between Sasha and her older sister, Gregorio had folded his arms. "Enjoy your evening."

In a huff, Adriana had picked up a metal pan and slammed it against a stainless steel counter before storming out.

For a moment, everyone had remained frozen in place.

Then her father had said, "Rosa, how about some espresso?"

To her mother, Sasha had tried to apologize for Gregorio's harshness, but Rosa waved her off. "This would have gone on forever if he hadn't put a stop to it."

After a few awkward minutes, they'd enjoyed a wonderful visit.

Her parents had sat at a table with them while her father had continued to order more food than they could eat in three days.

When they'd left the restaurant, they'd been loaded down with to-go boxes.

"I want my wedding ring here."

Bringing her back to the moment, Gregorio lifted her hand and he traced the outline of her engagement band.

She wanted nothing more, either.

Before she could respond, Damien and Catrina joined them. The couple was dressed as if they'd stepped out of a medieval fairytale—Damien in all black with a cape, Catrina in a flowing gown that made her look like a warrior queen.

"Still trying to convince her to set a date?" Damien asked, his usual commanding presence tempered by genuine warmth.

Catrina's skeptical expression had softened over the months as she'd watched Sasha and Gregorio together. Now there was acceptance in her eyes, maybe even happiness for them.

"Working on it." Gregorio reached for her and brushed his thumb across the pulse in her wrist. "Actually, since you're here..." He turned to his friend, and Sasha caught a flicker of vulnerability in his expression that few ever saw. "I was hoping you'd stand with me. As my best man."

Something powerful passed between the two men—years of friendship, shared battles, mutual respect. Damien's eyes glistened briefly before he masked it. "Try to stop me, brother."

As the two men hugged, Catrina pressed a hand to her heart. "You two deserve all the happiness in the world," she said softly to Sasha and Gregorio. "I'm sorry I doubted you at first."

"You were protecting someone you care about," Sasha replied. "I understand that."

"And how about you two?" Sasha asked when the moment was right. As far as she knew, Damien and Catrina hadn't set a date yet.

"Christmas," Catrina said.

Damien blinked.

"I take it this is a surprise?" Gregorio asked.

"About fucking time," Damien replied.

Standing, he pulled Catrina to her feet. "If you'll excuse us? My fiancée has something to answer for with surprising me like that."

Obviously proud of herself, Catrina smiled.

Then, seeing Damien's fierce expression, she pressed her lips together, even though her eyes danced with happiness.

"With me, wench," Damien demanded, clamping his hand around her upper arm.

"Yes, Sir." She flashed a triumphant shrug.

"I'd say he was surprised," Sasha mused once the pair had disappeared back inside the house.

"And that he wanted to be the first to know the news about his own wedding."

Like Catrina, Sasha grinned. "Never a good idea to let your Dominant think he always has the upper hand."

"No?"

Once more, he quirked a brow, this time in pseudo-threat.

"I mean…" She took a quick drink and choked on the spice. "Clearly, she clearly made a bad call, Sir."

"Right." He pulled her in closer.

"But, Sir!"

"Never a good call to let a sub think she has the upper hand."

She clenched her buttocks in response to the tone in his voice. This wasn't going to go well for her.

Also like Catrina, she couldn't be happier.

After depositing their glasses on the tray of a passing waiter dressed as Little Red Riding Hood, he helped her to stand then guided her through the Den and into the dungeon.

They chatted with a few people before he took her to a private room.

Inside, hundreds of candles created an intimate golden glow. Rose petals scattered across the floor led to a beautiful archway draped in fairy lights.

"Close your eyes, Petal."

She obeyed without hesitation, trusting him completely. When he told her to open them again, she gasped. The room had been transformed into an enchanted garden, with twinkling lights creating a canopy of stars above them.

"This is where I want to have a collaring ceremony first, if you're open to it," he said softly. "One month from today."

Her heart stuttered. "What?"

"I'll arrange everything with Damien." His voice was rough with emotion as he withdrew a small box from his pocket. Inside there was a delicate collar. "And then I want the wedding soon after. I want everyone to know you're mine completely, in every way." He looked at her even deeper. "The way I'm yours."

Tears spilled down her cheeks as she turned to face him. "Yes," she whispered. She'd been trying to make decisions, but there were so many of them. *Flowers. Venue. Gown.*

Him pushing her a little intensified the timeline, giving her a sense of urgency to get things done. "Yes," she repeated. "Yes, yes. *Yes.*"

"We can have another ceremony later for friends and family. But I don't want to wait any longer than absolutely necessary to make you mine."

His kiss was tender, reverent, full of promise. When he finally pulled back, his eyes shimmered with unshed tears of his own. "I love you, my Petal. My precious. My heart."

"And I love you." She touched his cheek gently. "My protector. My pirate. My forever."

As his arms wrapped around her, holding her close beneath their canopy of stars, Sasha knew with absolute certainty that this was exactly where she belonged. In weeks, she would marry her soulmate in this very spot. Their path hadn't been easy, but every step had led them here—to each other, to forever.

"Now…there's the tiny matter of your earlier sass."

Her mouth dried. "But—"

"And you thinking you had the upper hand."

"But, Sir—" she tried again.

"Anything you want to say for yourself before you get the spanking you deserve?"

She could apologize, but that wouldn't get her out of it. "Uhm…"

With his thumb and forefinger, he captured her chin and tilted it back. "You have a lot to answer for, sub."

"Yes, Sir." Her heart leapt, and she swallowed deeply. "I do." *And I wouldn't have it any other way.*

Want to see more from this author? Here's a taster for you to enjoy!

The Donovan Dynasty: Bind

Sierra Cartwright

Excerpt

"Let me help you with that."

At the sexy, intimate sound of a man's voice, Lara stopped shrugging into her coat and turned to glance over her shoulder. Her pulse slammed to a stop. *Connor Donovan.*

When he'd entered the hotel's ballroom an hour earlier, she'd immediately noticed him. Even at an event attended by Houston's power elite, the man had commanded attention.

Her friend Erin had introduced her to Connor, her older brother, and president of Donovan Worldwide.

He'd been polite, though courteously distant, as if his attention was focused elsewhere. She'd found that his icy demeanor was the perfect complement to his cool, intimidating gray eyes.

In spite of herself, she'd continued to watch him.

After only fifteen minutes, he and a couple of other men had made their excuses and left the ballroom. Since all were moguls, their absence had been noted.

Connor had been the first to return, and she'd seen the delicious way that he'd adjusted one of his starched, white cuffs.

And now, he was standing only inches behind her.

"May I?" he prompted.

His voice was friendly, but his implacable tone sent a shudder through her. She realized it wasn't really a request. "I'd appreciate that," she said.

When his fingers brushed hers, she felt his touch as if it were a sliver of lightning.

Their proximity felt intimate, making her aware of how devastatingly handsome he was. She made a conscious decision not to let him know how much he flustered her. She'd grown up around authoritative men, but he possessed a unique aura of command.

He continued to hold the jacket until she'd settled into it.

"Thank you," she said as she turned to face him. Though she was tall and wore cripplingly high stilettos, she had to tip her head back to meet his gaze.

He looked at her without blinking, and for a moment, she was the focus of his attention.

"It's my pleasure to help a beautiful woman."

She told herself not to take him seriously. The man hadn't been named president of Donovan Worldwide at such an early age without learning to consider the impact of his words. Still, his genteel Southern manners impressed her. No one could have faulted him for walking past the coat check area. But he hadn't.

He turned his hand palm up, indicating she should precede him through the revolving glass door.

Outside, a cold rain fell in wind-whipped torrents. Thank goodness the portico was covered but, of course, there were no vehicles waiting in the taxi lane.

A sedan pulled up, and Connor said, "I'll give you a ride."

"That won't be necessary."

Just then a valet hurried over. "Taxi, ma'am?"

She nodded as she brushed her hair back from her face.

The valet went to the curb and blew a whistle to summon the cab.

"Are you certain?" Connor asked.

The idea of being in the back of a vehicle with him even for a few minutes gave her shivers in a way that had nothing to do with the outside temperature. "I promise you, Mr. Donovan, I'll be okay."

The cab arrived.

Connor waved off the valet. Despite the weather, he opened the door to the taxi and handed her into the vehicle.

"I'll see you again soon," he said. The words were laced with promise.

His gaze lingered. His eyes no longer seemed as cold, yet they appeared ten times more dangerous.

With a decisive move, he closed the door then walked away, each stride purposeful.

In the scant few minutes they'd spent together, she'd felt the vortex of his authority. She knew she could have refused his help, but there had been something mesmerizing—something seductive—about the way he'd instinctively taken control of the situation.

She gave the driver her destination and tried to shake off Connor's effect.

* * * *

"You should ask my brother to marry you."

Shocked by the statement, Lara jerked her hand, causing wine to slosh over the rim of her glass. *"What?"* Even the thought of suggesting such a thing made her heart stop before rushing on in a fury. Absently, she reached for her napkin to blot at the red stain that was seeping across the white tablecloth.

"You should marry Connor. You remember him from the cocktail party, right?"

As if she'd ever forget.

"You two would make a fabulous couple." Erin Donovan reached for her glass of chardonnay and sat back, wearing a huge smile. "So there you are. It's the perfect solution."

"Perfect? I don't see how marriage changes anything."

"First of all, you'd have access to Connor's advice."

"I've already hired advisors."

"Who aren't running companies as successful as Donovan Worldwide."

"I can't argue that," Lara agreed.

"If he thinks it's worthwhile, he may help with the financial issues."

Which her father would never consider.

"Surely you could get him a seat on the board if he were your husband?" Erin persisted. "You'd have someone to back your position. And most of all, you'd have a lover to share the emotional burden with. Stop scowling. You'll give yourself frown lines."

Lara stared at Erin. They'd known each other since graduate school, and they'd continued to meet once a week to discuss business, as well as other issues in their lives. Years had made them more than friends, it had also made them confidantes.

Until this moment, Lara had considered Erin to be extremely intelligent and a gifted problem solver. But her suggestion that Lara marry someone she didn't love, especially the aloof and dynamic Connor? Even though her father's stubbornness meant BHI's situation was dire, marriage wasn't the way to solve the problems plaguing her family's business. "You've lost your mind."

After taking a sip of wine, Erin put the glass down and leaned forward. "You should think about it."

"Not in a million years." Even though her interaction with Connor had only been a few minutes long, its impact had stayed with her. The next day, she'd caught herself thinking about him, wondering what might have happened if she had let him drive her back to her bungalow.

Probably nothing, she'd told herself. Just because he'd offered a ride didn't mean he was sexually attracted to her.

Unfortunately, she'd been so turned on by him that it had taken several ridiculous days and lots of determination to free herself from the hold he had on her.

Now, more than three weeks later, the tendrils of the memory still unnerved her. "Rumor has it he's not in the market for a wife." Not only that, but according to reports, he rarely dated.

"Which means you looked him up!" Erin pronounced.

"I didn't say that," Lara protested.

"How else would you know?" Erin grinned cheekily. "I think you'd be ideal for him. You saw him. He's too damn serious about everything, always has been. Since Dad died, it's gotten worse. Not that I can blame him. But he's recently become even more of a hard-ass than he used to be, like he doesn't deserve to be happy. He needs a vacation. Or someone to shake up his careful little world. Aunt Kathryn agrees." She tipped her head to the side, as if considering Lara's suitability.

"Don't look at me," Lara said. "I'm not that woman. My life is complicated enough." When she went out, it was generally for happy hour with a group of friends.

She could kick back, have fun, have an occasional hook-up, but keep her time free. "Besides, I like a different kind of man."

"That's absolutely true," Erin agreed. "You like men who are milquetoasts."

"I prefer the word uncomplicated."

"Uh-huh," Erin said. "Remember Randy? He was milquetoast."

"He was a nice guy."

"It took him four dates to kiss you."

"Three," Lara corrected.

"Which is three too many."

Lara fought back a small smile. Erin would tease her relentlessly if Lara admitted the truth. She'd had to initiate the intimacy. And when it had happened, the kiss hadn't curled her toes or made her swoon. In fact, she'd been strangely unaroused. When they'd slept together, it had been perfunctory, leaving her unsatisfied. When she'd hinted that she'd wanted more, he'd scowled, obviously half offended, half puzzled.

She'd told herself that great sex—hell, even good sex—was overrated. Randy had been a good man, always understanding, never protesting when she'd worked late or canceled dates to deal with one of her father's dramatic pronouncements. In the end though, lack of sexual chemistry had made them drift apart.

One night at dinner, when they hadn't seen each other in more than a week, she'd suggested an amicable parting. He'd smiled, in relief, she imagined.

And since she was swamped with work, she'd opted not to pursue dating for a while. Her vivid imagination and her vibrator collection were enough. She might not have a man as a partner in her life, but she told herself that was okay, for now.

"Consider it," Erin encouraged.

Instead of responding, Lara reached for her wine.

"You should at least schedule a meeting with him," Erin persisted.

"Do you ever stop?"

"I could give you his cell phone number."

The image of him made her shiver. All that power and intensity? "No. Absolutely not. Thanks."

"In that case, I'll give you the secret code to get past his personal assistant in case you decide to call the office. You can find the number online."

"A secret code?"

"Don't laugh," Erin said. "A lot of enterprising reporters and salespeople will use all sorts of tactics to get past the gatekeeper."

"She must be tough."

"He," Erin corrected.

"Your brother's personal assistant is a man?" The information shouldn't have shocked Lara, but it did.

"Oh, yes."

"Oh?"

With her index finger, Erin skimmed the rim of her glass. "He's…interesting."

"In what way?"

"Uh-uh. You're not getting any information out of me. Go see for yourself."

"Stop it!" Lara protested. "Tell me."

"Not a chance." Erin made a show of fanning her face with her hand. "Okay. I'll tell you this much…Thompson is a gem. Gorgeous. Ex-military. I don't know, he's…forbidding."

"Forbidding? That's an interesting word."

"Like he has all these secrets. He doesn't talk about himself much. The man scares the hell out of me in the most exciting way possible."

"Now I'm intrigued."

"That was my point, exactly."

Forbidding. If you added handsome, enigmatic and powerful, the same description could apply to Connor.

The waiter brought them coffee and the slice of the renowned key lime pie they'd ordered to share.

"This'll cost me an hour on the treadmill," Erin said as she stuck her spoon in one side.

"It's worth every single minute," Lara pointed out.

After they'd paid the bill, they went outside. Humidity and heat from the unseasonably warm spring evening swamped Lara, settling over her, making her suddenly restless.

"Seven, seven, three, four," Erin said.

Lara scowled.

"That's the code so that you can contact Connor."

"I won't need it."

"I want you to be my sister-in-law." Erin waved a cheery goodbye and headed for her car while Lara walked back toward the skyscraper that housed her family's business, Bertrand Holdings, Inc. Since it was technically after hours, she shrugged off her black blazer then tucked it through the handle of her oversized bag.

Earlier she'd debated whether or not to cancel her dinner plans with Erin, but since she'd been working so many hours, Lara had decided to keep the appointment but go back to work to wrap up the day's final details, straighten her desk then stop by the workout center before heading home. Lately, it seemed as if she spent more time behind her desk than anywhere else.

Problem was, she couldn't see an end anytime soon. They needed more help than they had, but cutbacks had left all departments woefully understaffed. Doing more with less had become a mantra. Unfortunately for her, that resulted in a lot of twelve-hour days, and Saturday had become a regular workday.

She entered the high-rise through the revolving glass door and exhaled in relief as the air-conditioning cooled her damp skin. At least the brisk walk should have worked off part of the key lime pie.

As she strode across the marble floor toward a bank of elevators, she waved to the security guard.

"No rest for the wicked?"

"I'll have to make a note to be a saint in my next life," Lara said.

"You and me both, sister," the woman replied.

Since most workers had gone home hours before, the building was quiet. It amazed her how different downtown became after hours. The lack of energy was palpable, weighty. An elevator was even waiting to whisk Lara directly to the eighteenth floor.

She was deep in thought when she exited the car and almost walked directly into someone.

He reached for her, grabbing her upper arms to steady her.

"I beg your pardon," she said.

"Are you all right?"

Lara looked up. Electricity hummed through her when she realized Connor Donovan was holding her. For a breathless moment, time seemed to stop.

"Well, well," he said. "Ms. Bertrand." He continued to hold her.

Self-preservation instincts told her to pull away, but she didn't...couldn't.

Their gazes held. He drew his dark eyebrows together, making him look even more intimidating. Rather than scaring her, his frown, his presence, compelled her attention.

She wasn't sure how much time had passed before she found a thread of equilibrium. "I'm…surprised to see you here." And why was he?

In his dove-gray suit, starched shirt, red tie and polished wingtip shoes, the man was impossibly handsome, made even more so by the slight shadow of stubble on his strong jaw. And his voice… It wasn't just his words, but his deep, well-modulated tone that made her think of summer nights and hot, hot sex.

His eyes, though, accentuated by the color of his clothing, were as chilly as she recalled.

Slowly, slowly, he released her. She took two small steps back. Where he'd touched her, she throbbed.

"I was sorry you didn't let me give you a lift home a few weeks ago."

"I'm sure you're a busy man."

"I always take time for the important things and people."

Was she ridiculous for thinking that he, too, felt the attraction between them? She shook her head. He was a powerful man, of course he had a strong sex drive. It didn't mean anything.

Under his scrutiny, she was hyperaware of her bare skin, the damp tendrils of hair curling against her nape, the way her silk shirt showed her silhouette. She wished she'd kept her blazer on.

Lara mentally took hold of herself before his power consumed her. "I was having dinner with your sister. If I'd known you had business with BHI, I would have rescheduled."

Something dark ghosted across his eyes. "I had understood I'd be meeting with the board of directors. Or at least with you *and* Pernell."

She adjusted her grip on her bag to cover the shock that her father hadn't said a word to her.

"At any rate, my proposal is no longer on the table."

"What proposal?"

"Regarding your communications division."

One that had been losing money, one she wanted to sell. Lara took in his pricey leather briefcase, no doubt containing a file folder with papers, or, more likely, a flash drive. "And you've changed your mind?"

"Pernell made it clear he wasn't open to discussion."

"I see." Her knees went weak. Was this another instance of her father's stubbornness? "I wish I had been there."

"I do, as well. Things might have worked out differently. Better."

She scrambled for time. Perhaps her father had been out of line. On the other hand, maybe Connor's offer had been a bad one. And she needed time to sort it out, learn what was going on, and mostly, think it through. "Are you open to continuing the negotiation?"

"Under my original terms? No."

Connor took another step closer to her, and she remained in place, waiting, wondering.

He was close enough that she could once again inhale his scent...that of relentless determination spiced with masculine power.

Her heart seemed to pause then raced when he reached for the elevator call button.

"If you're interested in hearing more, contact me." He paused long enough to pull out a business card. "My personal cell number is on there."

She accepted the card.

"Good evening," he said when the doors slid open.

Her voice suddenly constricted by the thundering of her pulse, she nodded and watched him enter the car.

Within seconds, he disappeared from view.

She exhaled, feeling simultaneously relieved and disappointed. What had she expected?

Lara straightened her shoulders and headed down the hallway to her father's office.

Lara knocked sharply then pushed the door open without waiting for an invitation.

Pernell raised his eyebrows as he glanced up. "Lara, darling." He cleared his throat. "I didn't expect you back today."

"Obviously." She took a seat across from him and dropped her bag onto the thick carpeting. The unyielding green leather, high-back chair squeaked as she sat. The rest of his office was just as uncomfortable. Dark mahogany bookshelves overflowed with civic awards, mementos and antique clocks. His gigantic desk had a huge phone, a blotter, a few fine pens and a cup of pencils. Begrudgingly, he'd allowed the IT team to install a computer, but it was behind him on a credenza. If he'd ever turned it on, she'd be astounded. His entire space reeked of old-world tradition or, in her opinion, an outdated way of doing business.

In contrast, her work area was minimalistic, equipped with modern electronics. It was designed for focus as well as flexibility. Its small, sparse confines were accented only by a shocking arrangement of red flowers displayed in an artistically shaped alloy metal vase, all designed to encourage creativity.

Their offices were only the beginning of the differences between Lara and her father.

"I just ran into Connor Donovan."

"Oh?" He glanced away, as if to avoid her gaze.

She gripped the chair arms. "He thought he had a meeting with both of us."

"Did he, now?"

"Dad, please. Don't patronize me." She held on to the tendril of frustration that threatened to unravel inside her. "Why didn't you mention we had an appointment with him?"

"I thought I'd see if he had anything interesting to say first."

How long had it been this way, the thrust and parry as she tried to dig necessary information from him? When she'd been young, he'd doted on her. Lara would hurry to him every chance she had. He'd encouraged it. Every time he'd had to work on a weekend, he'd brought her along. He'd allowed her to work summers while she was in high school, and he'd been her greatest mentor. Even while she'd been in college, she'd looked forward to the opportunity to spend time with him.

It wasn't until after grad school that she'd realized he was attached to outdated ways of doing business, and she'd started to challenge his decisions.

More and more, he'd begun to leave her out of conversations, and the wedge seemed as unbridgeable as it was wide. Now she understood the frustrations that had led her mother to divorce him five years ago. The man was stubborn.

Opting for the direct route, Lara stated, "Connor said the offer is off the table."

"It was never on it," her father replied, relaxing back in his seat, obviously once again feeling in control.

"Meaning?"

"He has some ideas on how we can work together on some projects. But essentially he's arrogant enough to think we should sell the communications division to him."

"Did you look at his proposition?"

"It was missing a comma and some zeroes. I never even looked at it." He clapped his hands together and left them steepled. "I tossed him out on his ass. Told him to take his insulting offer with him."

"You did *what?*" Energy ripped through her, bringing her to her feet.

"Sit down," Pernell instructed. "I don't like tipping my head back to see you." For the first time in weeks, he smiled. It erased years from his face, banished the shadows from beneath his eyes. His eyes, dark like her own, all but twinkled.

"You're enjoying this."

"Lara, you should have seen his face."

Since BHI was a private firm, they didn't answer to shareholders, just a seven-member board of directors. She and her father both held seats, along with her mother, Helene who had retained her position as part of her impressive divorce settlement. But because of her annoyances with Pernell, her mother hadn't been to a meeting in at least a year. Occasionally she threatened to show up, mostly to irritate him, Lara assumed.

The other four members had been appointed by Pernell over the years. They were colleagues and of a similar age and mindset.

Lara believed the company's financial problems could be solved with a steady, firm hand, a compelling five-year plan, some management shake-ups and, above all, getting rid of certain divisions.

At the last board meeting, she'd presented the dismal financial report, for the third quarter in a row. They could not afford for this spiral to continue.

Despite her passionate entreaty urging them to make changes, they'd voted to continue on the course they'd set.

One of the board members had stated that they had weathered decades of market fluctuations. Things would come back. They always had. Pernell's ever-steady philosophy had served the company in good stead.

Now, her father's stubbornness was damaging BHI's valuation, and he refused to see the truth.

For the past eighteen months, she'd been steadfast in her conviction that they needed to make changes immediately. The resulting tension coiled between them, gnawing away at their relationship. "Dad—"

"Go home," he interrupted. "Get some rest. You've earned it. Have a glass of wine."

From experience, she knew she'd get no further with him. He could be right that the offer had been an intentional lowball, but she didn't know that.

"Go home, Lara Marie," he said softly.

"Only if you will," she countered.

"Donald will be coming for me in half an hour."

His driver, confidant, butler. She nodded. "We are not finished with this conversation."

"Believe me, Lara. I know." He sighed. Then, obviously realizing he'd revealed a weakness, he stood. "I'll see you tomorrow."

She was being thrown out. Like Connor had been.

Her father waited for her to pick up her bag before escorting her to the door.

Once she was out, he snapped it shut.

Frustration churned through her. Instead of cleaning up her desk, she exited the building and headed for the parking garage. She knew she should follow her original plan and hit the gym, but she wanted to go home, have some peace to think things through. It'd been a hell of an evening.

Her fast pace didn't alleviate any of her anxiety, and she was still simmering as she slid behind the wheel of her sedan.

Her car was cool, and she took a moment to unpin her hair and roll her shoulders, trying to ease some of the knots there. Unfortunately they seemed to have become permanent.

This evening there was no baseball game or concert, so traffic was as light as it ever was in Houston, and it took her less than twenty minutes to reach her historic bungalow in the Heights.

All the way home, she turned over Erin's words and the unexpected meeting with Connor.

Before going inside, she stopped long enough to water the bougainvillea and the potted plants that looked as wilted as she felt.

She headed straight for the bedroom to stow her bag, kick off her shoes, remove her thigh-high stockings then pull her shirt over her head. As usual, she left everything in a discarded heap. At times she was grateful she lived alone and wasn't dating anyone. There were benefits.

After she'd changed into a pair of shorts, a tank top and flip-flops, she went into the kitchen for that glass of wine her father had suggested. Since the day had been so frustrating, she added sparkling water to the glass to cut the alcohol in half. She had a feeling she'd be wanting at least one refill.

Glass in hand, she grabbed her iPad from the counter and went into the backyard, her favorite retreat. The outdoor space was the feature that had convinced her to offer full price for the house. In addition to the covered deck, there was a small vegetable garden, numerous oleander trees, lush banana plants, several types of palms and a fishpond that she had to constantly replenish thanks to the hungry local bird population. It was a small oasis in a busy city.

In cooler months, she had a heater on the deck, but today, she needed the overhead fan to churn through the humidity-laced air.

Lara sat on the porch swing and took a long drink before putting down the glass. Then she powered up the tablet. While she waited for it to connect, she used her toes to push off and set the swing into motion.

She became aware of children playing in the yard behind her. And soon after, the sounds of dogs running around. Mrs. Fuhrman, her next-door neighbor, must have let her five rescue animals outside.

Their excited yips and barks soothed her.

Without conscious thought, she did a search on Connor's name.

Not for the first time, she scrolled through a few articles about him. Most of it, she knew from Erin, so Lara only read the first couple of paragraphs before moving on.

After their father's death, Connor had been called home from his graduate school studies back east to take the helm of Donovan Worldwide. Though his grandfather, William, referred to as the Colonel, still served as CEO, Connor was president, and he was responsible for most of the decisions. According to unconfirmed reports, the Colonel had recently had a stroke, which meant that Connor had assumed even more obligations.

Lara saw a couple of references to Erin's role as a human resources guru, while Connor's younger brother handled research. According to Erin, they had a step-brother, Cade, who was the eldest child. Though she seemed to adore him, he wasn't around much, and there were only hints about the scandal of his birth. He ran a ranching operation—or, as it was referred to deeper in the story, the family's agribusiness interests—in west Texas.

As she'd mentioned to Erin, Lara had previously looked Connor up online, searching for any indication he had a girlfriend. She hadn't seen recent pictures of him with any women, though he'd been photographed at a Boston event with Julien Bonds, the renowned technology genius. But there was frustratingly little to give her a glimpse of who he really was or what mattered to him.

Without conscious thought, she pulled up the bookmarked images of him. All of them were mouth-watering. No matter what he was wearing, from khakis and a polo shirt with deck shoes, to a suit like he'd worn today, the man looked delicious. Tall and handsome, he had the lean frame of a runner or bicyclist. He was powerful and sexy. And he tripped all her physical responses.

She glanced up from the screen and stared into the distance, replaying their unexpected meeting near the elevator.

As a professional, she'd understood that Connor had been visiting on business, but the woman in her had pulsed with awareness.

Unbidden, Erin's words returned to tumble through Lara's mind.

Marry Connor?

The idea was absurd.

But for a moment, the idea of being with him tantalized. She wondered what it would be like to be with him, to surrender to his kiss. Would he be as bold in the bedroom as he was outside it? For a moment, she pictured him with his fingertips poised to open the top button on her favorite blouse. Would he skim her skin as he bared it, or would he move aggressively to the next button?

How restrained was he?

Would he tear the material in his haste to have her? That thought was followed by another, and she imagined him undressing, taking off his belt then looping it around his hand as he approached her.

She shook her head.

What was wrong with her? She wasn't sure where the unbidden fantasy had come from. And, as she'd found out, men thought she was too kinky as it was. She'd do better to banish the thoughts.

Adding Connor Donovan to her evening fantasies was a prescription for disaster.

Determinedly, she shoved her musings away.

She had real issues she needed to focus on, a family business that needed serious attention. And Connor had already indicated his willingness to help.

The idea of approaching him made rockets of ice shoot up her spine to settle at the back of her neck.

Lara reached for her glass and took a deep drink, contemplating. No doubt her father would see her action as disloyal. But her job as CFO was to advise and make recommendations, even if the owner didn't want to hear them.

Resolved, she went to shut down the tablet, but was once again riveted by a picture of Connor, this time adjusting one of his starched cuffs.

Damn, everything he did radiated appeal.

She headed inside and deposited her iPad and unfinished drink on the counter, telling herself she wasn't going to use her shower massager to masturbate while she thought of Connor.

But as she turned on the water in the bathroom, Lara admitted she was lying to herself. She was aroused—consumed by naughty thoughts of him—and she needed relief.

About the Author

Born in northern England and raised in the Wild West, Sierra Cartwright pens books that are as untamed as the Rockies she calls home.

She's an award-winning, multi-published writer who wrote her first book at age nine and hasn't stopped since.

Sierra invites you to share the complex journey of love and desire, of surrender and commitment. Her own journey has taught her that trusting takes guts and courage, and her work is a celebration for everyone who is willing to take that risk.

Sierra loves to hear from readers. You can find her contact information, website details and author profile page at https://www.firstforromance.com